THE HARDY BOYS®

UNDERCOVER BROTHERS™

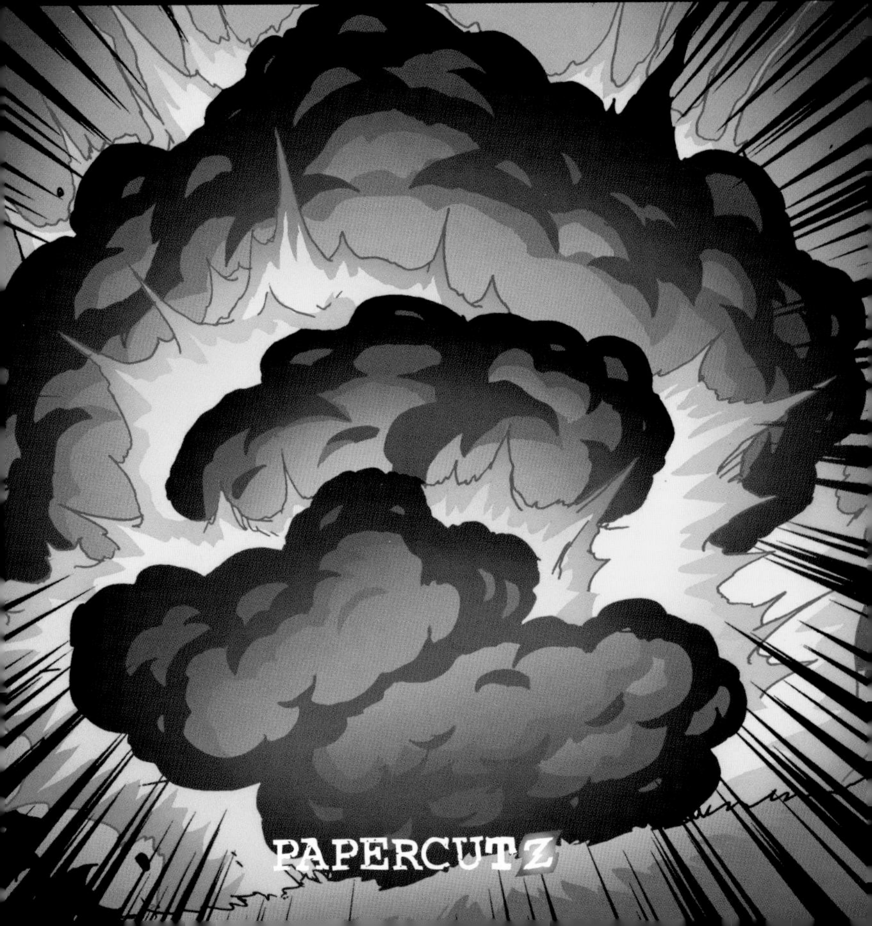

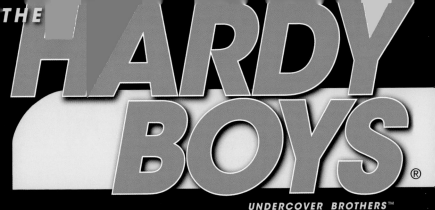

PAPERCUTZ

THE HARDY BOYS

#10

BOYS®

UNDERCOVER BROTHERS™

A Hardy Day's Night

SCOTT LOBDELL • Writer

PAULO H. MARCONDES

with MARCEL ZERO • Artists

Based on the series by
FRANKLIN W. DIXON

PAPERCUTZ™

New York

J-GN
HARDY BOYS

369-9298

A Hardy Day's Night
SCOTT LOBDELL – Writer
PAULO H. MARCONDES
with MARCEL ZERO — Artists
MARK LERER – Letterer
LAURIE E. SMITH — Colorist
JIM SALICRUP — Editor-in-Chief

ISBN 10: 1-59707-070-X paperback edition
ISBN 13: 978-1-59707-070-6 paperback edition
ISBN 10: 1-59707-071-8 hardcover edition
ISBN 13: 978-1-59707-071-3 hardcover edition

Printed in China

10   9   8   7   6   5   4   3   2   1

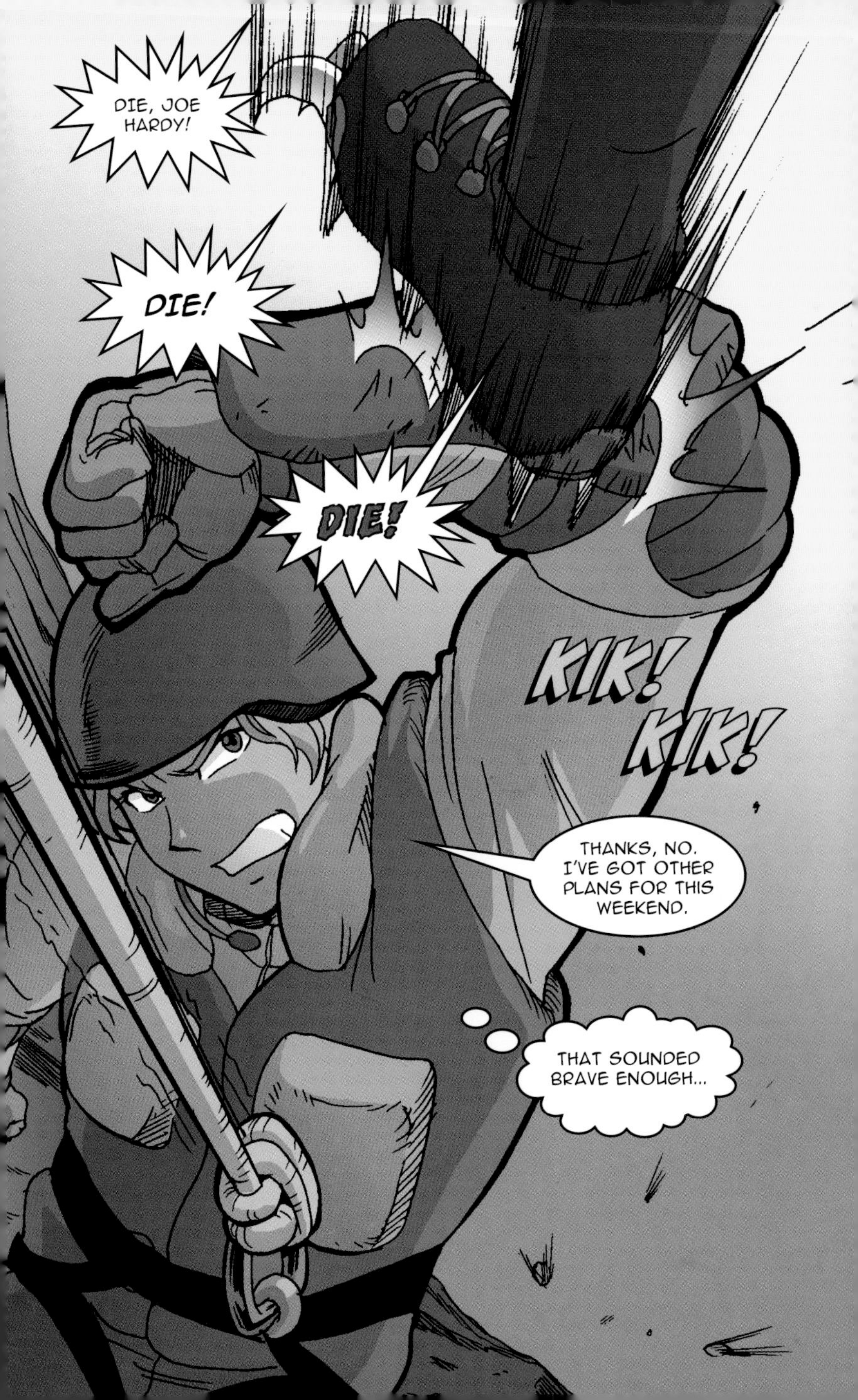
DIE, JOE HARDY!
DIE!
DIE!
KIK! KIK!
THANKS, NO. I'VE GOT OTHER PLANS FOR THIS WEEKEND.
THAT SOUNDED BRAVE ENOUGH...

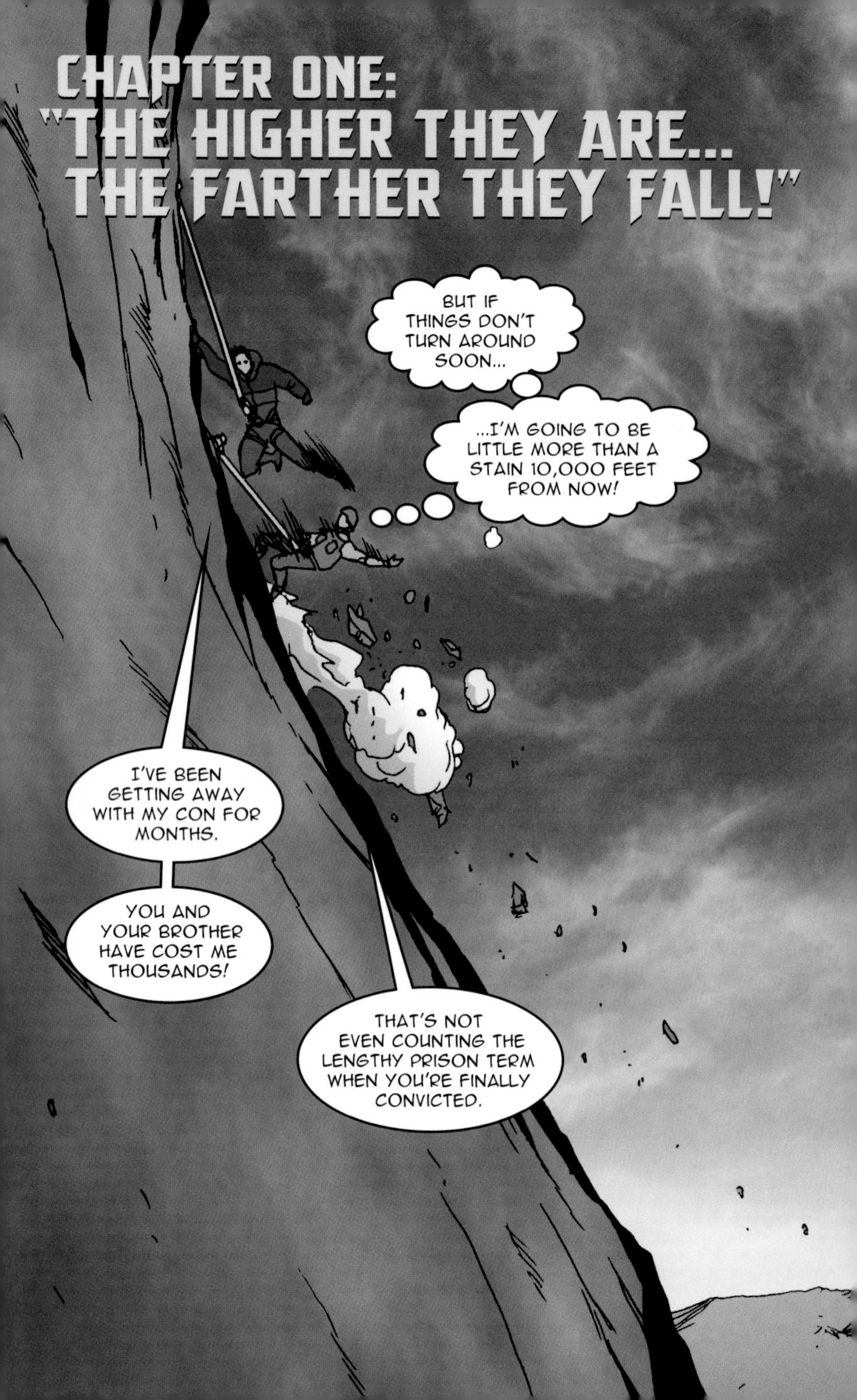
CHAPTER ONE:
"THE HIGHER THEY ARE... THE FARTHER THEY FALL!"
BUT IF THINGS DON'T TURN AROUND SOON...
...I'M GOING TO BE LITTLE MORE THAN A STAIN 10,000 FEET FROM NOW!
I'VE BEEN GETTING AWAY WITH MY CON FOR MONTHS.
YOU AND YOUR BROTHER HAVE COST ME THOUSANDS!
THAT'S NOT EVEN COUNTING THE LENGTHY PRISON TERM WHEN YOU'RE FINALLY CONVICTED.

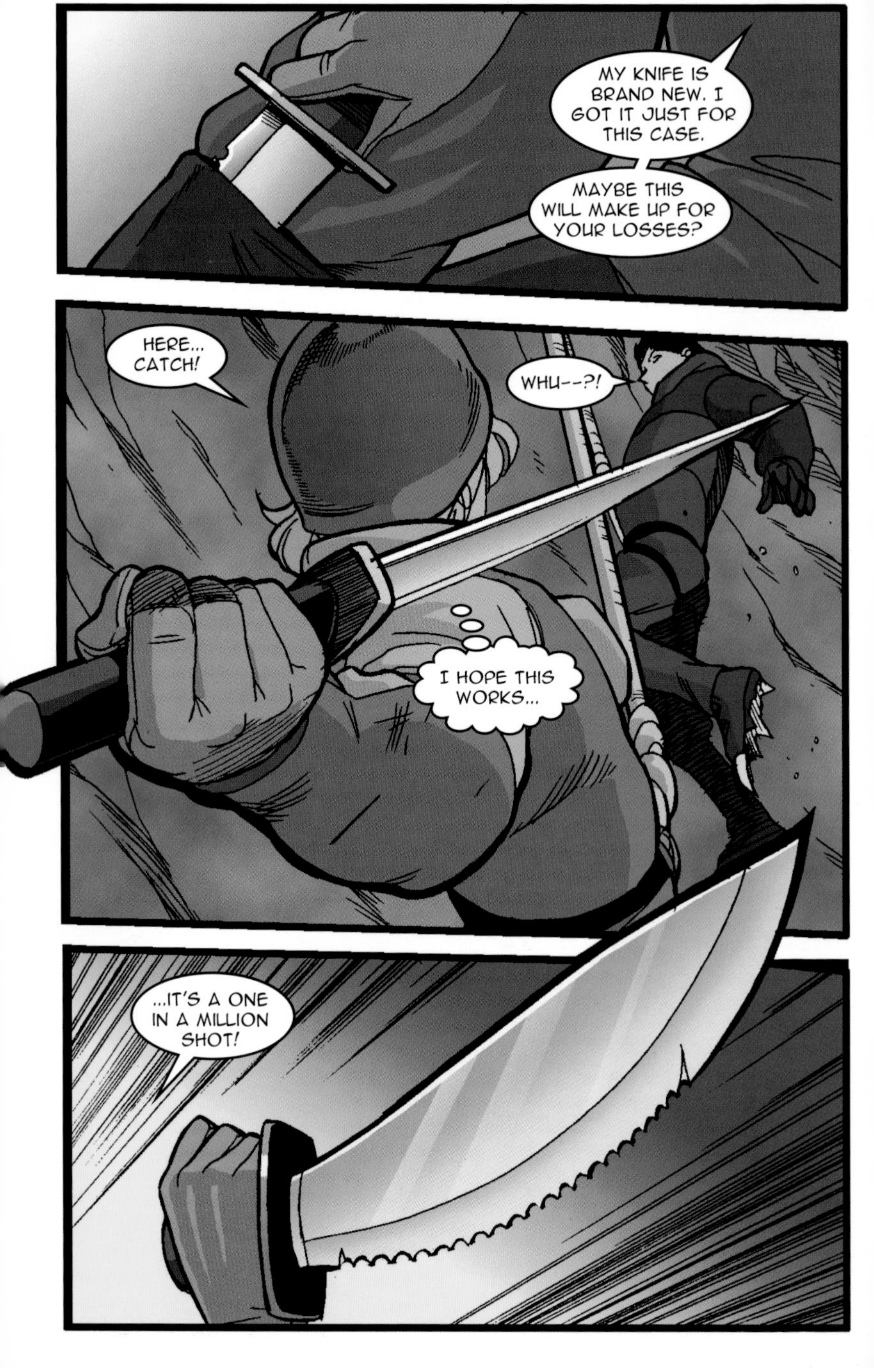
MY KNIFE IS BRAND NEW. I GOT IT JUST FOR THIS CASE.
MAYBE THIS WILL MAKE UP FOR YOUR LOSSES?
HERE... CATCH!
WHU--?!
I HOPE THIS WORKS...
...IT'S A ONE IN A MILLION SHOT!

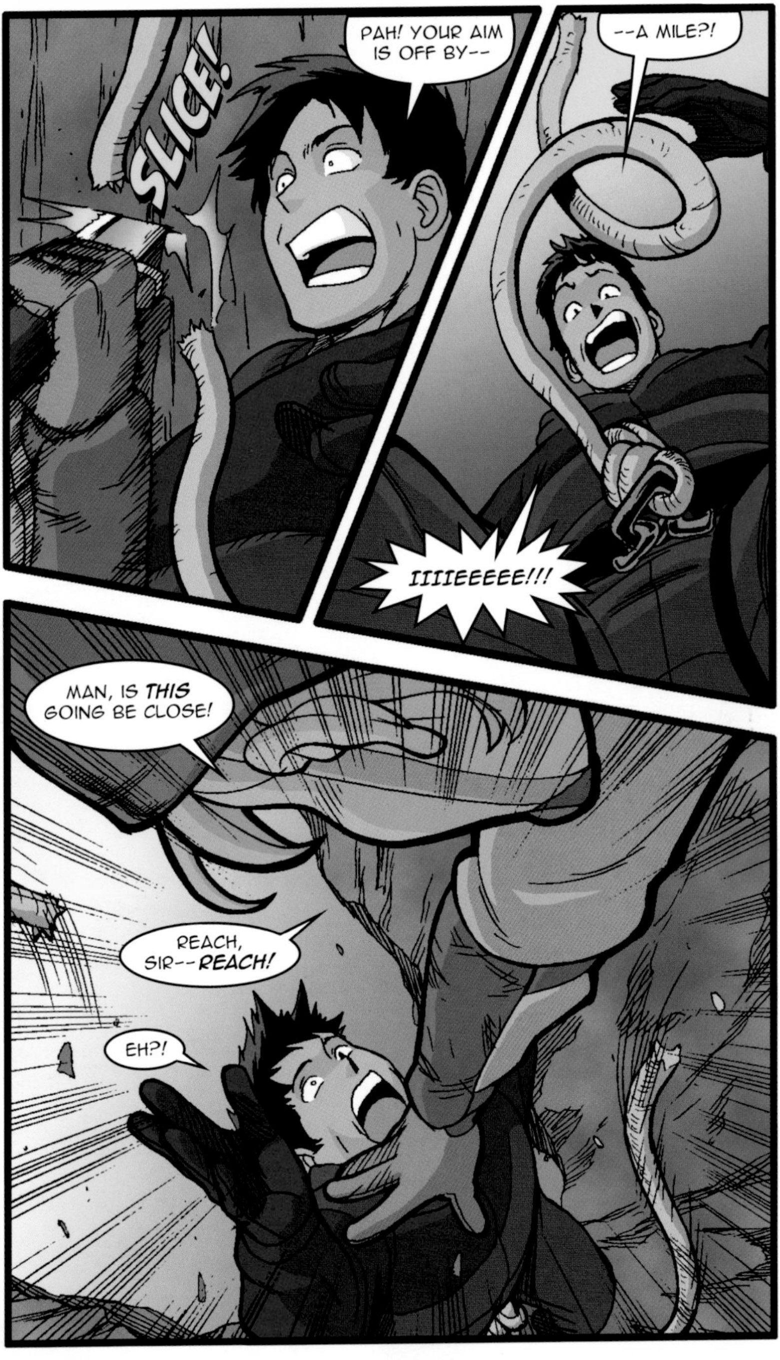
SLICE!
PAH! YOUR AIM IS OFF BY--
--A MILE?!
IIIIEEEEE!!!
MAN, IS THIS GOING BE CLOSE!
REACH, SIR--REACH!
EH?!

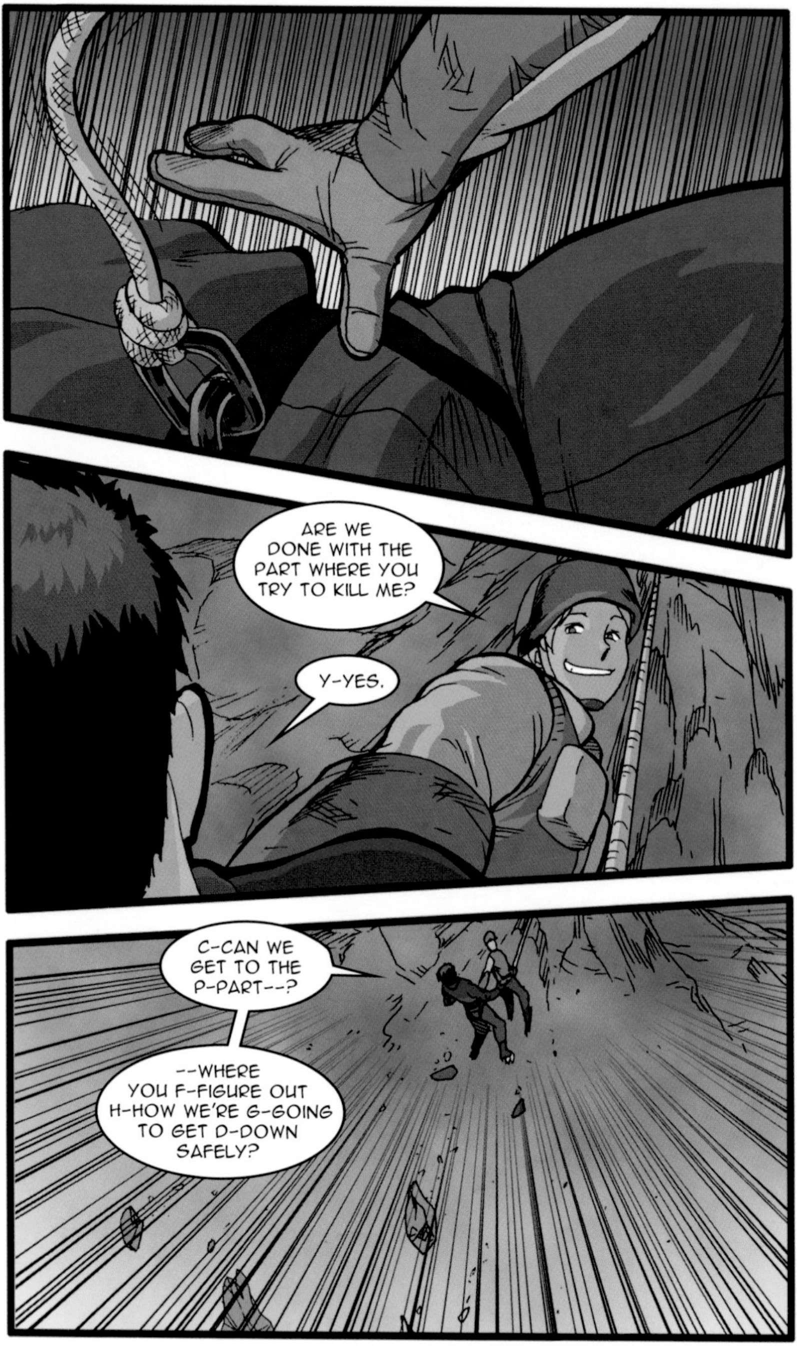
ARE WE DONE WITH THE PART WHERE YOU TRY TO KILL ME?
Y-YES.
C-CAN WE GET TO THE P-PART--?
--WHERE YOU F-FIGURE OUT H-HOW WE'RE G-GOING TO GET D-DOWN SAFELY?

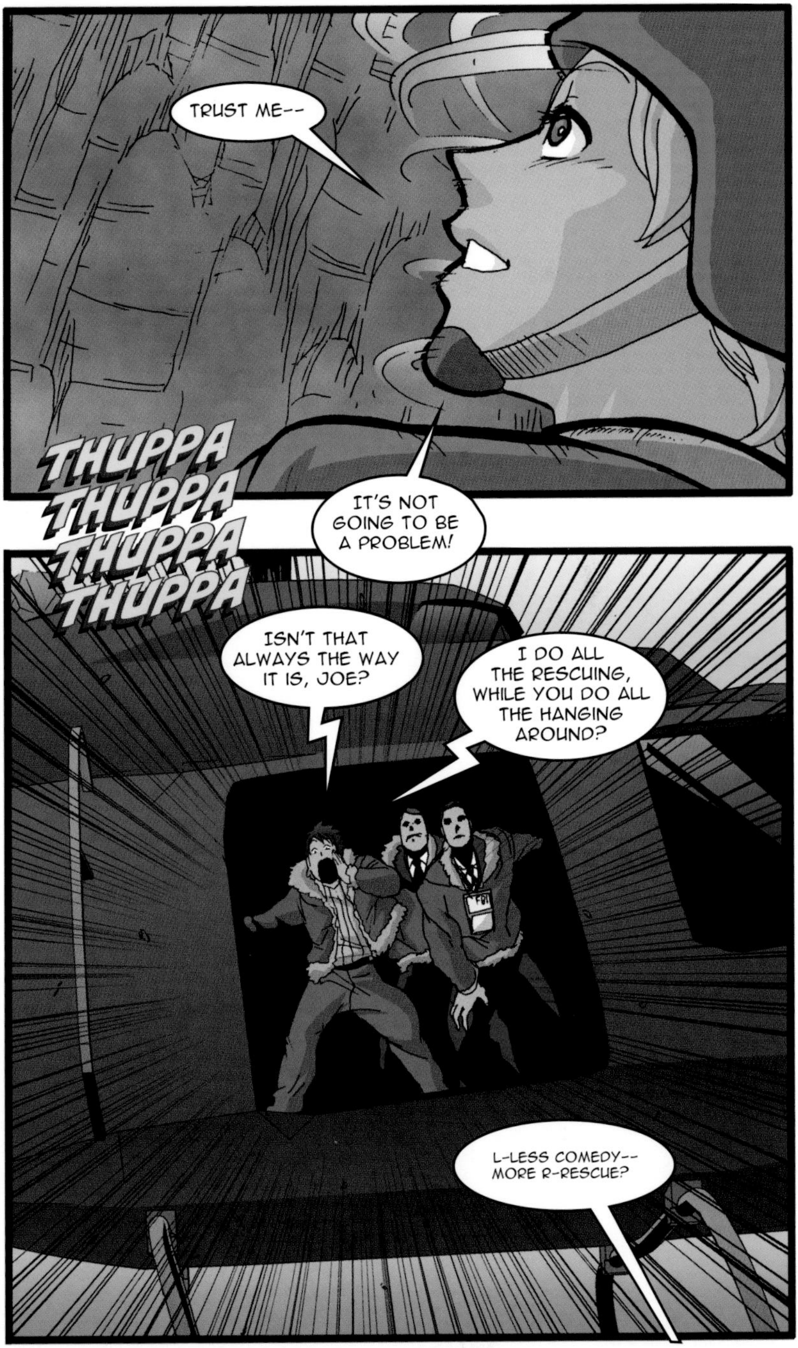
TRUST ME--
THUPPA THUPPA THUPPA THUPPA
IT'S NOT GOING TO BE A PROBLEM!
ISN'T THAT ALWAYS THE WAY IT IS, JOE?
I DO ALL THE RESCUING, WHILE YOU DO ALL THE HANGING AROUND?
L-LESS COMEDY-- MORE R-RESCUE?

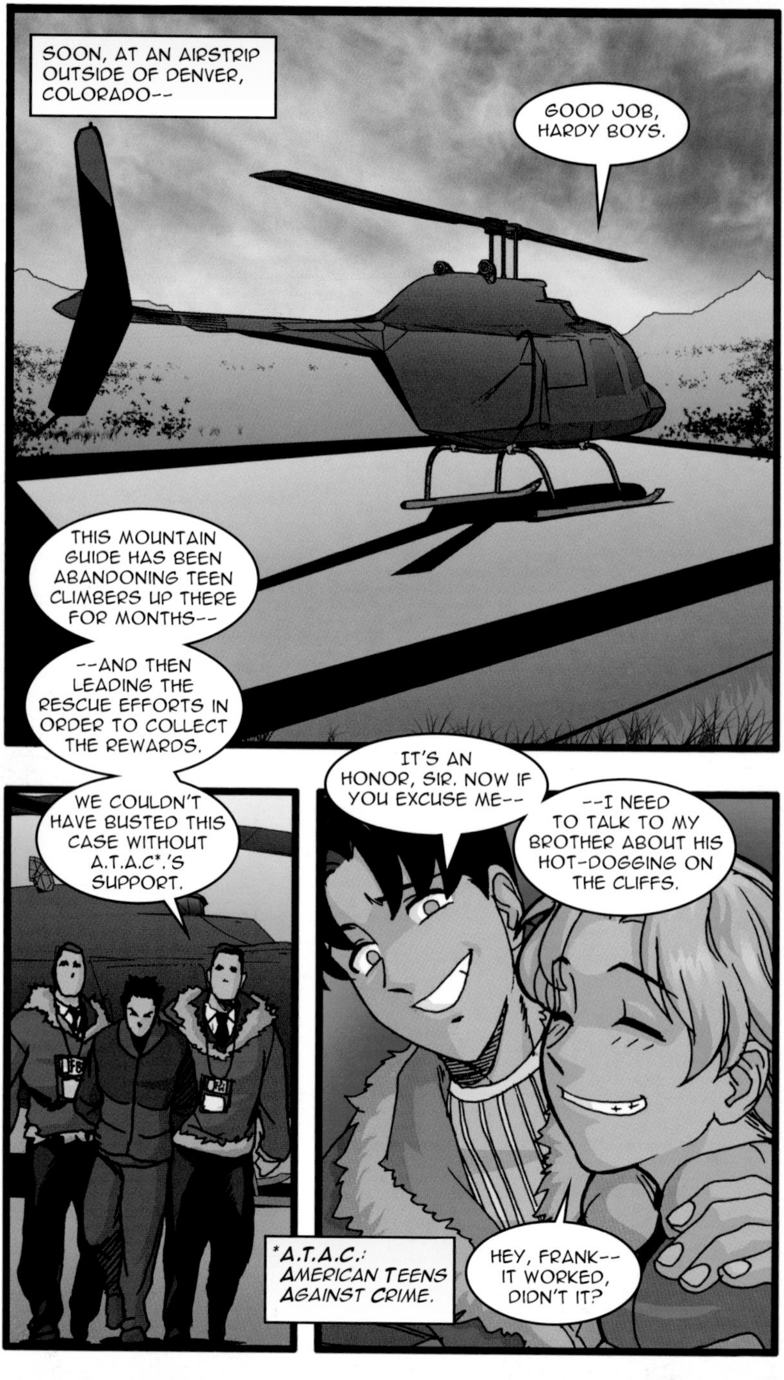
SOON, AT AN AIRSTRIP OUTSIDE OF DENVER, COLORADO--
GOOD JOB, HARDY BOYS.
THIS MOUNTAIN GUIDE HAS BEEN ABANDONING TEEN CLIMBERS UP THERE FOR MONTHS--
--AND THEN LEADING THE RESCUE EFFORTS IN ORDER TO COLLECT THE REWARDS.
WE COULDN'T HAVE BUSTED THIS CASE WITHOUT A.T.A.C*.'S SUPPORT.
*A.T.A.C.: AMERICAN TEENS AGAINST CRIME.
IT'S AN HONOR, SIR. NOW IF YOU EXCUSE ME--
--I NEED TO TALK TO MY BROTHER ABOUT HIS HOT-DOGGING ON THE CLIFFS.
HEY, FRANK-- IT WORKED, DIDN'T IT?

CHAPTER TWO: "DANCE 'TIL YOU DROP!"

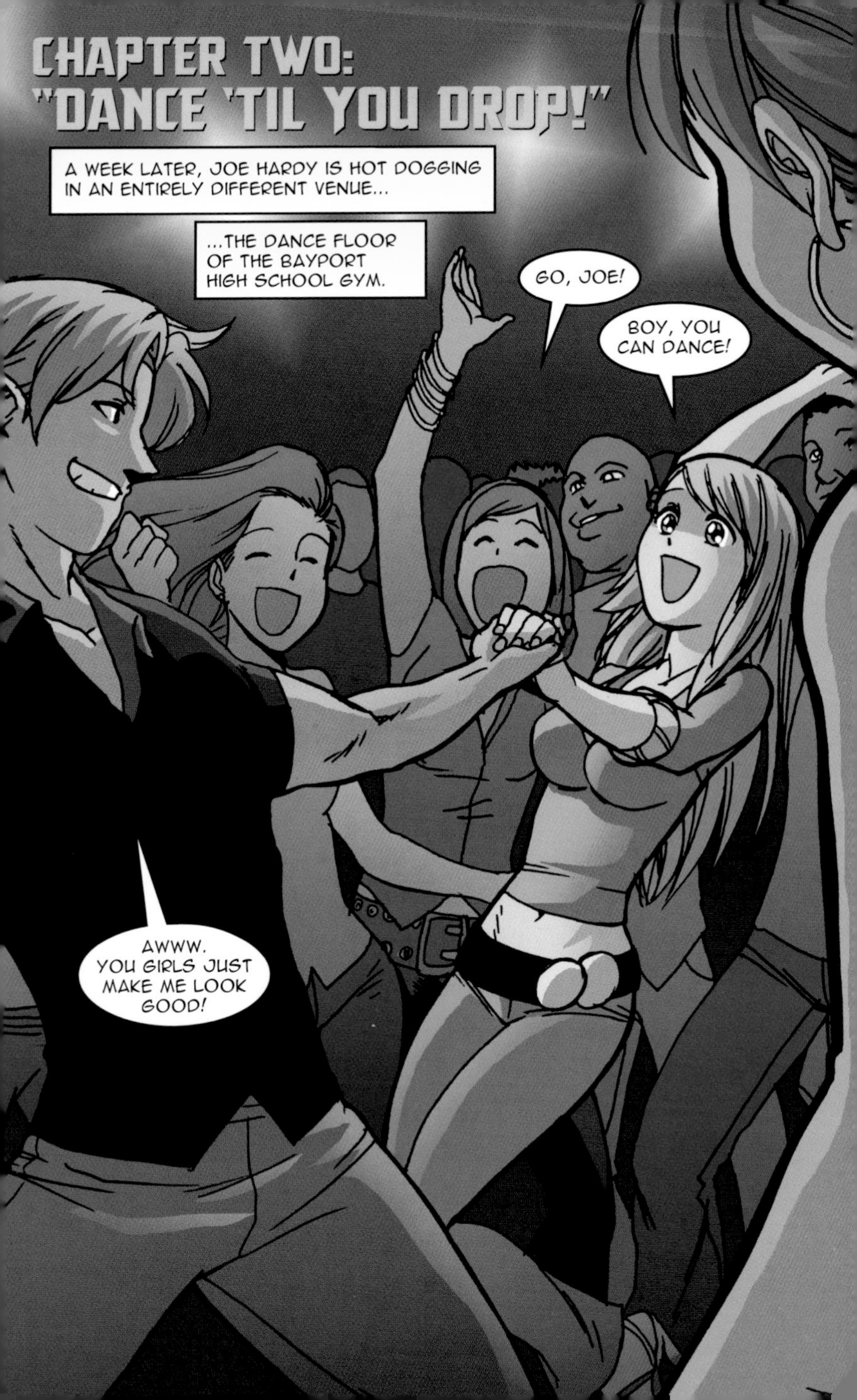
A WEEK LATER, JOE HARDY IS HOT DOGGING IN AN ENTIRELY DIFFERENT VENUE...
...THE DANCE FLOOR OF THE BAYPORT HIGH SCHOOL GYM.
GO, JOE!
BOY, YOU CAN DANCE!
AWWW. YOU GIRLS JUST MAKE ME LOOK GOOD!

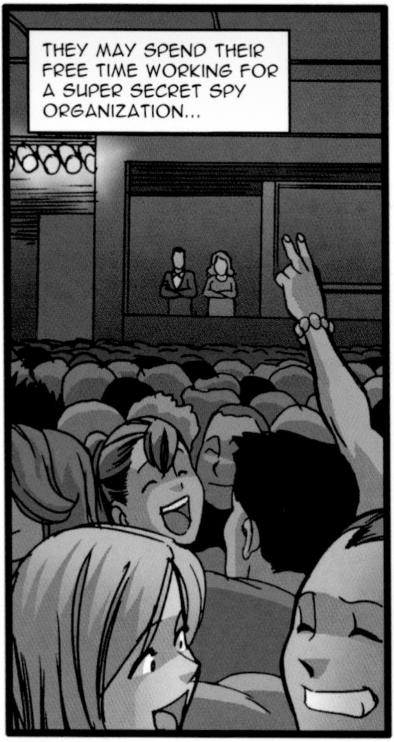
THEY MAY SPEND THEIR FREE TIME WORKING FOR A SUPER SECRET SPY ORGANIZATION...

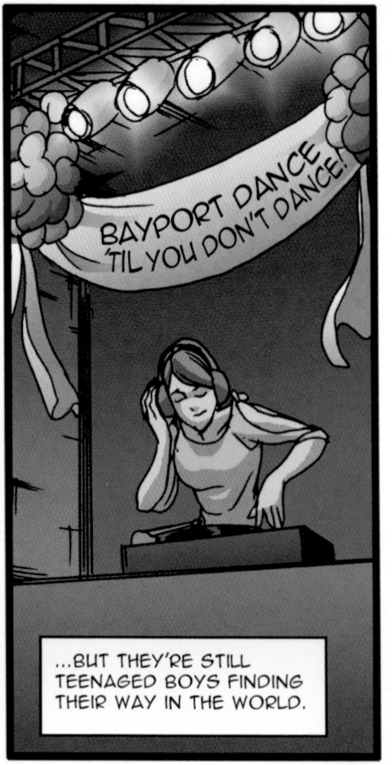
BAYPORT DANCE 'TIL YOU DON'T DANCE!
...BUT THEY'RE STILL TEENAGED BOYS FINDING THEIR WAY IN THE WORLD.

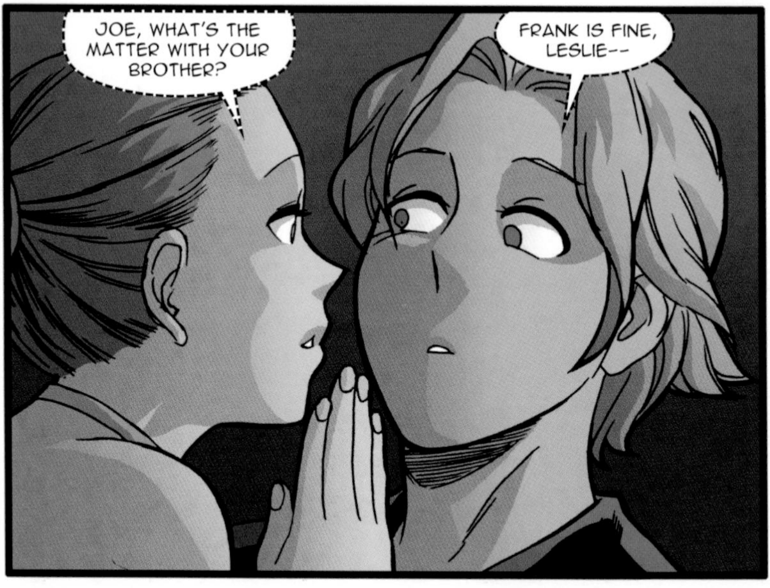
JOE, WHAT'S THE MATTER WITH YOUR BROTHER?
FRANK IS FINE, LESLIE--

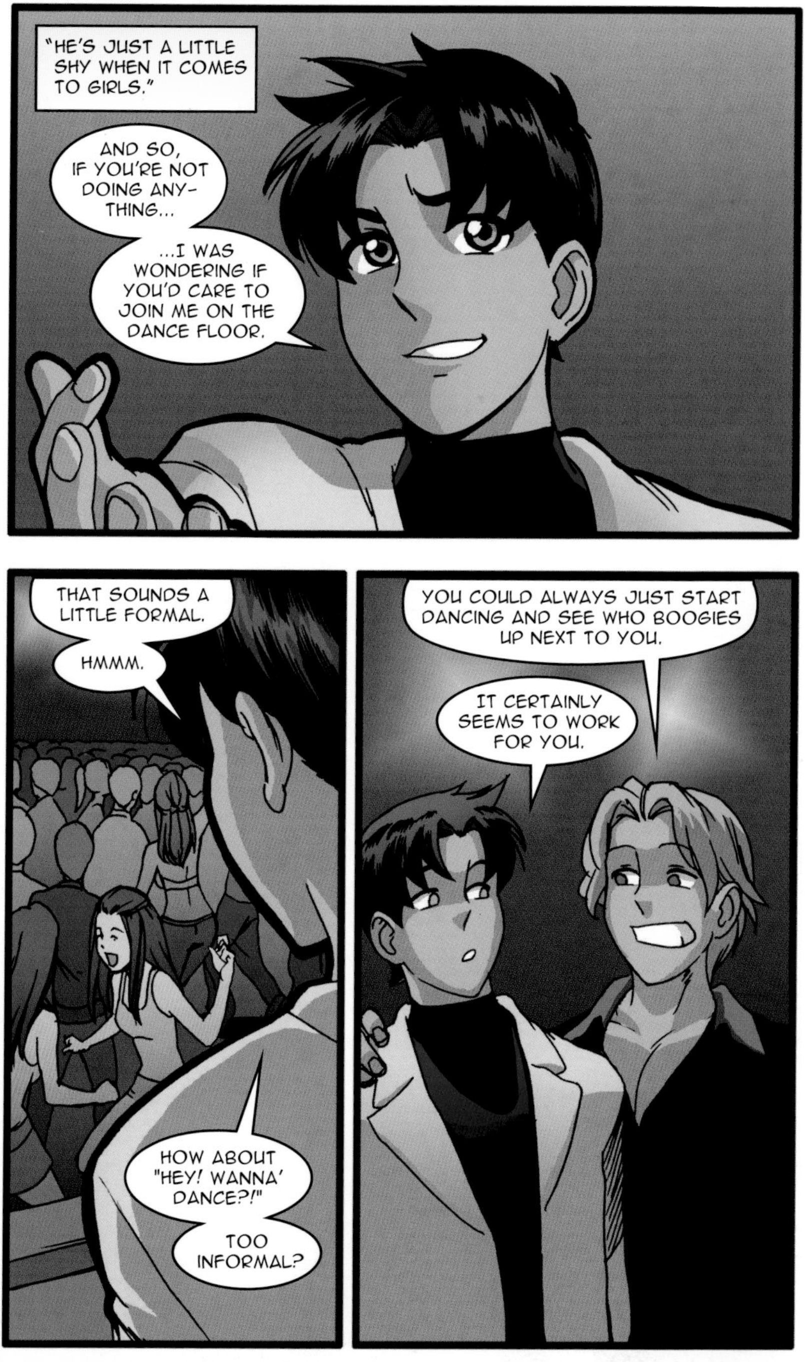
"HE'S JUST A LITTLE SHY WHEN IT COMES TO GIRLS."
AND SO, IF YOU'RE NOT DOING ANY-THING...
...I WAS WONDERING IF YOU'D CARE TO JOIN ME ON THE DANCE FLOOR.
THAT SOUNDS A LITTLE FORMAL.
HMMM.
HOW ABOUT "HEY! WANNA' DANCE?!"
TOO INFORMAL?
YOU COULD ALWAYS JUST START DANCING AND SEE WHO BOOGIES UP NEXT TO YOU.
IT CERTAINLY SEEMS TO WORK FOR YOU.

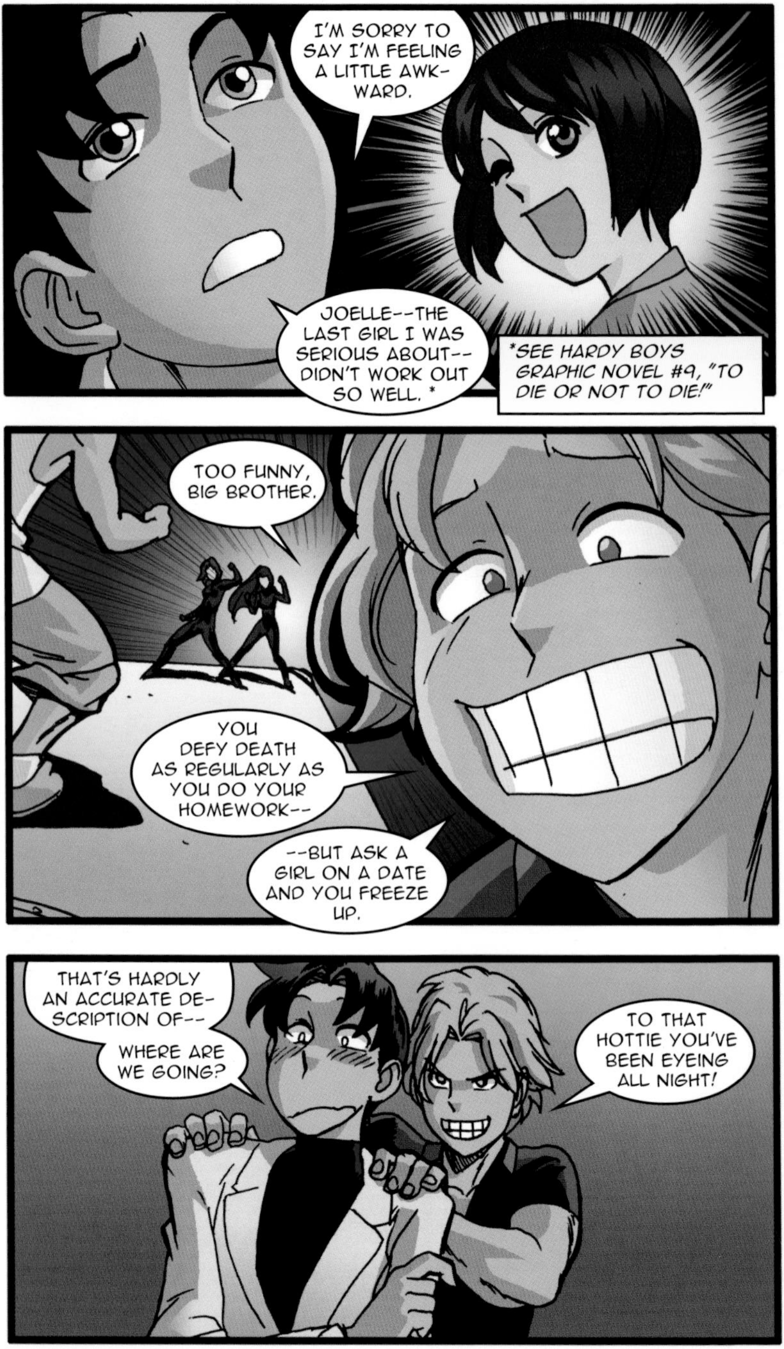
I'M SORRY TO SAY I'M FEELING A LITTLE AWK-WARD.
JOELLE--THE LAST GIRL I WAS SERIOUS ABOUT--DIDN'T WORK OUT SO WELL. *
*SEE HARDY BOYS GRAPHIC NOVEL #9, "TO DIE OR NOT TO DIE!"
TOO FUNNY, BIG BROTHER.
YOU DEFY DEATH AS REGULARLY AS YOU DO YOUR HOMEWORK--
--BUT ASK A GIRL ON A DATE AND YOU FREEZE UP.
THAT'S HARDLY AN ACCURATE DE-SCRIPTION OF--
WHERE ARE WE GOING?
TO THAT HOTTIE YOU'VE BEEN EYEING ALL NIGHT!

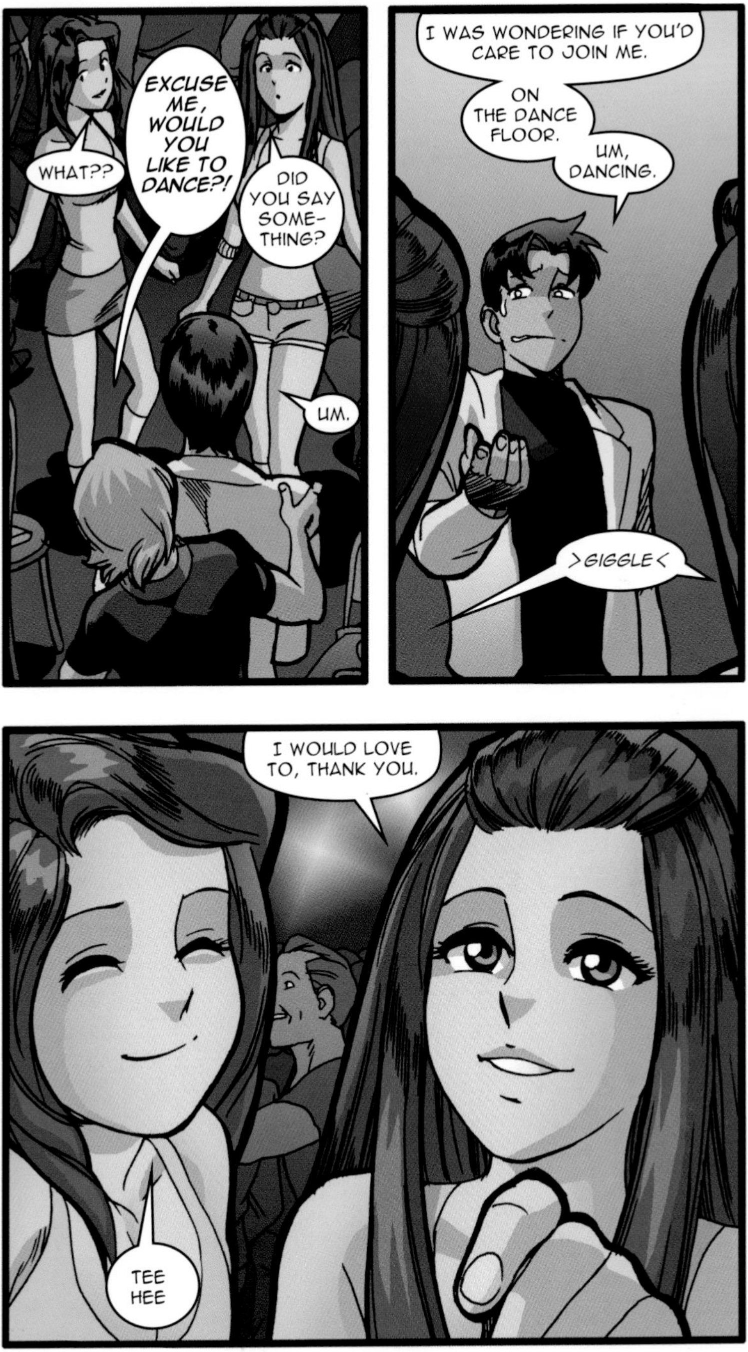
EXCUSE ME, WOULD YOU LIKE TO DANCE?!
WHAT??
DID YOU SAY SOME-THING?
UM.
I WAS WONDERING IF YOU'D CARE TO JOIN ME.
ON THE DANCE FLOOR.
UM, DANCING.
>GIGGLE<
I WOULD LOVE TO, THANK YOU.
TEE HEE

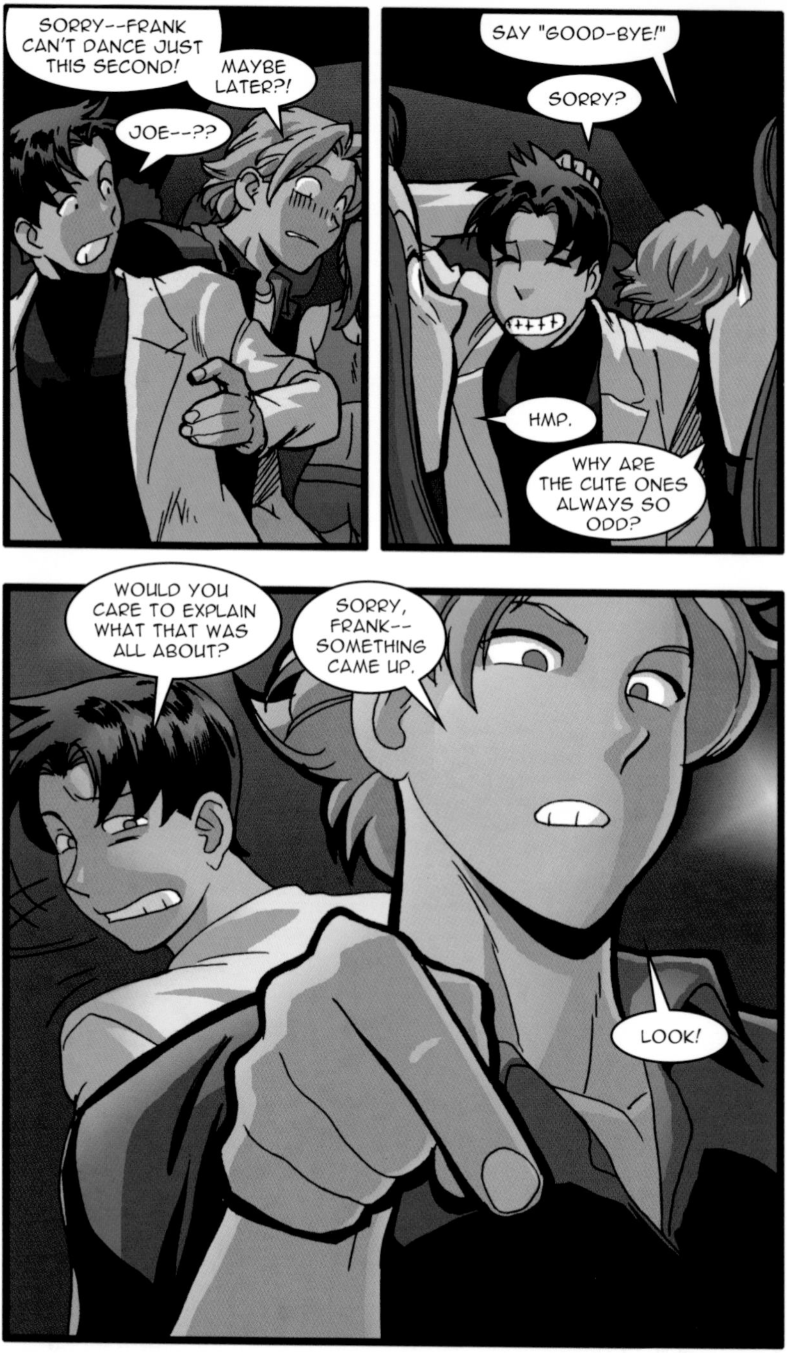
SORRY--FRANK CAN'T DANCE JUST THIS SECOND!
MAYBE LATER?!
JOE--??
SAY "GOOD-BYE!"
SORRY?
HMP.
WHY ARE THE CUTE ONES ALWAYS SO ODD?
WOULD YOU CARE TO EXPLAIN WHAT THAT WAS ALL ABOUT?
SORRY, FRANK-- SOMETHING CAME UP.
LOOK!

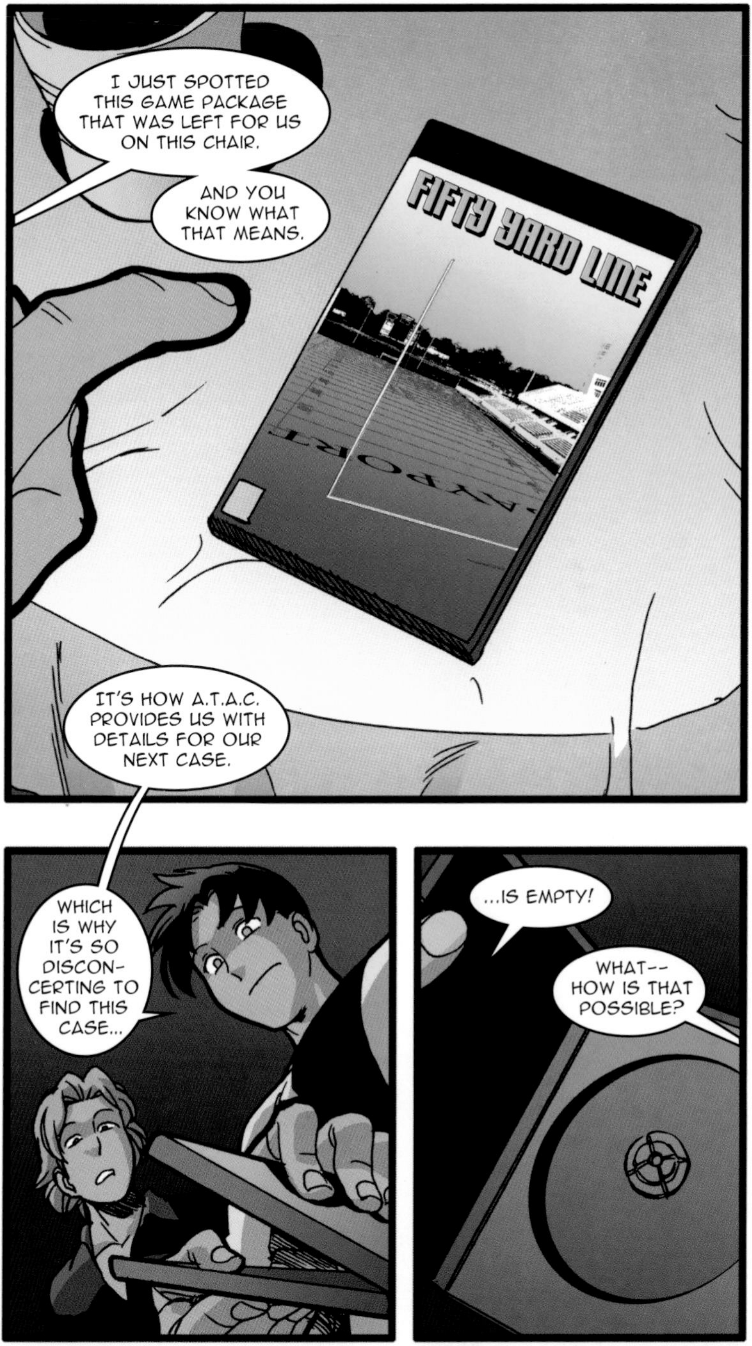
I JUST SPOTTED THIS GAME PACKAGE THAT WAS LEFT FOR US ON THIS CHAIR.
AND YOU KNOW WHAT THAT MEANS.
FIFTY YARD LINE
IT'S HOW A.T.A.C. PROVIDES US WITH DETAILS FOR OUR NEXT CASE.
WHICH IS WHY IT'S SO DISCON-CERTING TO FIND THIS CASE...
...IS EMPTY!
WHAT-- HOW IS THAT POSSIBLE?

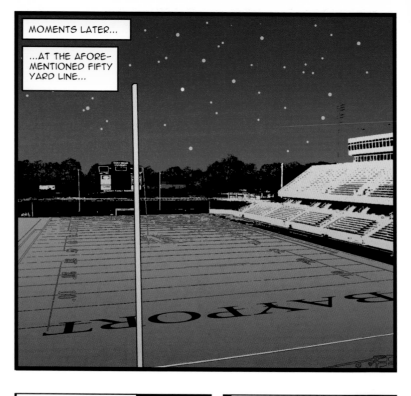

MOMENTS LATER...

...AT THE AFORE-MENTIONED FIFTY YARD LINE...

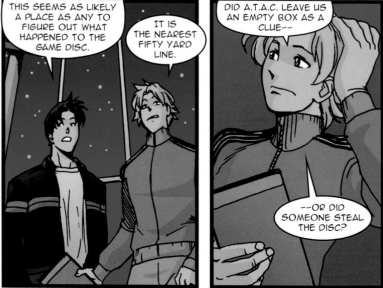

THIS SEEMS AS LIKELY A PLACE AS ANY TO FIGURE OUT WHAT HAPPENED TO THE GAME DISC.

IT IS THE NEAREST FIFTY YARD LINE.

DID A.T.A.C. LEAVE US AN EMPTY BOX AS A CLUE--

--OR DID SOMEONE STEAL THE DISC?

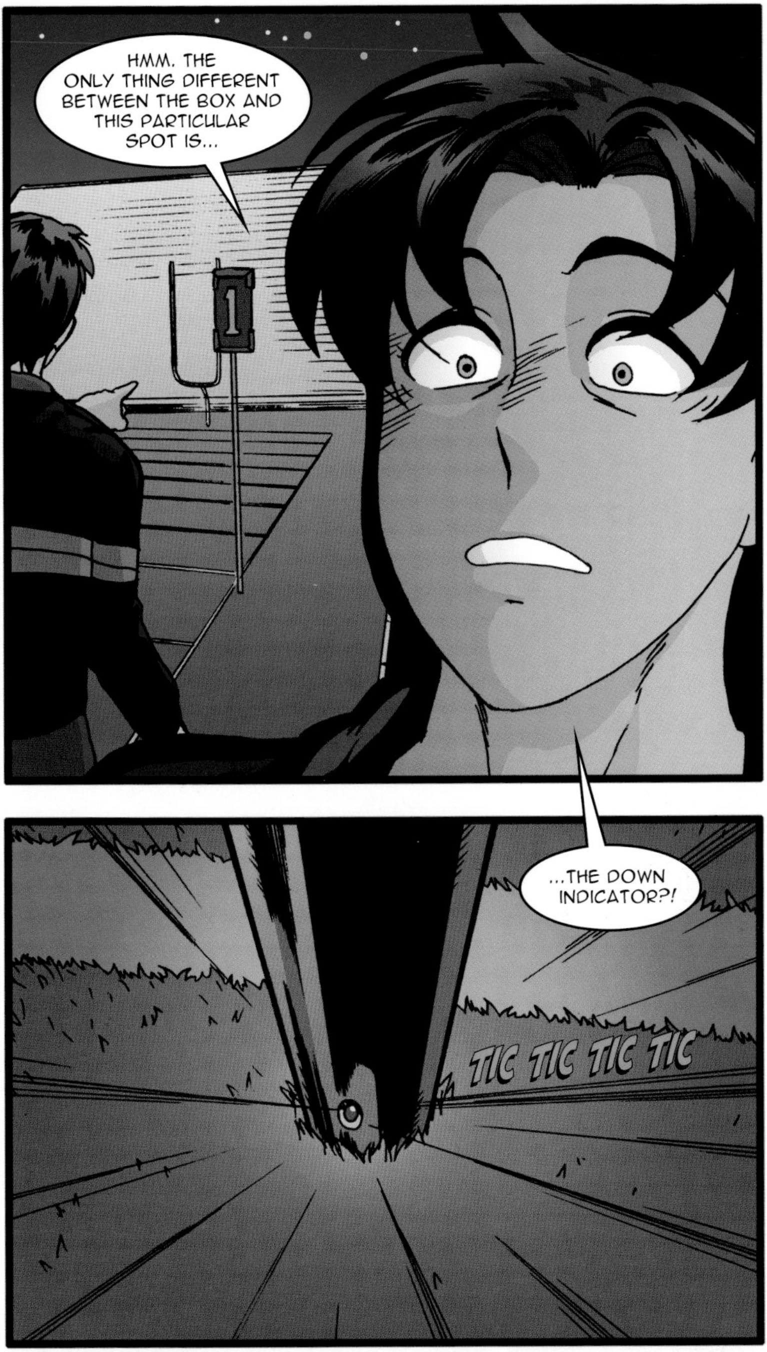
HMM. THE ONLY THING DIFFERENT BETWEEN THE BOX AND THIS PARTICULAR SPOT IS...
1
...THE DOWN INDICATOR?!
TIC TIC TIC TIC

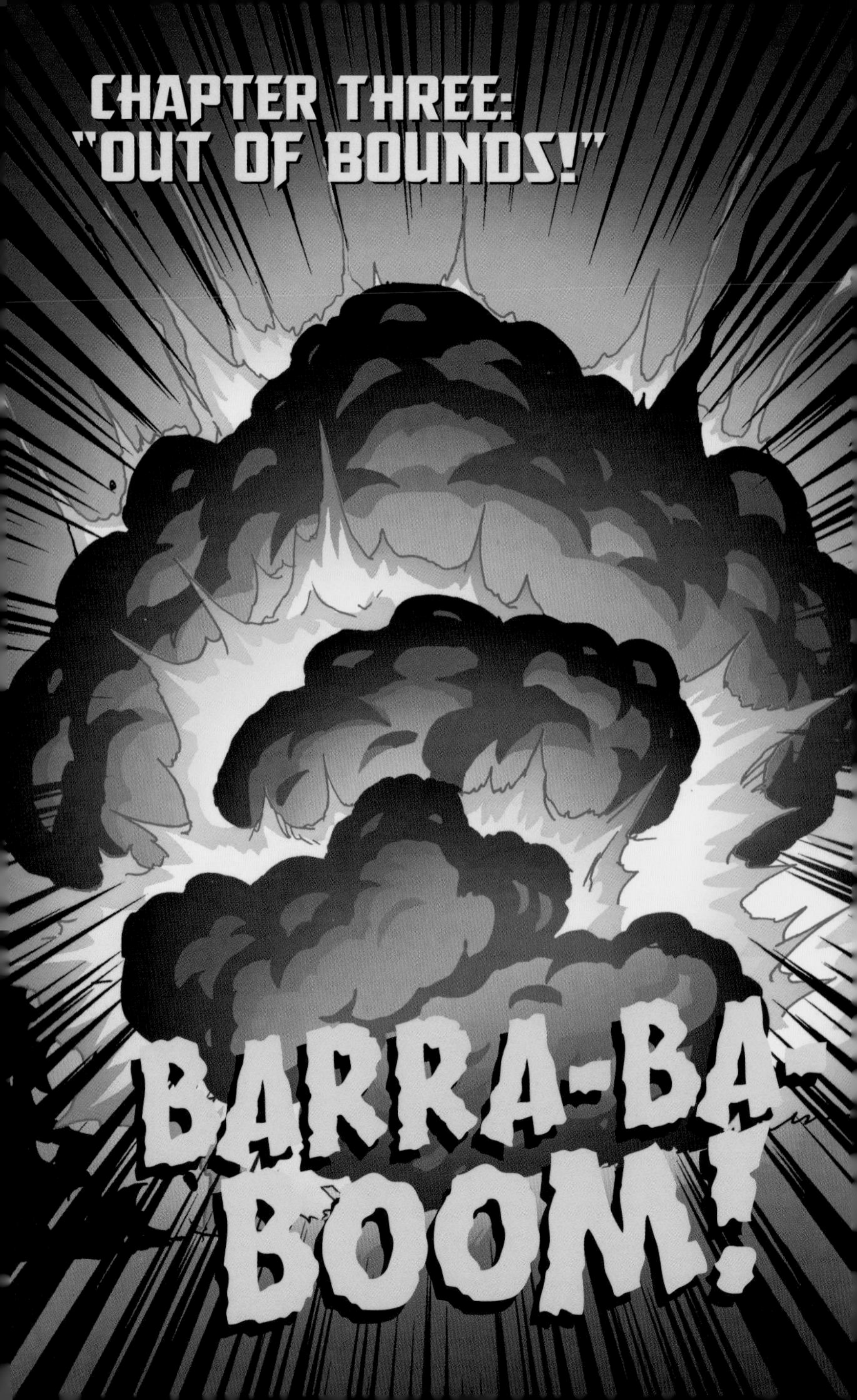
CHAPTER THREE:
"OUT OF BOUNDS!"
BARRA-BA-
BOOM!

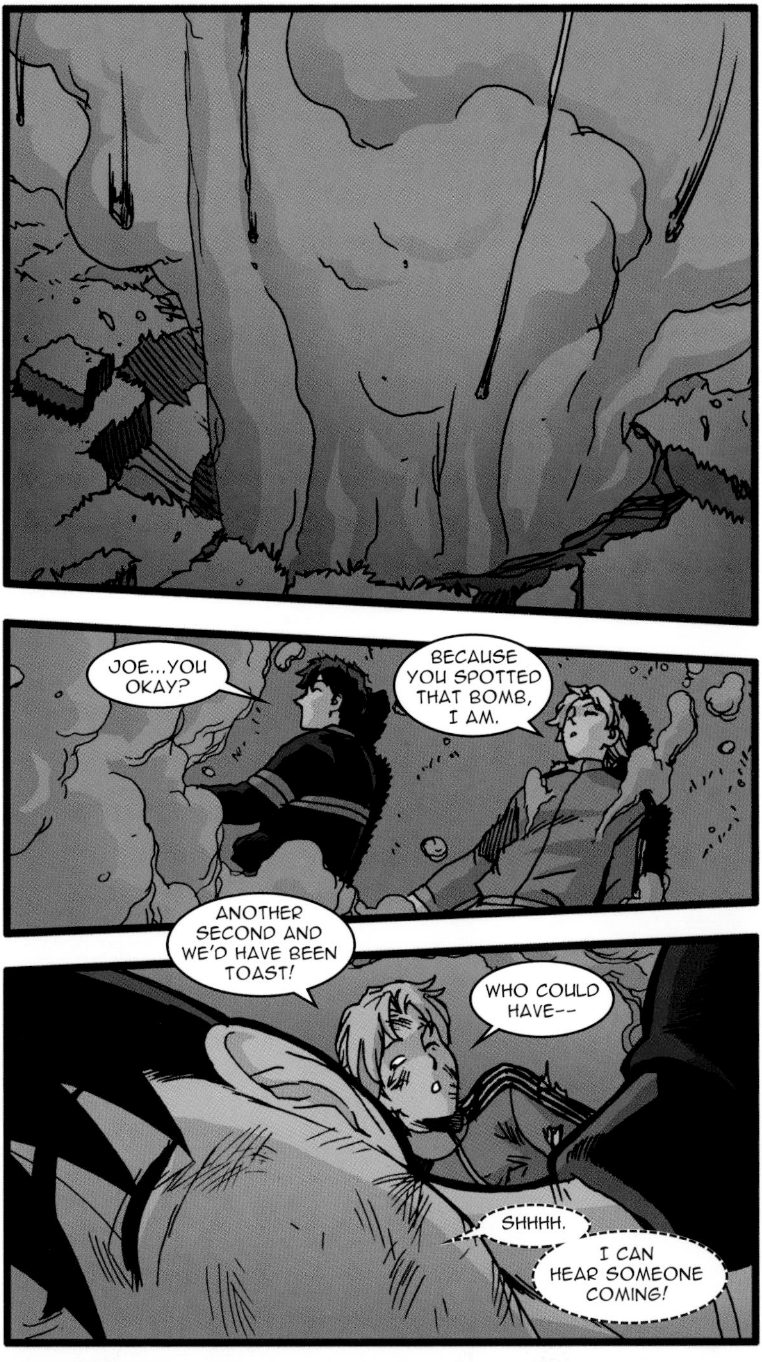
JOE...YOU OKAY?
BECAUSE YOU SPOTTED THAT BOMB, I AM.
ANOTHER SECOND AND WE'D HAVE BEEN TOAST!
WHO COULD HAVE--
SHHHH.
I CAN HEAR SOMEONE COMING!

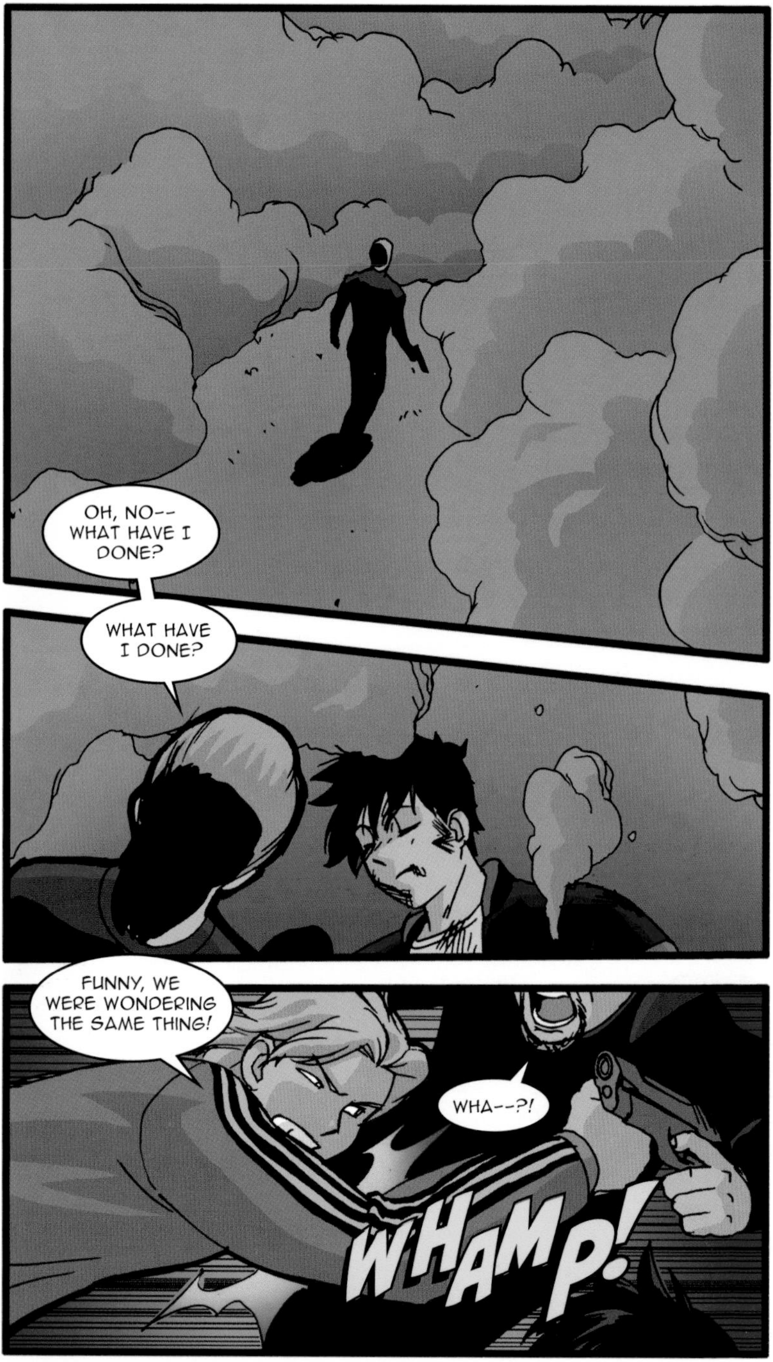
OH, NO--
WHAT HAVE I
DONE?
WHAT HAVE
I DONE?
FUNNY, WE
WERE WONDERING
THE SAME THING!
WHA--?!
WHAMP!

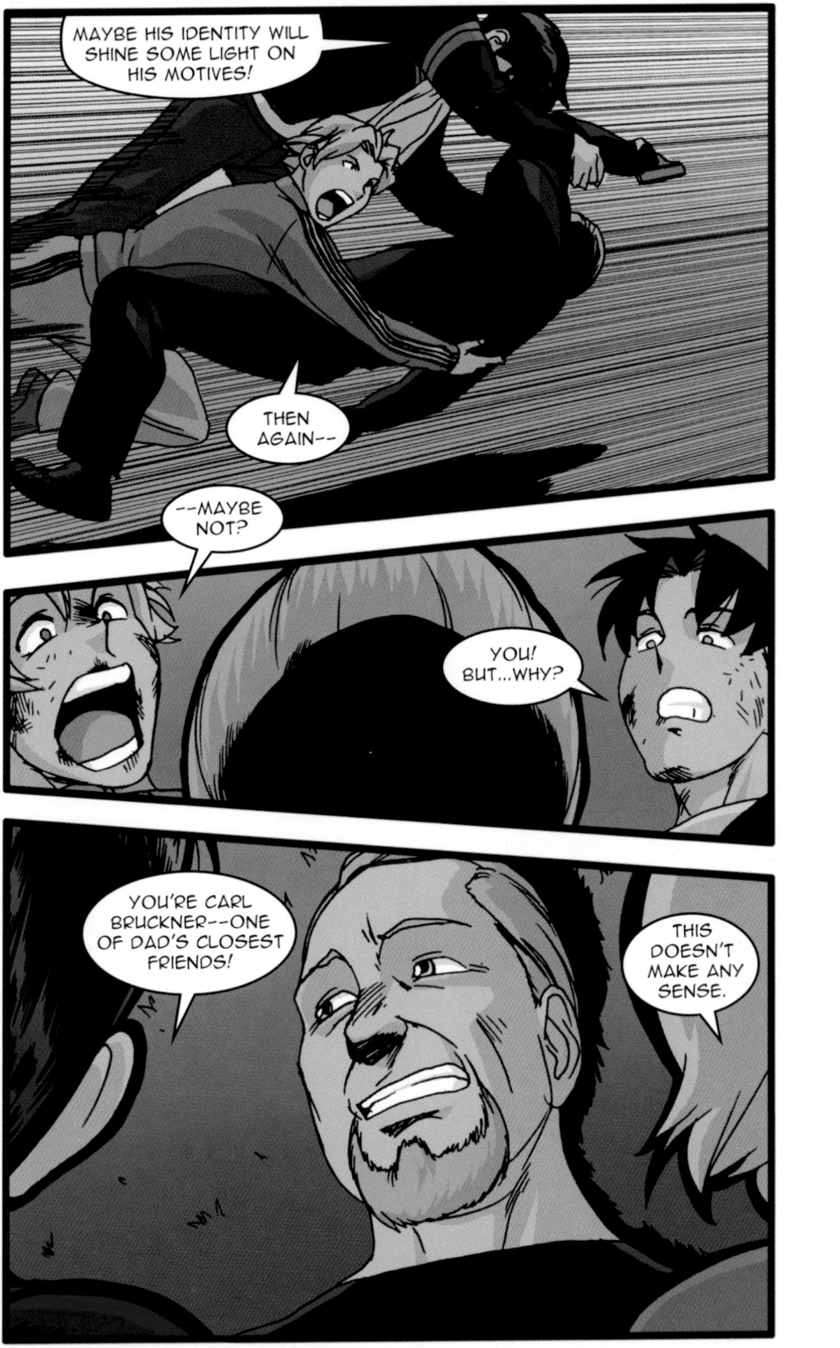
MAYBE HIS IDENTITY WILL SHINE SOME LIGHT ON HIS MOTIVES!
THEN AGAIN--
--MAYBE NOT?
YOU! BUT...WHY?
YOU'RE CARL BRUCKNER--ONE OF DAD'S CLOSEST FRIENDS!
THIS DOESN'T MAKE ANY SENSE.

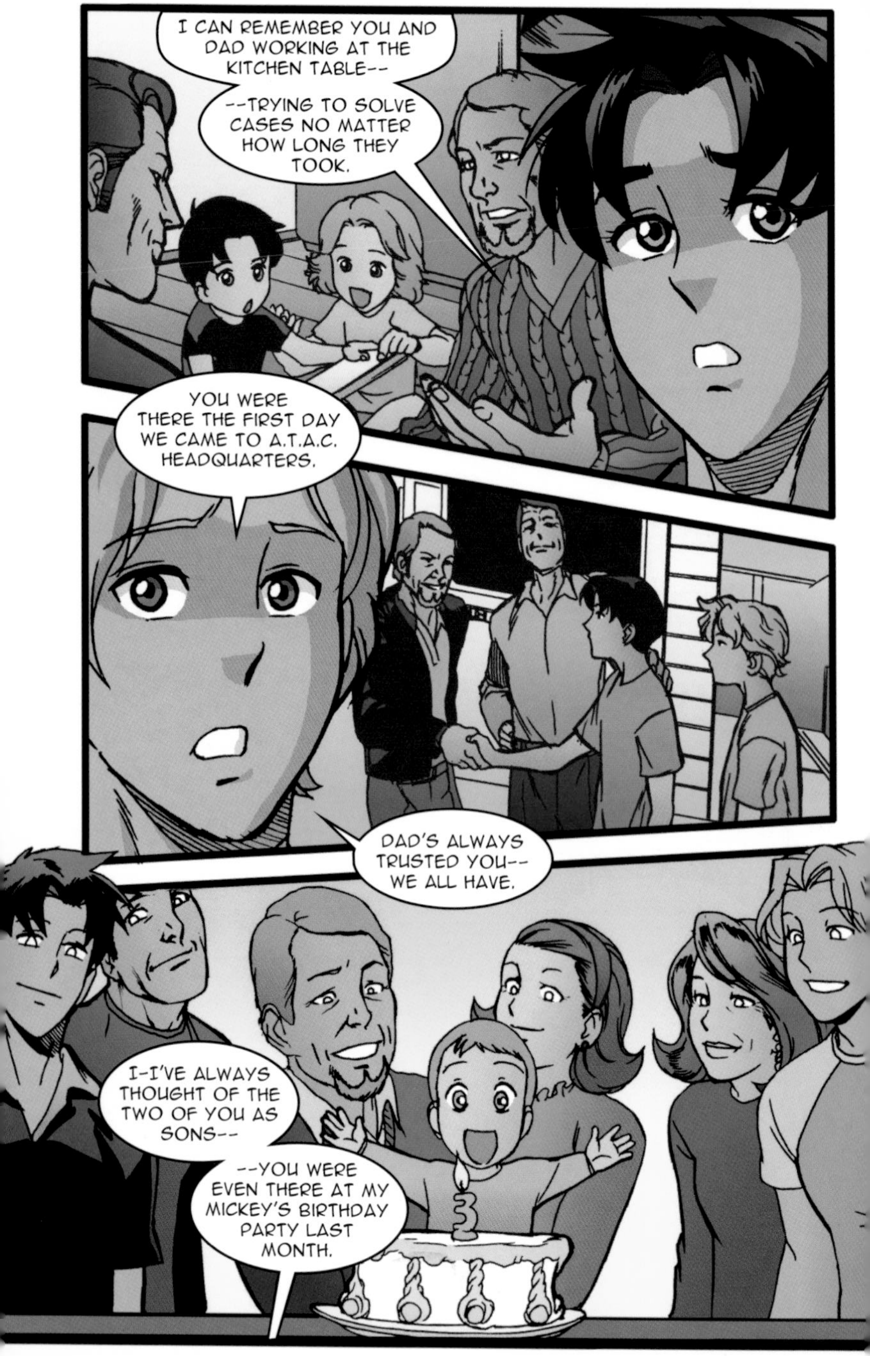
I CAN REMEMBER YOU AND DAD WORKING AT THE KITCHEN TABLE--
--TRYING TO SOLVE CASES NO MATTER HOW LONG THEY TOOK.
YOU WERE THERE THE FIRST DAY WE CAME TO A.T.A.C. HEADQUARTERS.
DAD'S ALWAYS TRUSTED YOU-- WE ALL HAVE.
I-I'VE ALWAYS THOUGHT OF THE TWO OF YOU AS SONS--
--YOU WERE EVEN THERE AT MY MICKEY'S BIRTHDAY PARTY LAST MONTH.

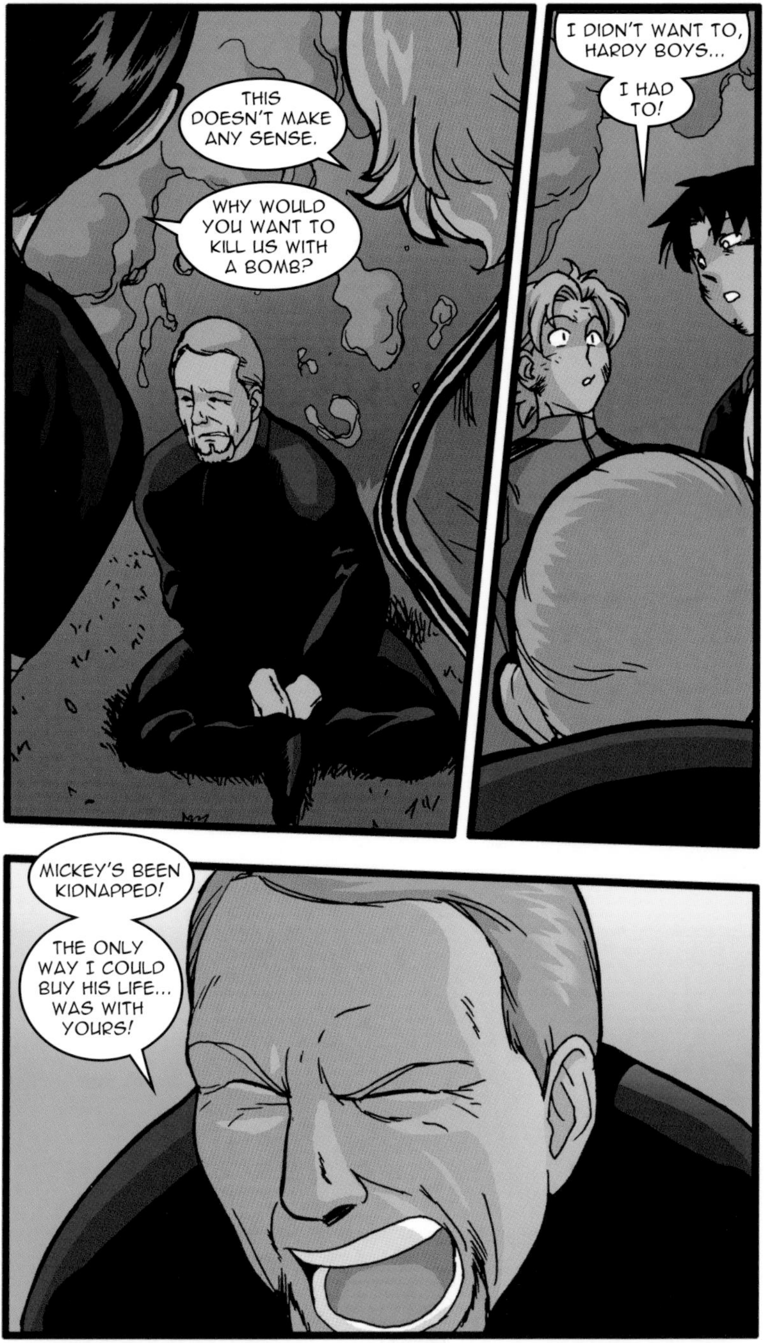
THIS DOESN'T MAKE ANY SENSE.
WHY WOULD YOU WANT TO KILL US WITH A BOMB?
I DIDN'T WANT TO, HARDY BOYS...
I HAD TO!
MICKEY'S BEEN KIDNAPPED!
THE ONLY WAY I COULD BUY HIS LIFE... WAS WITH YOURS!

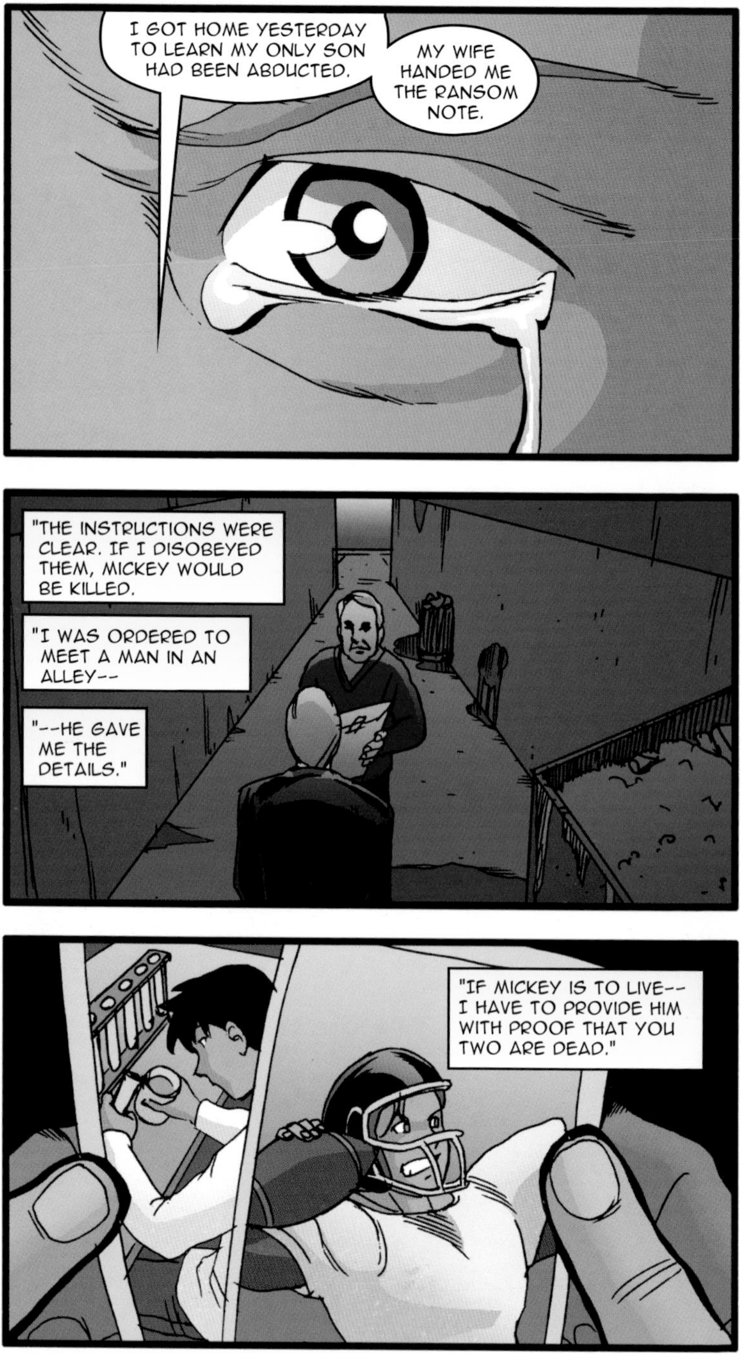
I GOT HOME YESTERDAY TO LEARN MY ONLY SON HAD BEEN ABDUCTED.
MY WIFE HANDED ME THE RANSOM NOTE.
"THE INSTRUCTIONS WERE CLEAR. IF I DISOBEYED THEM, MICKEY WOULD BE KILLED.
"I WAS ORDERED TO MEET A MAN IN AN ALLEY--
"--HE GAVE ME THE DETAILS."
"IF MICKEY IS TO LIVE--I HAVE TO PROVIDE HIM WITH PROOF THAT YOU TWO ARE DEAD."

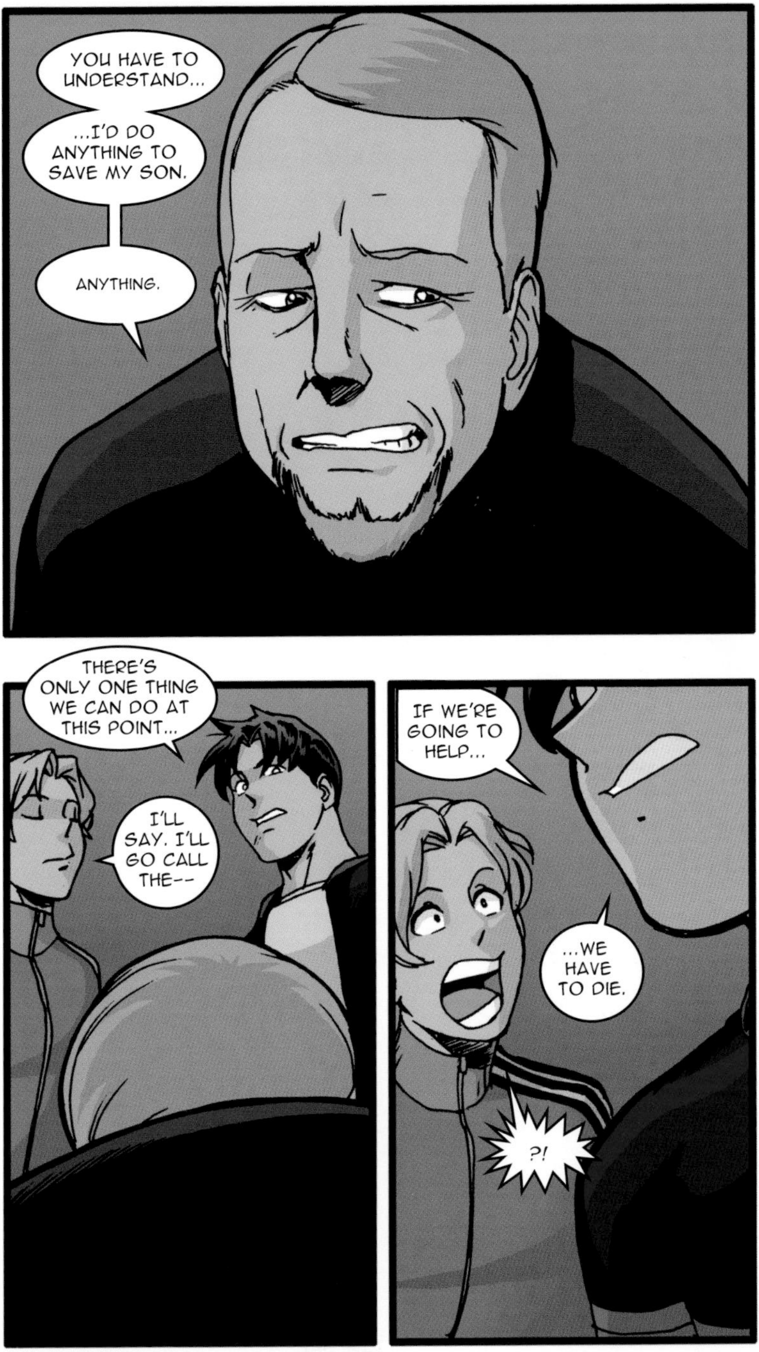
YOU HAVE TO UNDERSTAND...
...I'D DO ANYTHING TO SAVE MY SON.
ANYTHING.
THERE'S ONLY ONE THING WE CAN DO AT THIS POINT...
I'LL SAY. I'LL GO CALL THE--
IF WE'RE GOING TO HELP...
...WE HAVE TO DIE.
?!

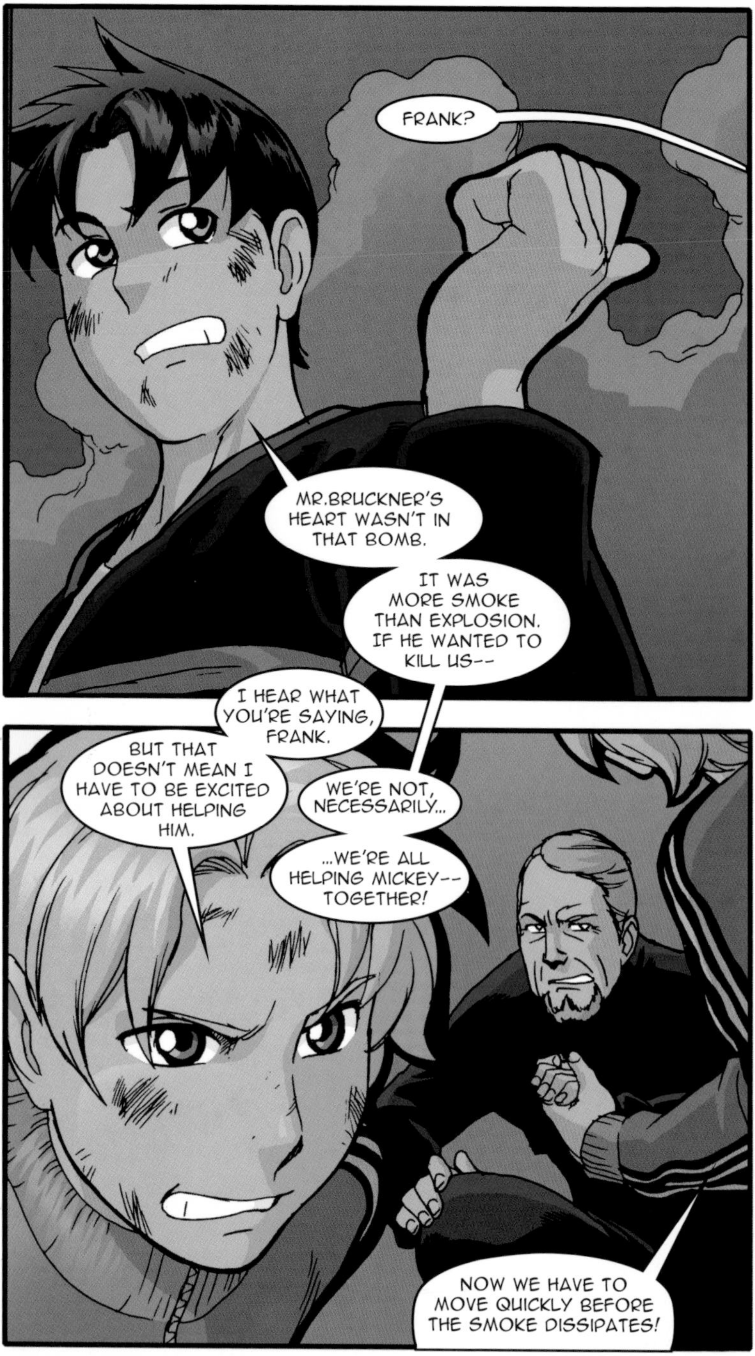
FRANK?
MR.BRUCKNER'S HEART WASN'T IN THAT BOMB.
IT WAS MORE SMOKE THAN EXPLOSION. IF HE WANTED TO KILL US--
I HEAR WHAT YOU'RE SAYING, FRANK.
BUT THAT DOESN'T MEAN I HAVE TO BE EXCITED ABOUT HELPING HIM.
WE'RE NOT, NECESSARILY...
...WE'RE ALL HELPING MICKEY-- TOGETHER!
NOW WE HAVE TO MOVE QUICKLY BEFORE THE SMOKE DISSIPATES!

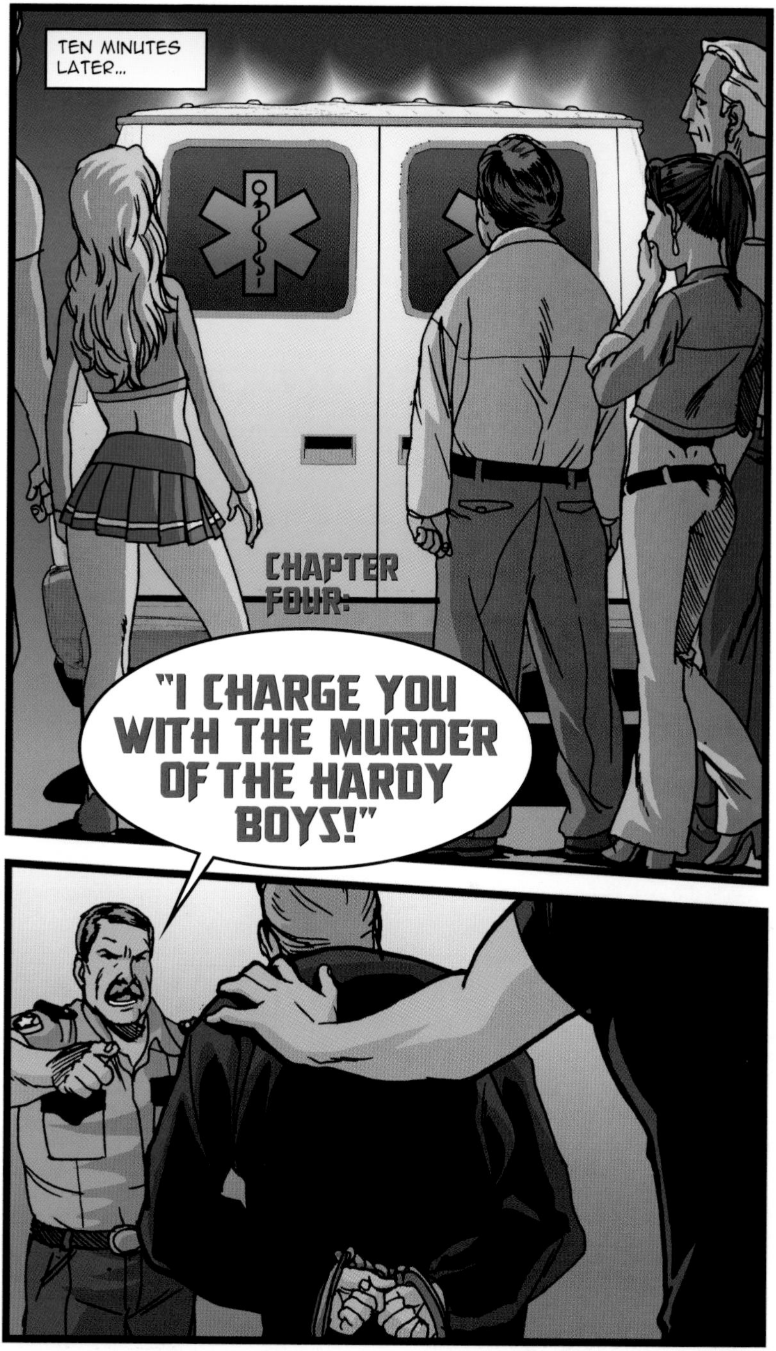
TEN MINUTES LATER...
CHAPTER FOUR:
"I CHARGE YOU WITH THE MURDER OF THE HARDY BOYS!"

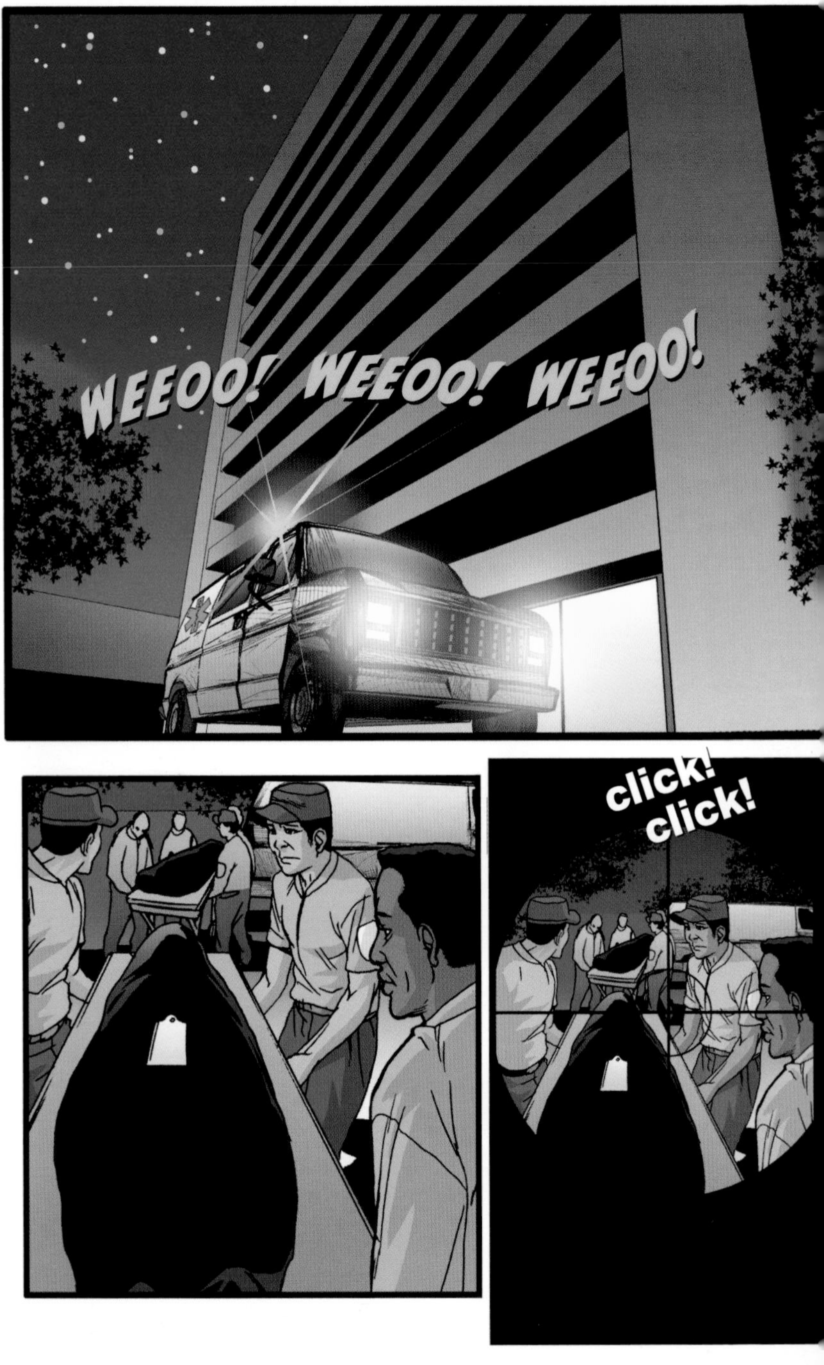
WEEOO! WEEOO! WEEOO!
click!
click!

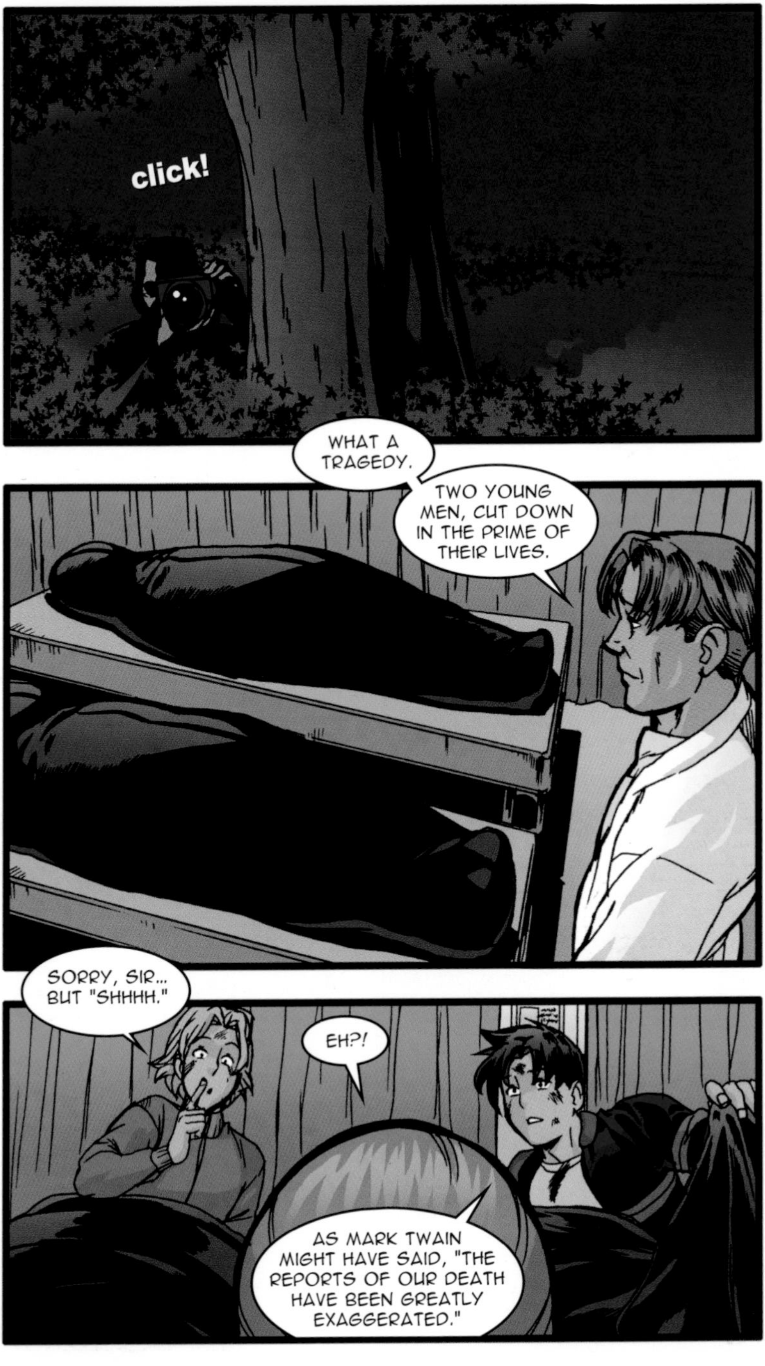
click!
WHAT A TRAGEDY.
TWO YOUNG MEN, CUT DOWN IN THE PRIME OF THEIR LIVES.
SORRY, SIR... BUT "SHHHH."
EH?!
AS MARK TWAIN MIGHT HAVE SAID, "THE REPORTS OF OUR DEATH HAVE BEEN GREATLY EXAGGERATED."

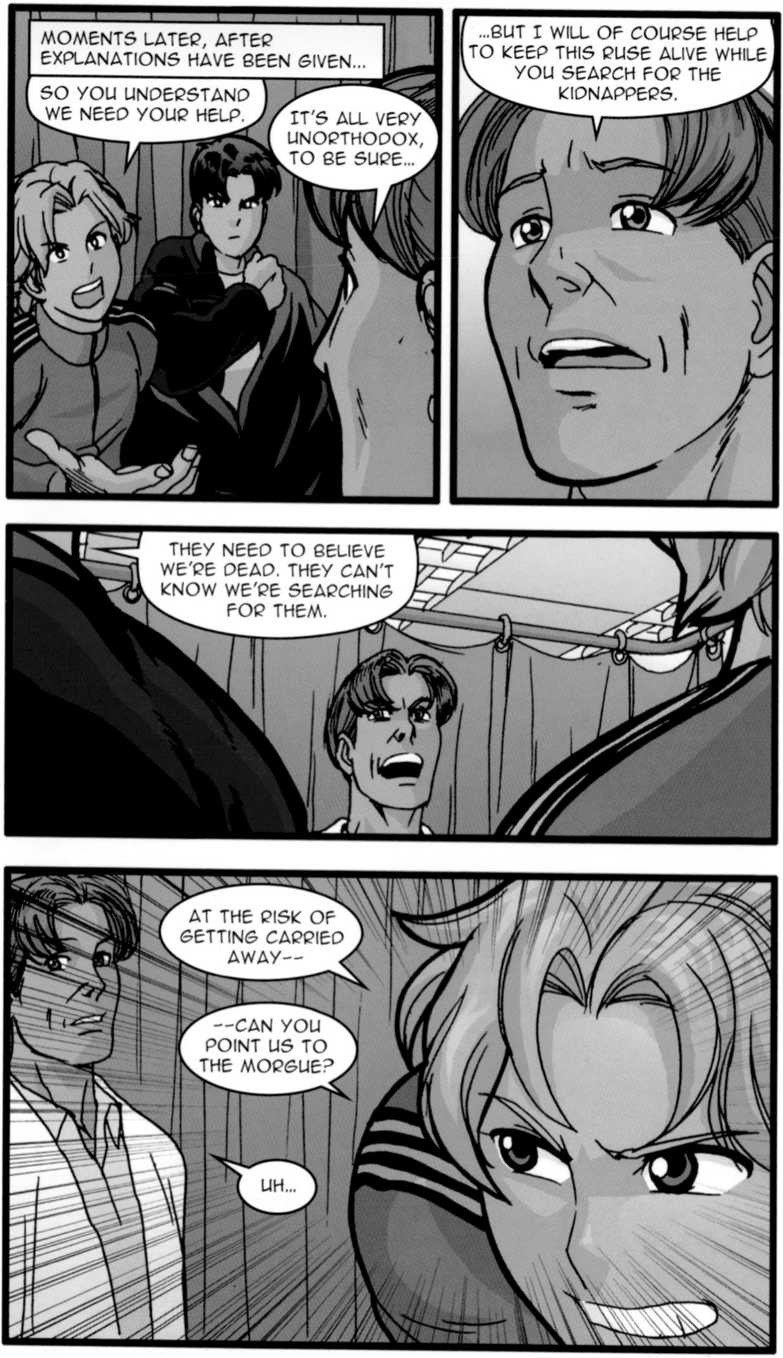
MOMENTS LATER, AFTER EXPLANATIONS HAVE BEEN GIVEN...
SO YOU UNDERSTAND WE NEED YOUR HELP.
IT'S ALL VERY UNORTHODOX, TO BE SURE...
...BUT I WILL OF COURSE HELP TO KEEP THIS RUSE ALIVE WHILE YOU SEARCH FOR THE KIDNAPPERS.
THEY NEED TO BELIEVE WE'RE DEAD. THEY CAN'T KNOW WE'RE SEARCHING FOR THEM.
AT THE RISK OF GETTING CARRIED AWAY--
--CAN YOU POINT US TO THE MORGUE?
UH...

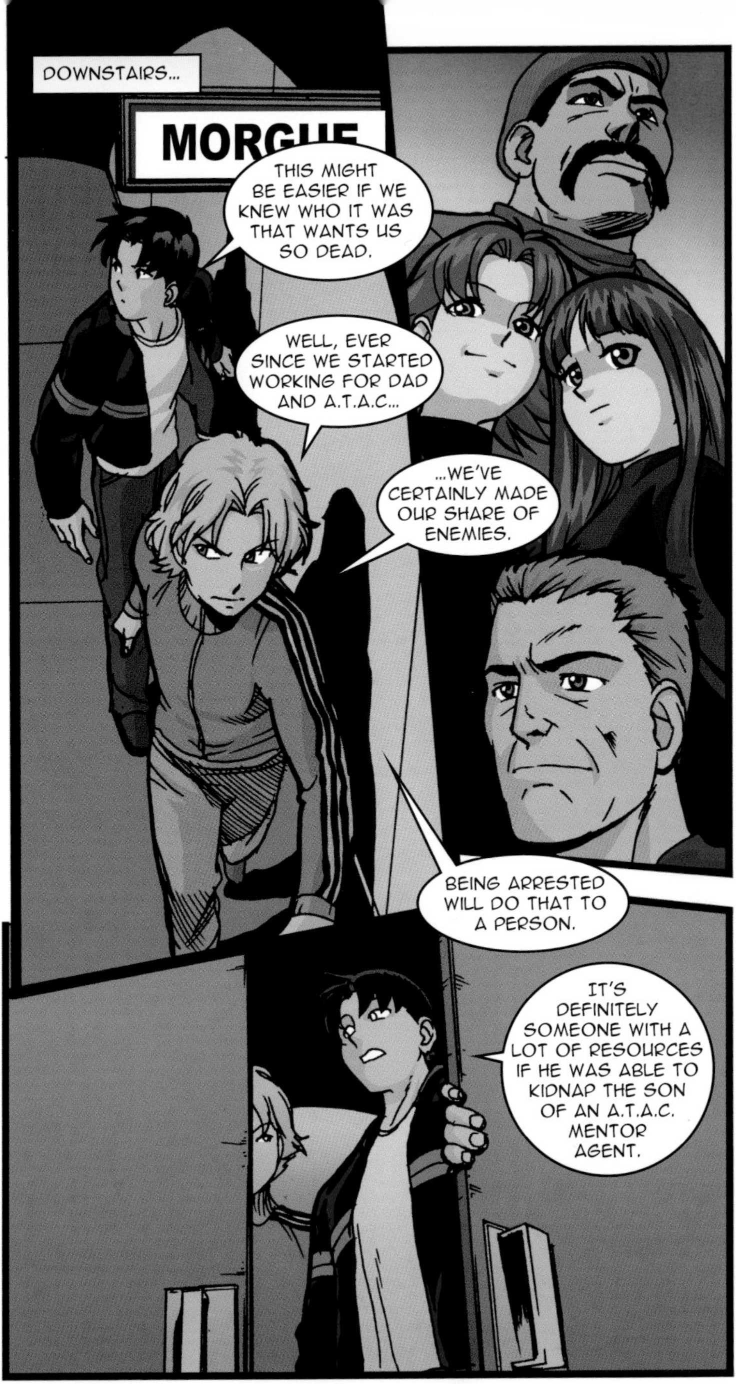
DOWNSTAIRS...
MORGUE
THIS MIGHT BE EASIER IF WE KNEW WHO IT WAS THAT WANTS US SO DEAD.
WELL, EVER SINCE WE STARTED WORKING FOR DAD AND A.T.A.C...
...WE'VE CERTAINLY MADE OUR SHARE OF ENEMIES.
BEING ARRESTED WILL DO THAT TO A PERSON.
IT'S DEFINITELY SOMEONE WITH A LOT OF RESOURCES IF HE WAS ABLE TO KIDNAP THE SON OF AN A.T.A.C. MENTOR AGENT.

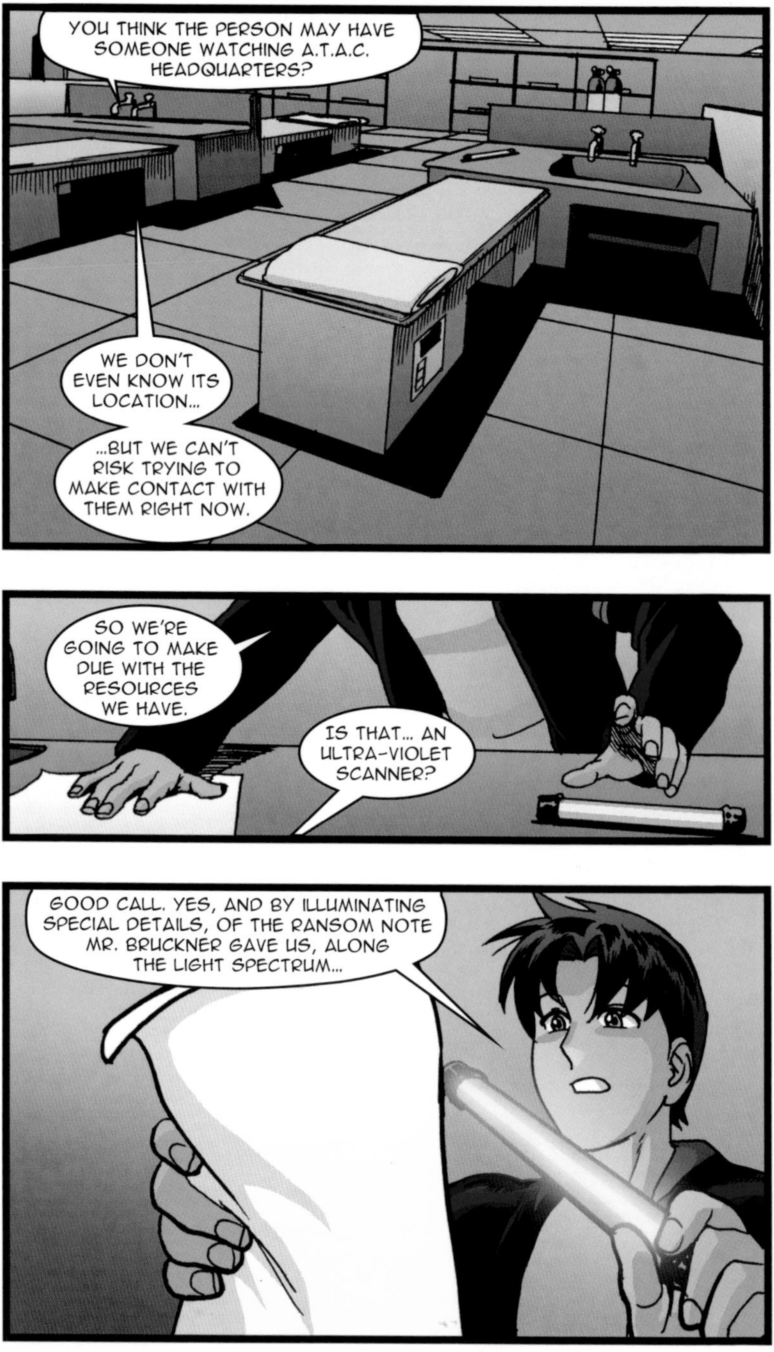
YOU THINK THE PERSON MAY HAVE SOMEONE WATCHING A.T.A.C. HEADQUARTERS?
WE DON'T EVEN KNOW ITS LOCATION...
...BUT WE CAN'T RISK TRYING TO MAKE CONTACT WITH THEM RIGHT NOW.
SO WE'RE GOING TO MAKE DUE WITH THE RESOURCES WE HAVE.
IS THAT... AN ULTRA-VIOLET SCANNER?
GOOD CALL. YES, AND BY ILLUMINATING SPECIAL DETAILS, OF THE RANSOM NOTE MR. BRUCKNER GAVE US, ALONG THE LIGHT SPECTRUM...

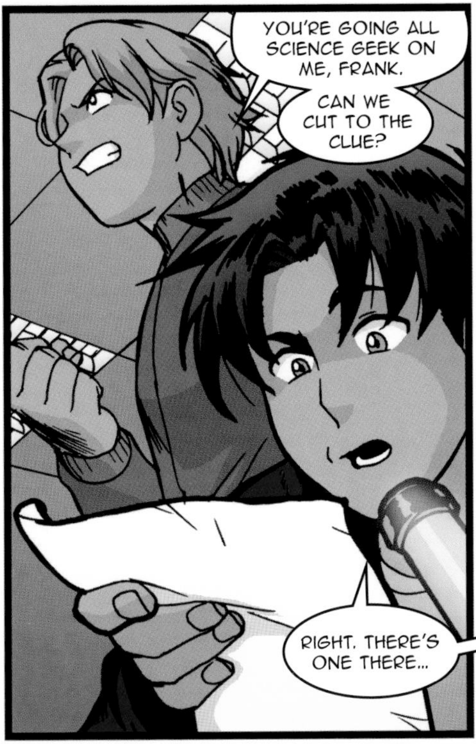
YOU'RE GOING ALL SCIENCE GEEK ON ME, FRANK.
CAN WE CUT TO THE CLUE?
RIGHT. THERE'S ONE THERE...

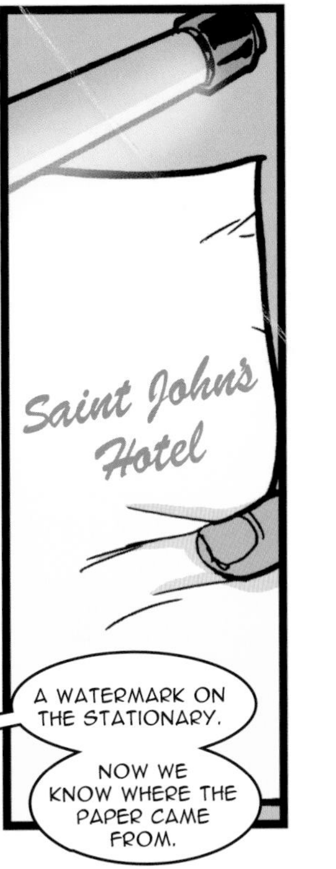
Saint Johns Hotel
A WATERMARK ON THE STATIONARY.
NOW WE KNOW WHERE THE PAPER CAME FROM.

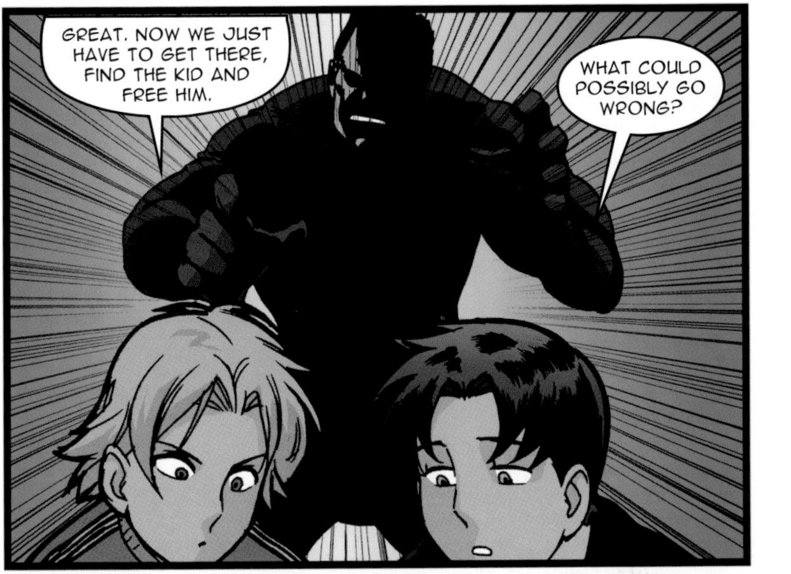
GREAT. NOW WE JUST HAVE TO GET THERE, FIND THE KID AND FREE HIM.
WHAT COULD POSSIBLY GO WRONG?

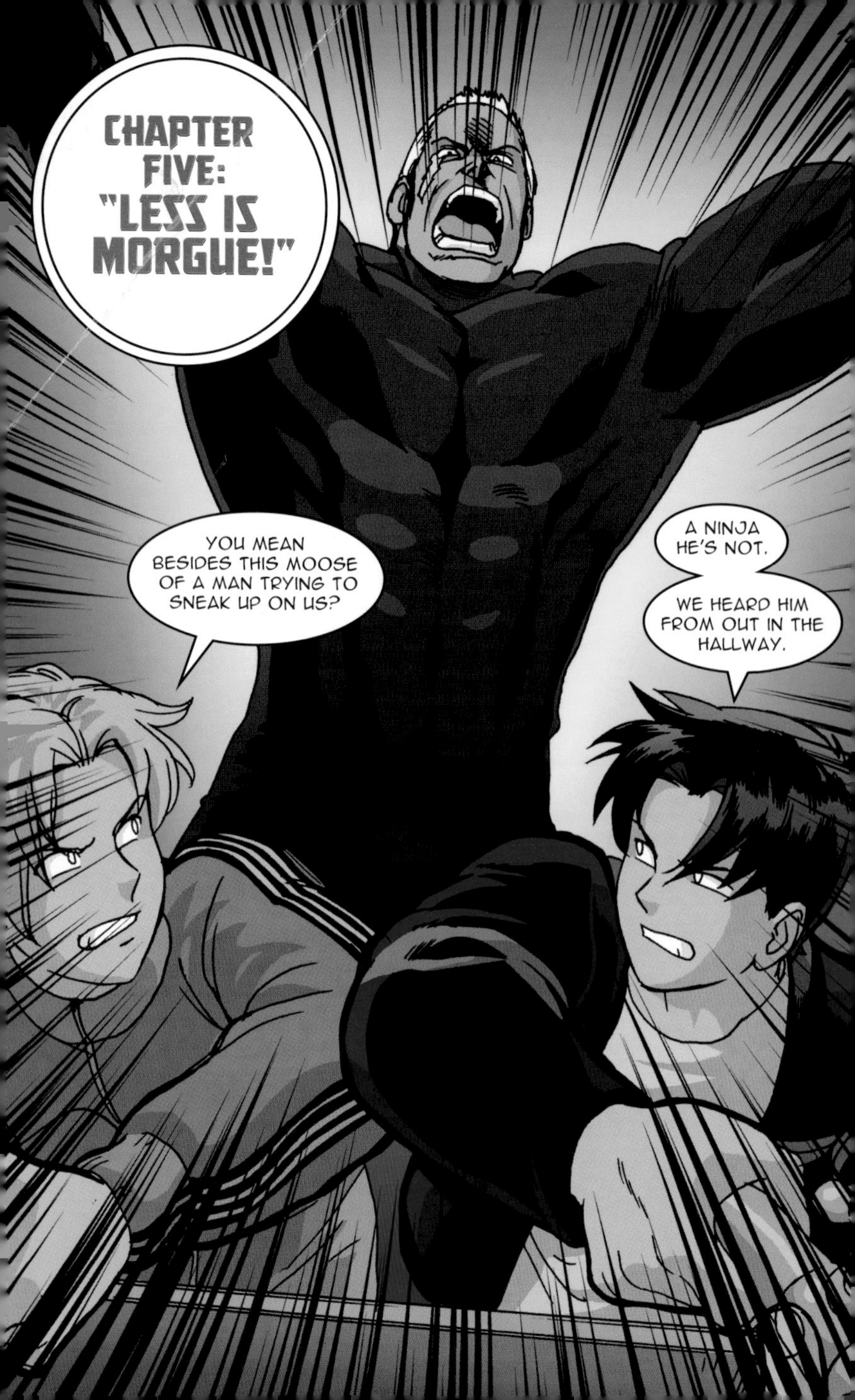
CHAPTER FIVE: "LESS IS MORGUE!"
YOU MEAN BESIDES THIS MOOSE OF A MAN TRYING TO SNEAK UP ON US?
A NINJA HE'S NOT.
WE HEARD HIM FROM OUT IN THE HALLWAY.

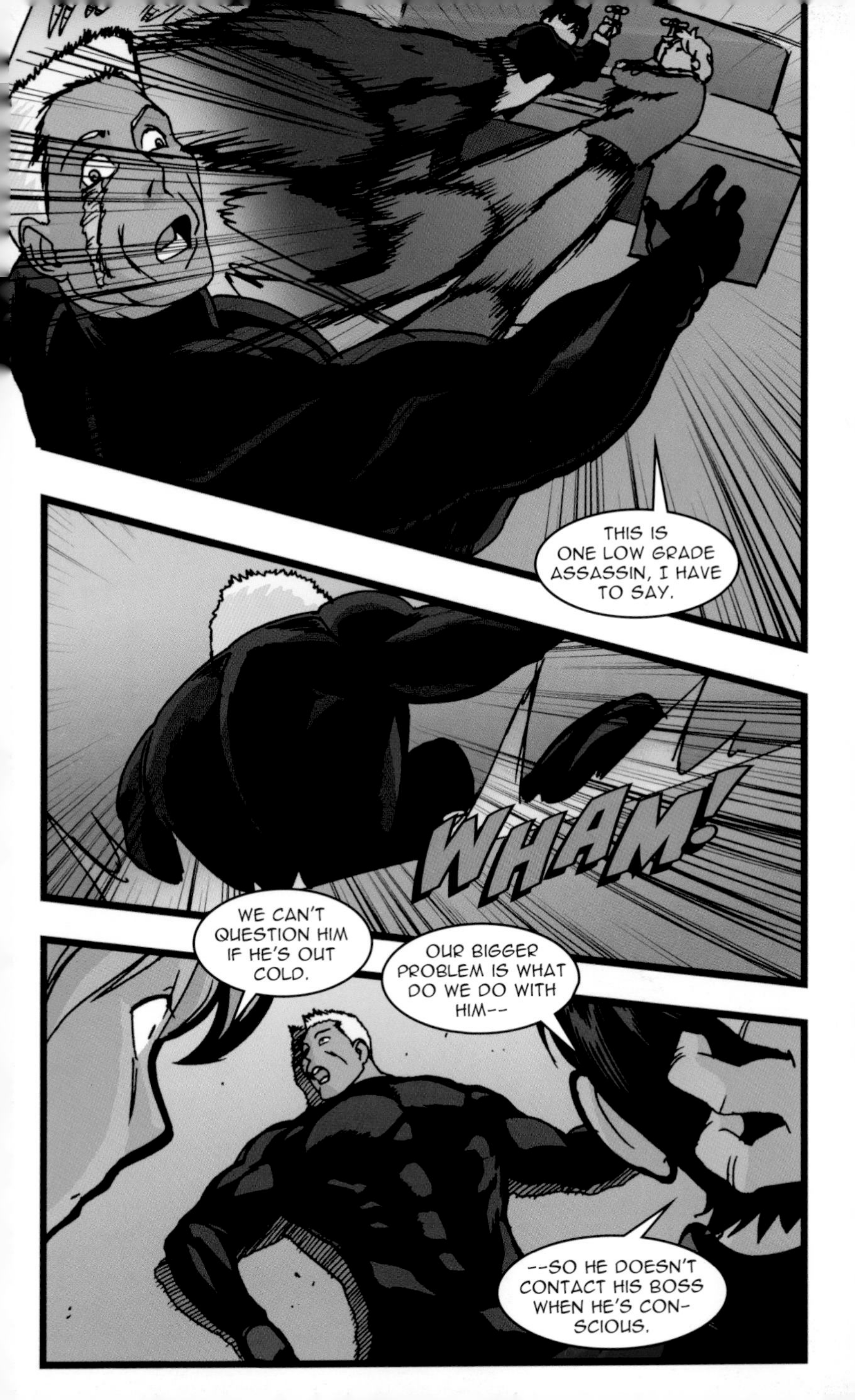
THIS IS ONE LOW GRADE ASSASSIN, I HAVE TO SAY.
WHAM!
WE CAN'T QUESTION HIM IF HE'S OUT COLD.
OUR BIGGER PROBLEM IS WHAT DO WE DO WITH HIM--
--SO HE DOESN'T CONTACT HIS BOSS WHEN HE'S CON-SCIOUS.

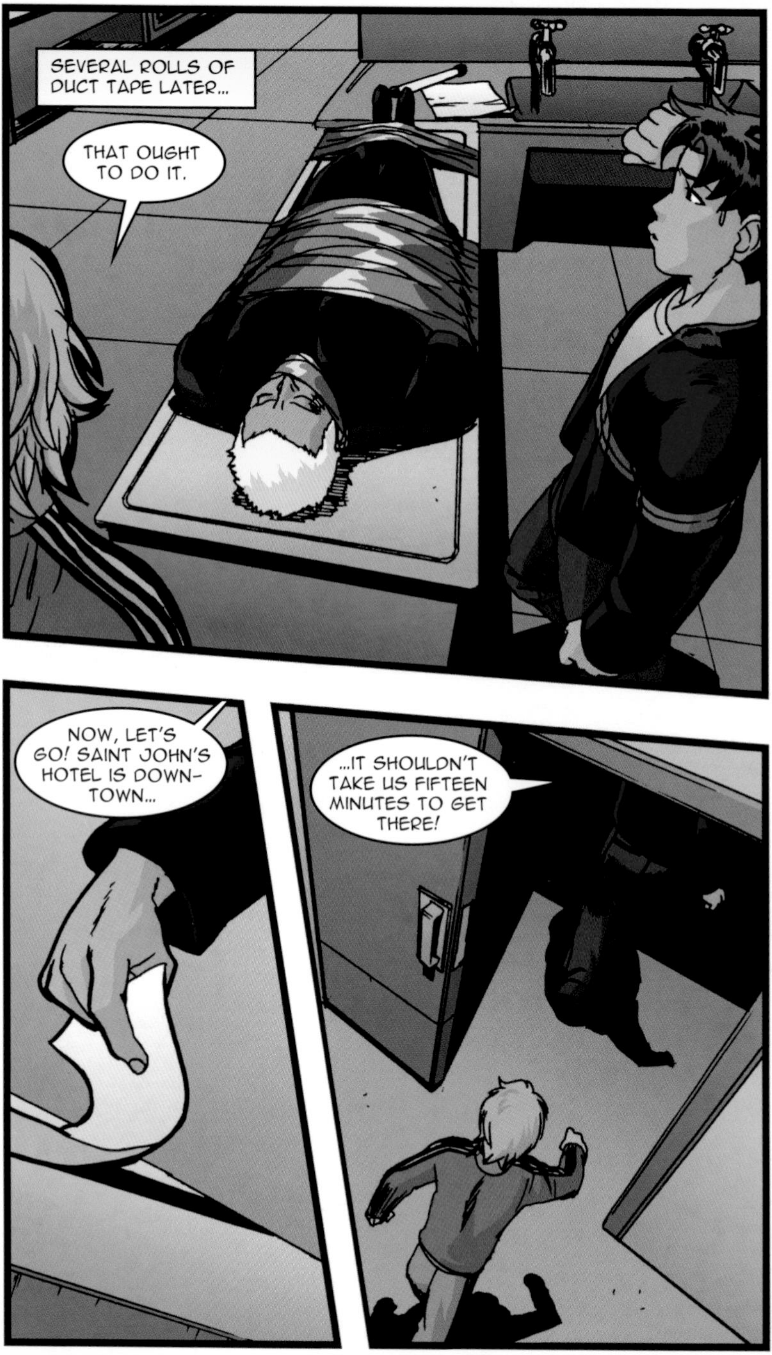
SEVERAL ROLLS OF DUCT TAPE LATER...
THAT OUGHT TO DO IT.
NOW, LET'S GO! SAINT JOHN'S HOTEL IS DOWN-TOWN...
...IT SHOULDN'T TAKE US FIFTEEN MINUTES TO GET THERE!

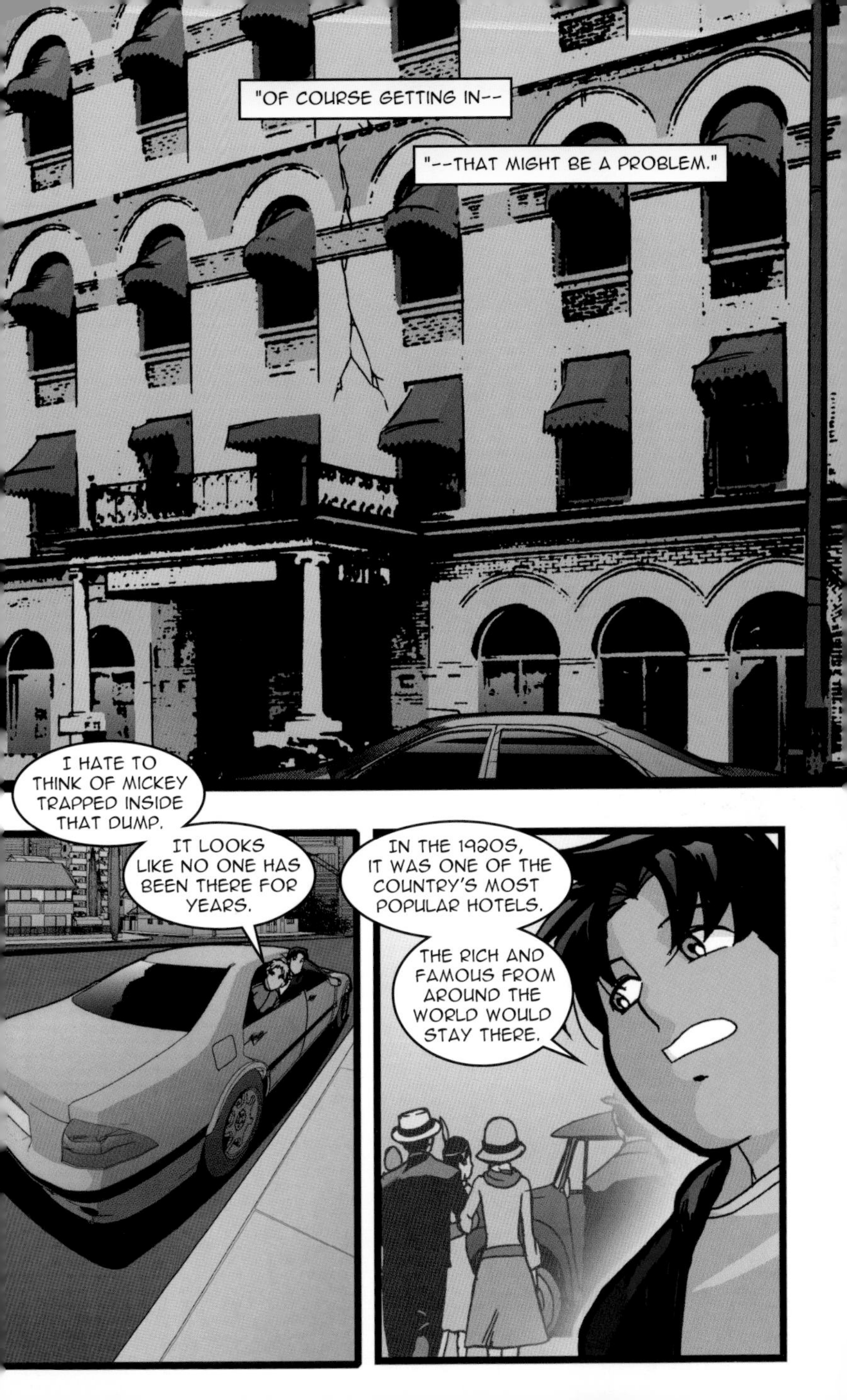
"OF COURSE GETTING IN--
"--THAT MIGHT BE A PROBLEM."
I HATE TO THINK OF MICKEY TRAPPED INSIDE THAT DUMP.
IT LOOKS LIKE NO ONE HAS BEEN THERE FOR YEARS.
IN THE 1920S, IT WAS ONE OF THE COUNTRY'S MOST POPULAR HOTELS.
THE RICH AND FAMOUS FROM AROUND THE WORLD WOULD STAY THERE.

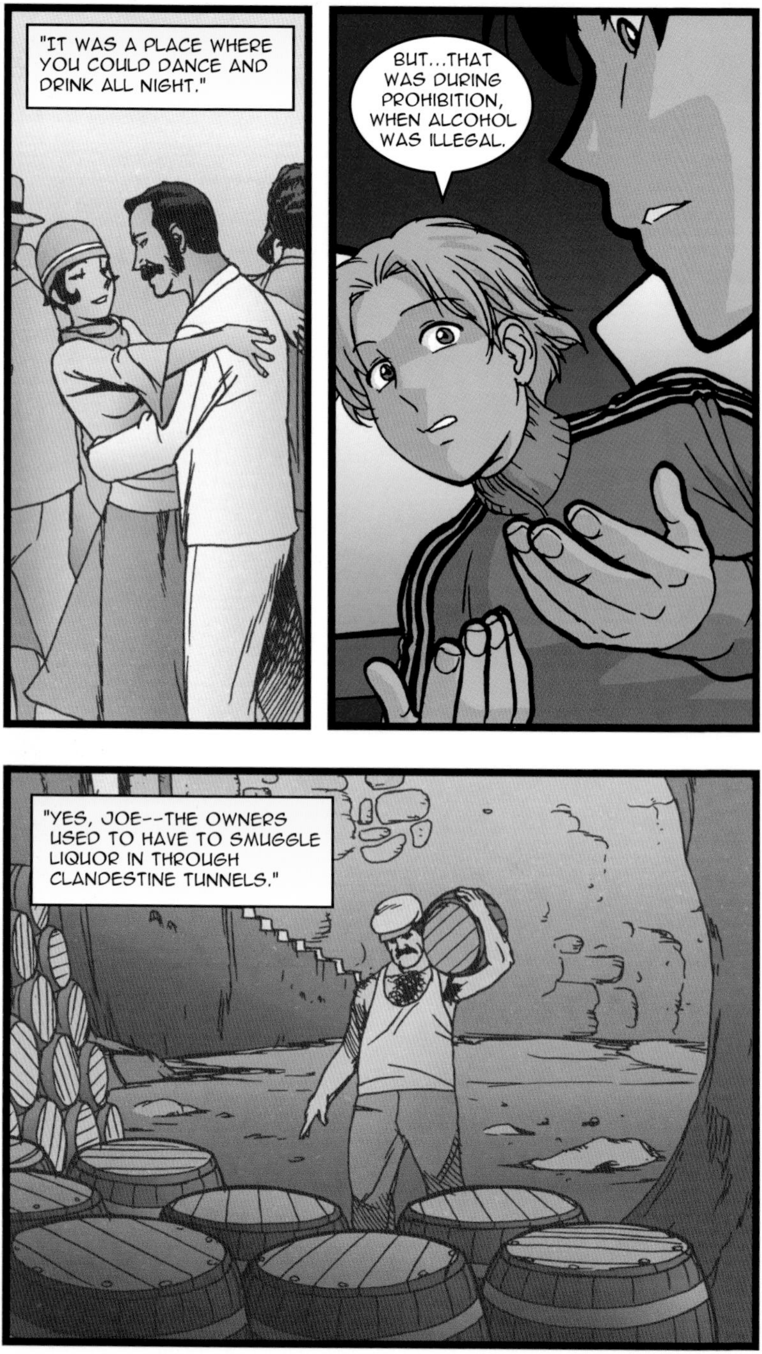
"IT WAS A PLACE WHERE YOU COULD DANCE AND DRINK ALL NIGHT."
BUT...THAT WAS DURING PROHIBITION, WHEN ALCOHOL WAS ILLEGAL.
"YES, JOE--THE OWNERS USED TO HAVE TO SMUGGLE LIQUOR IN THROUGH CLANDESTINE TUNNELS."

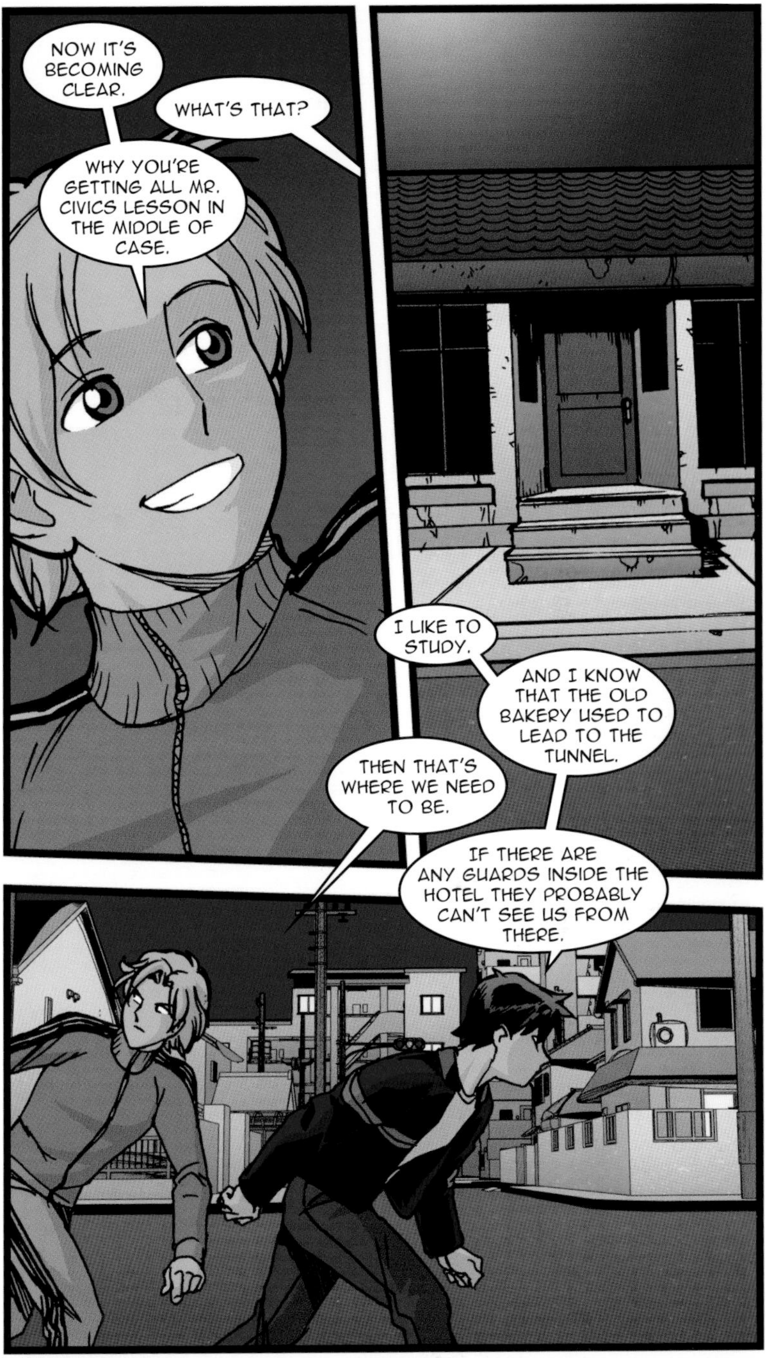
NOW IT'S BECOMING CLEAR.
WHAT'S THAT?
WHY YOU'RE GETTING ALL MR. CIVICS LESSON IN THE MIDDLE OF CASE.
I LIKE TO STUDY.
AND I KNOW THAT THE OLD BAKERY USED TO LEAD TO THE TUNNEL.
THEN THAT'S WHERE WE NEED TO BE.
IF THERE ARE ANY GUARDS INSIDE THE HOTEL THEY PROBABLY CAN'T SEE US FROM THERE.

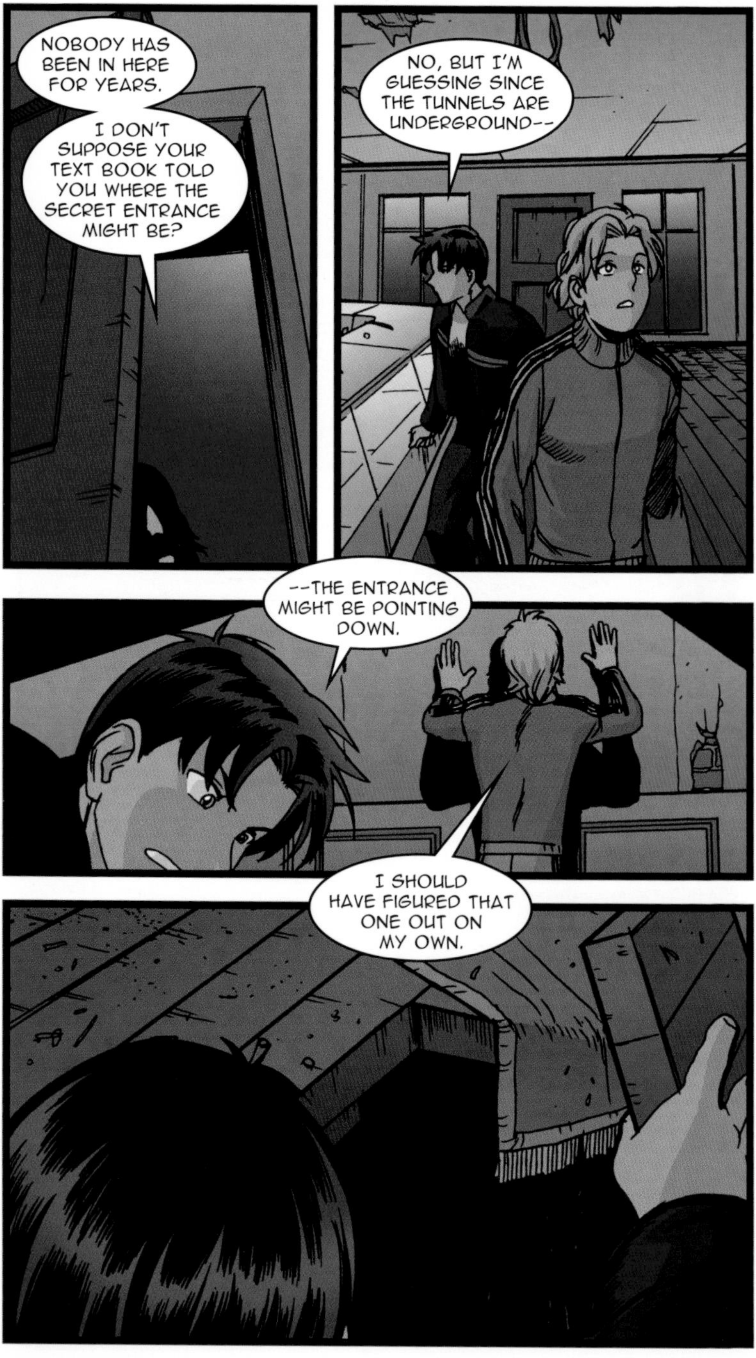
NOBODY HAS BEEN IN HERE FOR YEARS.
I DON'T SUPPOSE YOUR TEXT BOOK TOLD YOU WHERE THE SECRET ENTRANCE MIGHT BE?
NO, BUT I'M GUESSING SINCE THE TUNNELS ARE UNDERGROUND--
--THE ENTRANCE MIGHT BE POINTING DOWN.
I SHOULD HAVE FIGURED THAT ONE OUT ON MY OWN.

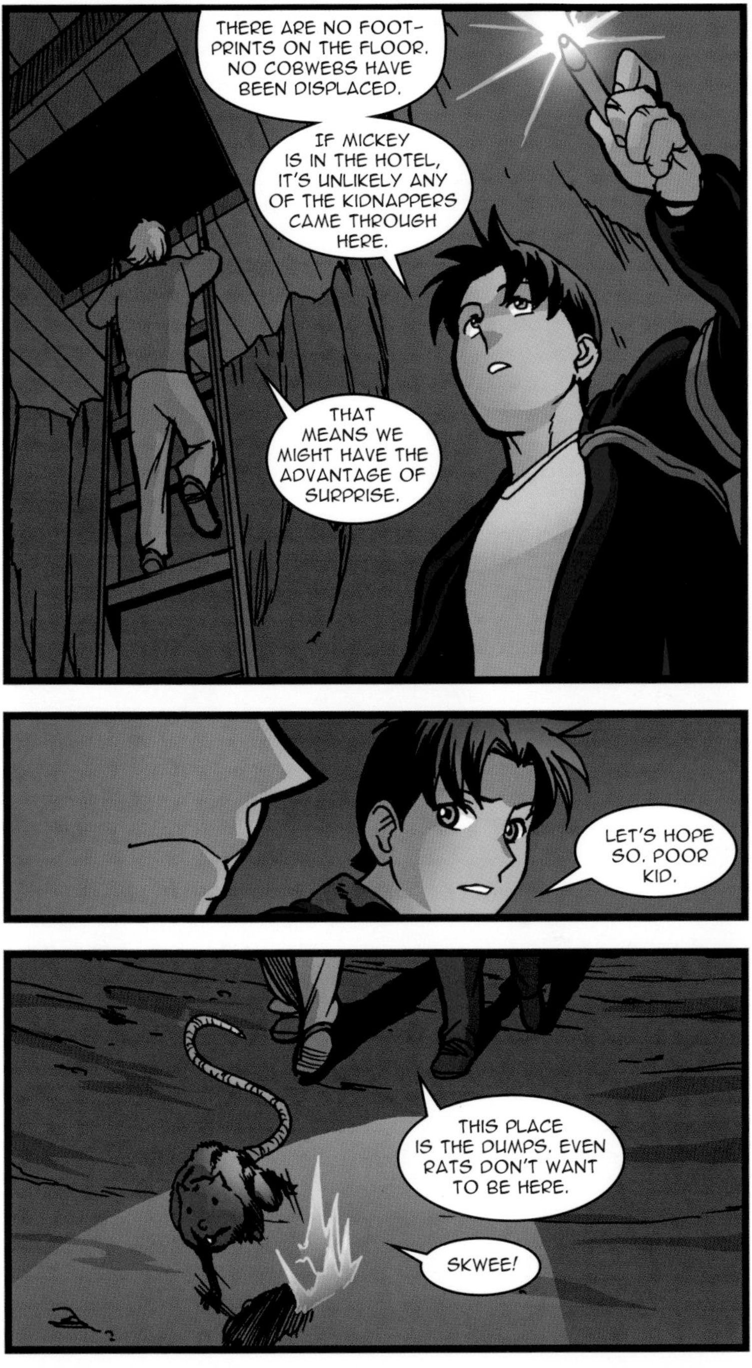
THERE ARE NO FOOT-PRINTS ON THE FLOOR. NO COBWEBS HAVE BEEN DISPLACED.
IF MICKEY IS IN THE HOTEL, IT'S UNLIKELY ANY OF THE KIDNAPPERS CAME THROUGH HERE.
THAT MEANS WE MIGHT HAVE THE ADVANTAGE OF SURPRISE.
LET'S HOPE SO. POOR KID.
THIS PLACE IS THE DUMPS. EVEN RATS DON'T WANT TO BE HERE.
SKWEE!

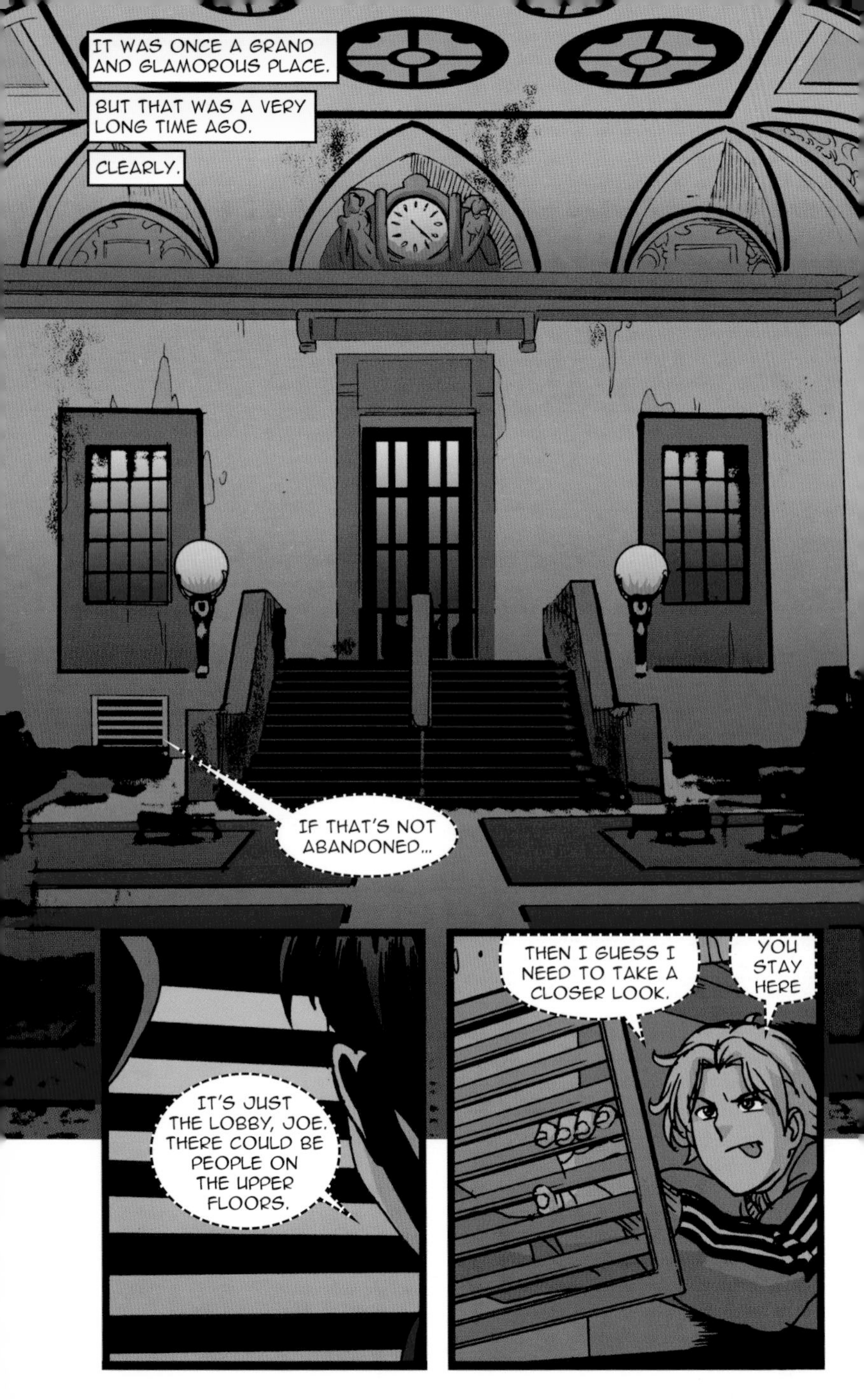
IT WAS ONCE A GRAND AND GLAMOROUS PLACE.
BUT THAT WAS A VERY LONG TIME AGO.
CLEARLY.
IF THAT'S NOT ABANDONED...
IT'S JUST THE LOBBY, JOE. THERE COULD BE PEOPLE ON THE UPPER FLOORS.
THEN I GUESS I NEED TO TAKE A CLOSER LOOK.
YOU STAY HERE

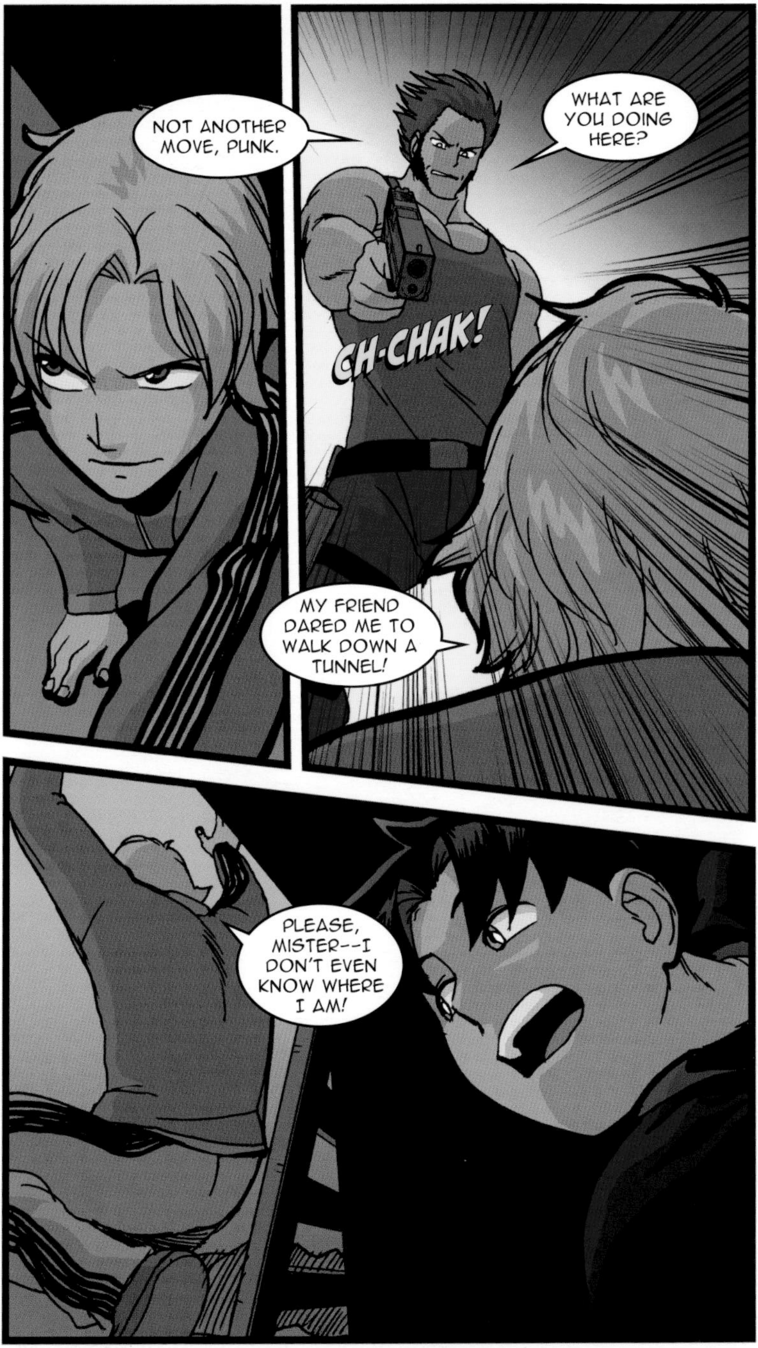
NOT ANOTHER MOVE, PUNK.
WHAT ARE YOU DOING HERE?
CH-CHAK!
MY FRIEND DARED ME TO WALK DOWN A TUNNEL!
PLEASE, MISTER--I DON'T EVEN KNOW WHERE I AM!

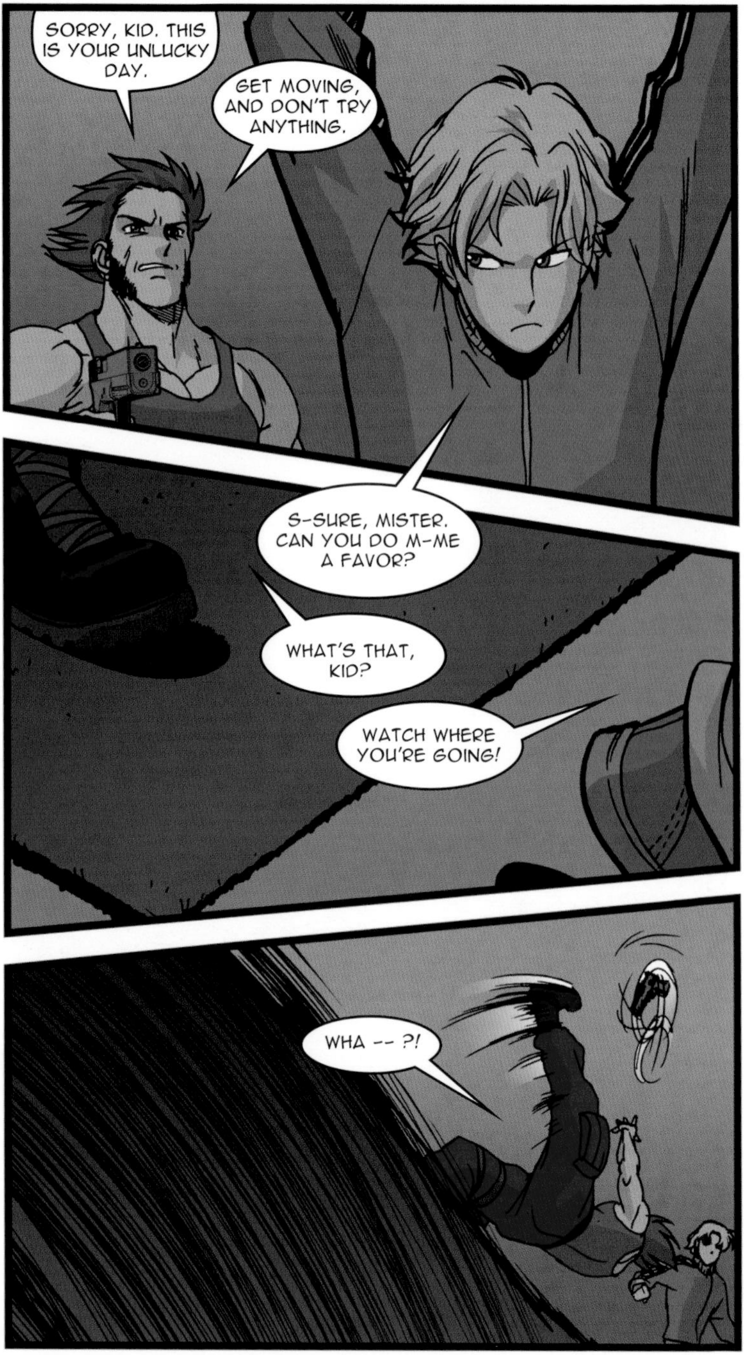
SORRY, KID. THIS IS YOUR UNLUCKY DAY.
GET MOVING, AND DON'T TRY ANYTHING.
S-SURE, MISTER. CAN YOU DO M-ME A FAVOR?
WHAT'S THAT, KID?
WATCH WHERE YOU'RE GOING!
WHA -- ?!

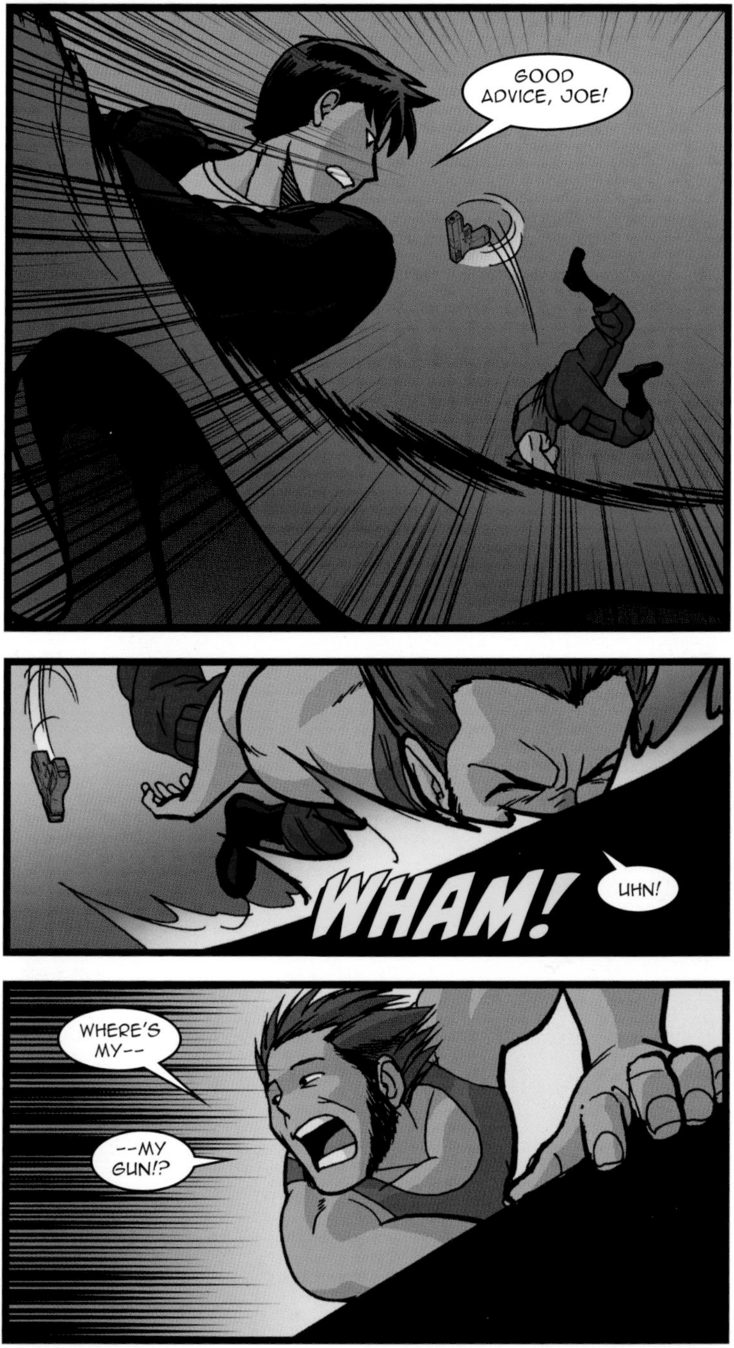
GOOD ADVICE, JOE!
WHAM!
UHN!
WHERE'S MY--
--MY GUN!?

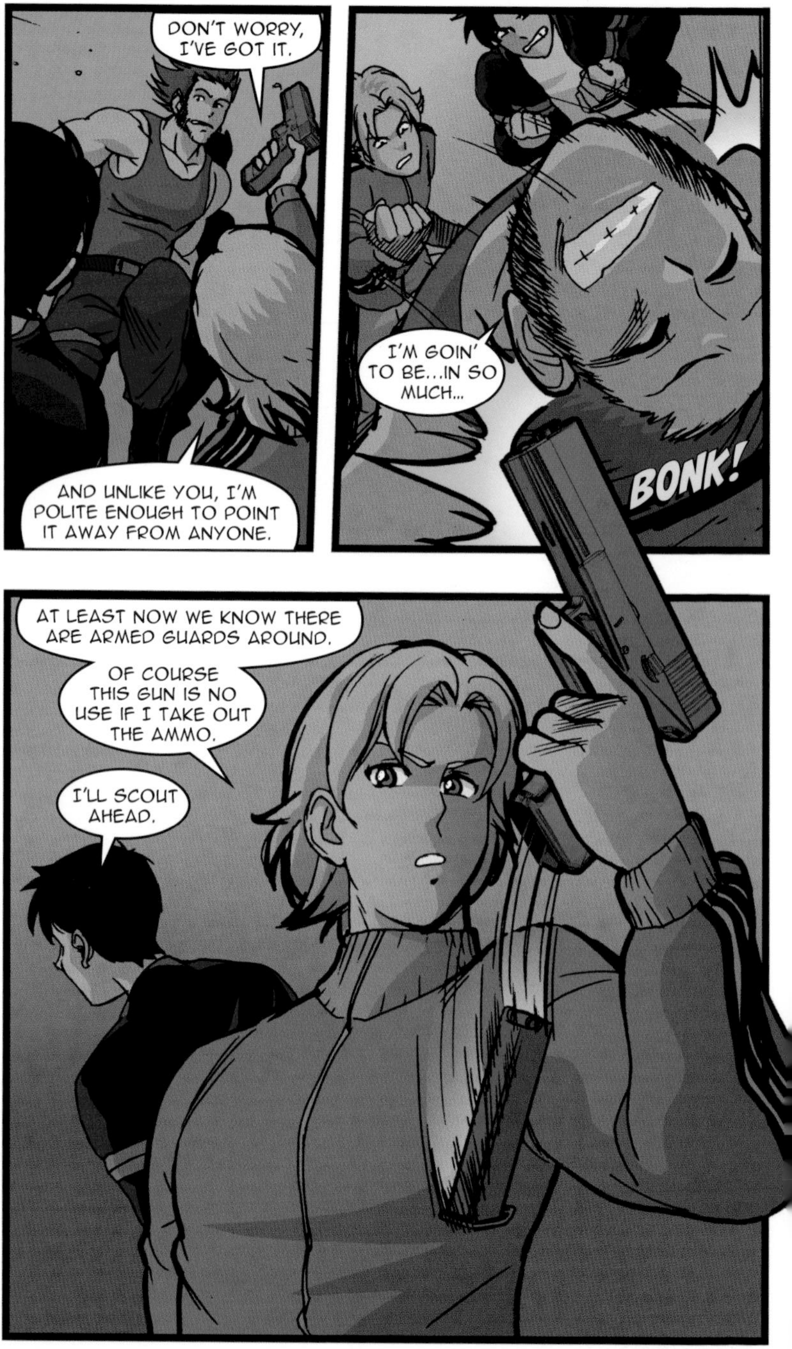
DON'T WORRY, I'VE GOT IT.
AND UNLIKE YOU, I'M POLITE ENOUGH TO POINT IT AWAY FROM ANYONE.
I'M GOIN' TO BE...IN SO MUCH...
BONK!
AT LEAST NOW WE KNOW THERE ARE ARMED GUARDS AROUND.
OF COURSE THIS GUN IS NO USE IF I TAKE OUT THE AMMO.
I'LL SCOUT AHEAD.

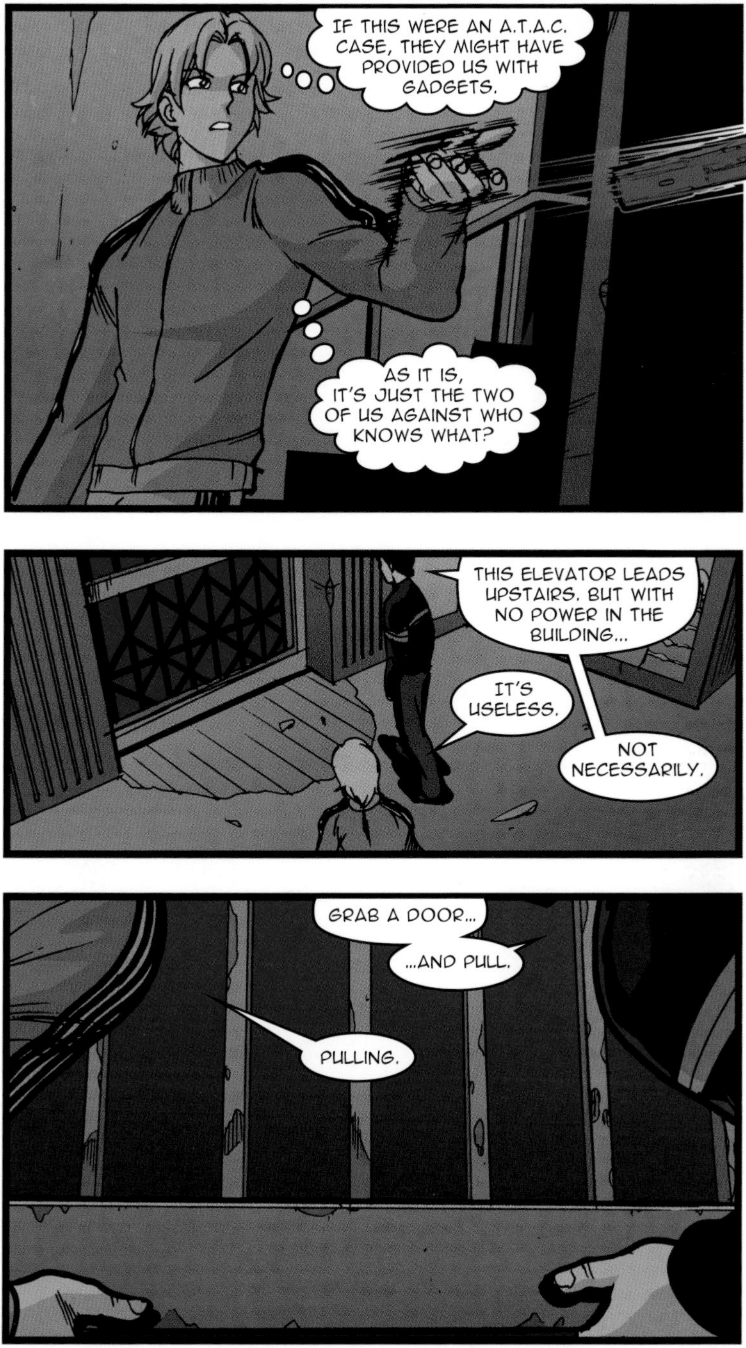
IF THIS WERE AN A.T.A.C. CASE, THEY MIGHT HAVE PROVIDED US WITH GADGETS.
AS IT IS, IT'S JUST THE TWO OF US AGAINST WHO KNOWS WHAT?
THIS ELEVATOR LEADS UPSTAIRS. BUT WITH NO POWER IN THE BUILDING...
IT'S USELESS.
NOT NECESSARILY.
GRAB A DOOR...
...AND PULL.
PULLING.

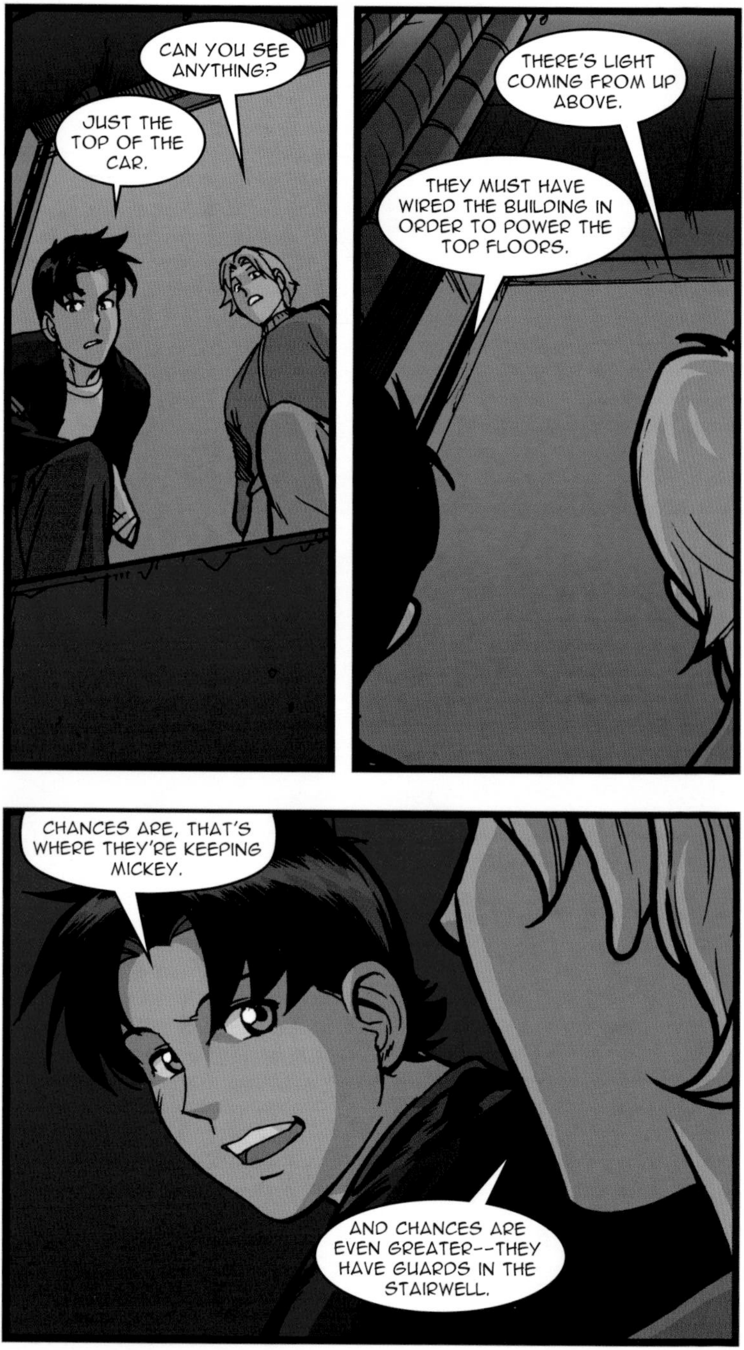
CAN YOU SEE ANYTHING?
JUST THE TOP OF THE CAR.
THERE'S LIGHT COMING FROM UP ABOVE.
THEY MUST HAVE WIRED THE BUILDING IN ORDER TO POWER THE TOP FLOORS.
CHANCES ARE, THAT'S WHERE THEY'RE KEEPING MICKEY.
AND CHANCES ARE EVEN GREATER--THEY HAVE GUARDS IN THE STAIRWELL.

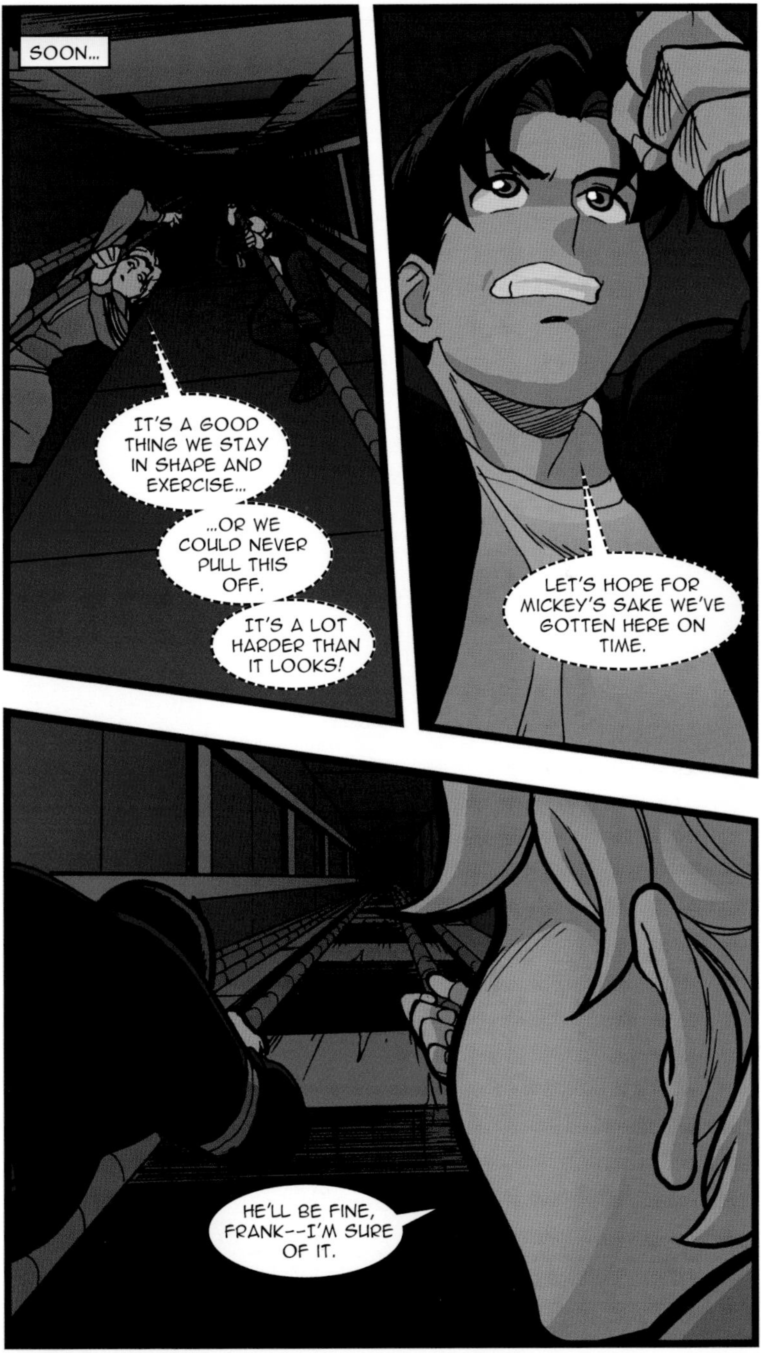
SOON...
IT'S A GOOD THING WE STAY IN SHAPE AND EXERCISE...
...OR WE COULD NEVER PULL THIS OFF.
IT'S A LOT HARDER THAN IT LOOKS!
LET'S HOPE FOR MICKEY'S SAKE WE'VE GOTTEN HERE ON TIME.
HE'LL BE FINE, FRANK--I'M SURE OF IT.

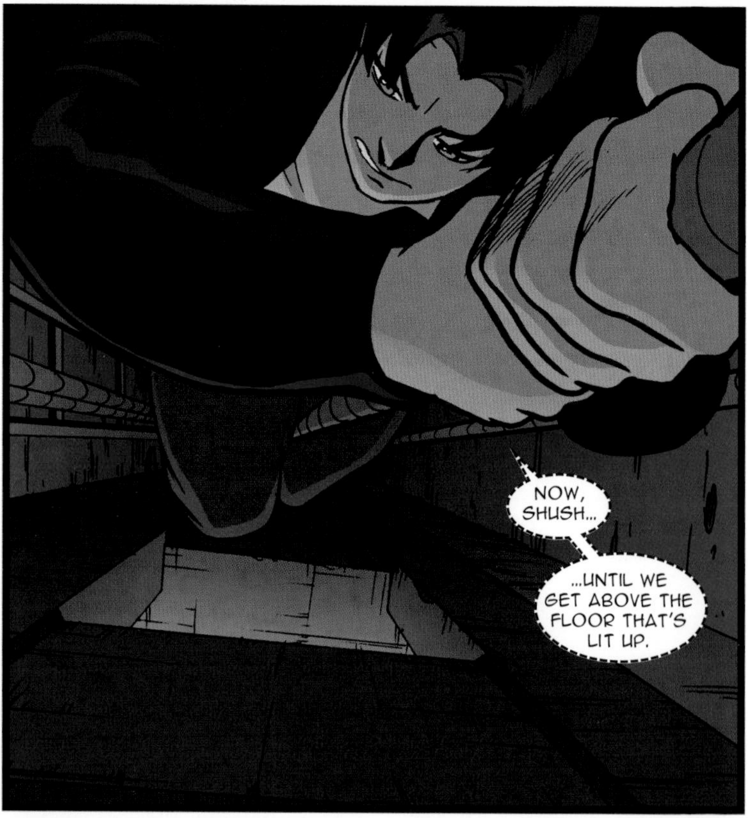
NOW, SHUSH...
...UNTIL WE GET ABOVE THE FLOOR THAT'S LIT UP.

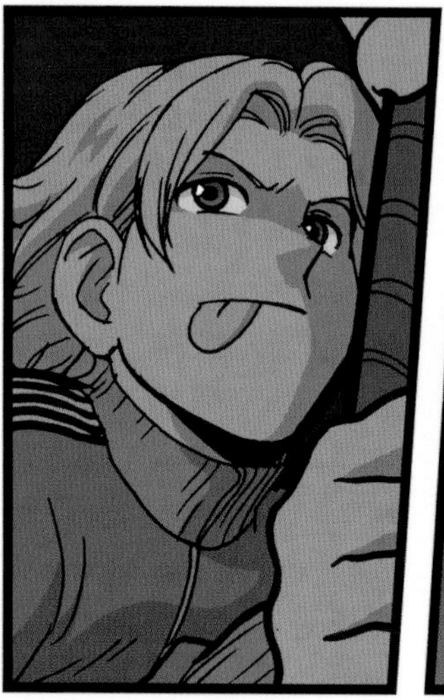

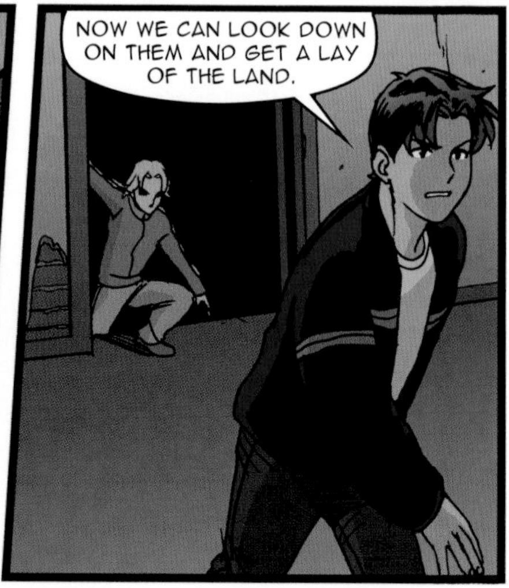
NOW WE CAN LOOK DOWN ON THEM AND GET A LAY OF THE LAND.

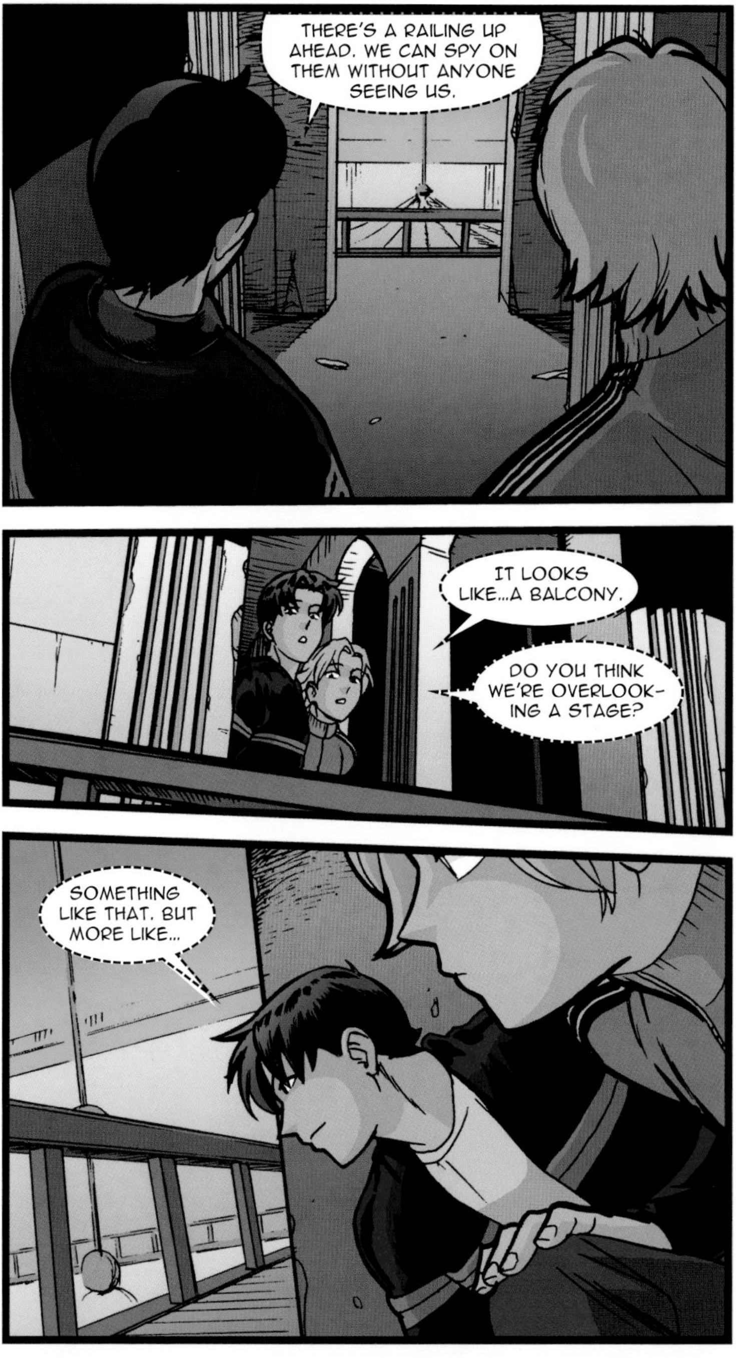
THERE'S A RAILING UP AHEAD. WE CAN SPY ON THEM WITHOUT ANYONE SEEING US.
IT LOOKS LIKE...A BALCONY.
DO YOU THINK WE'RE OVERLOOKING A STAGE?
SOMETHING LIKE THAT. BUT MORE LIKE...

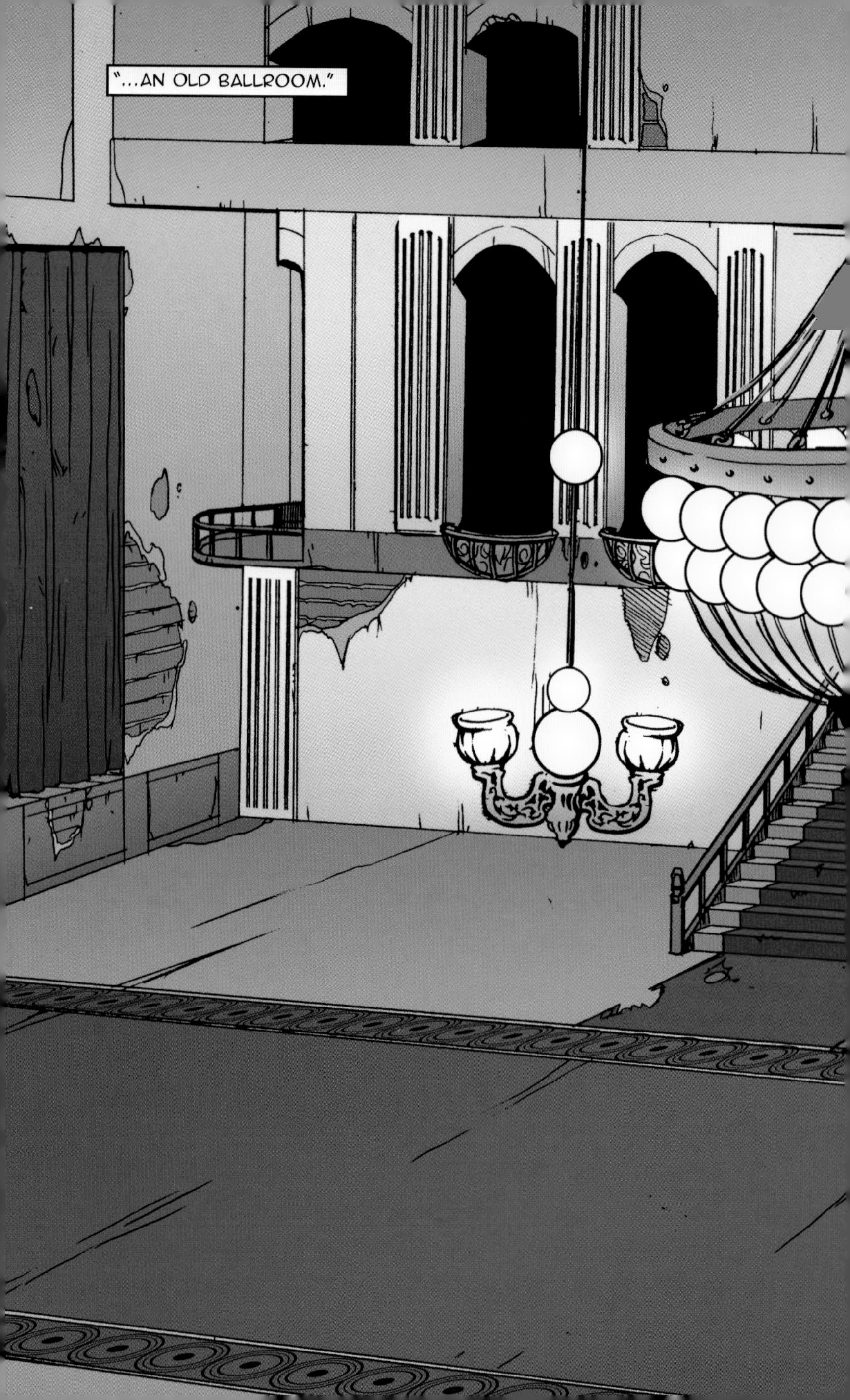
"...AN OLD BALLROOM."

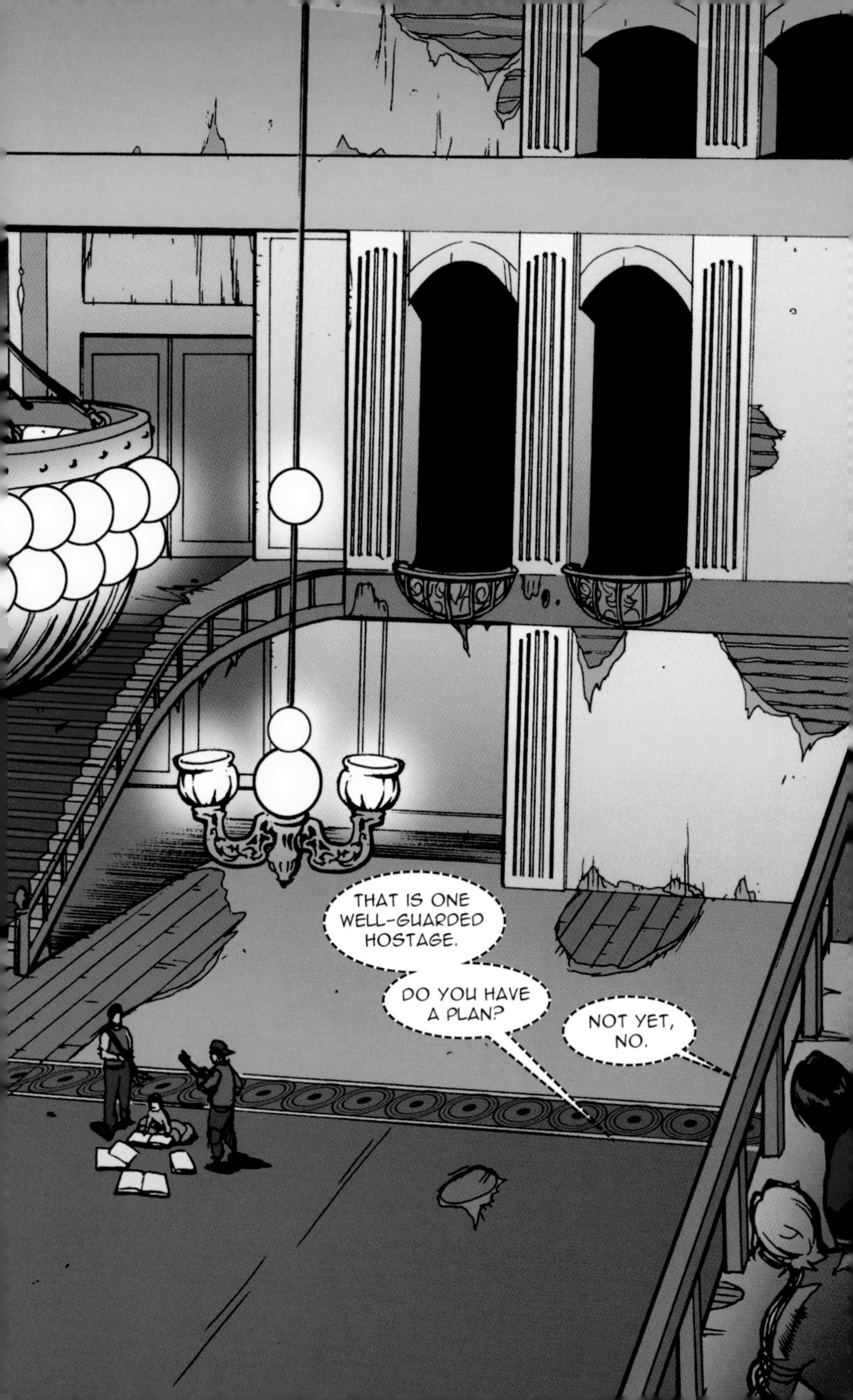
THAT IS ONE WELL-GUARDED HOSTAGE.
DO YOU HAVE A PLAN?
NOT YET, NO.

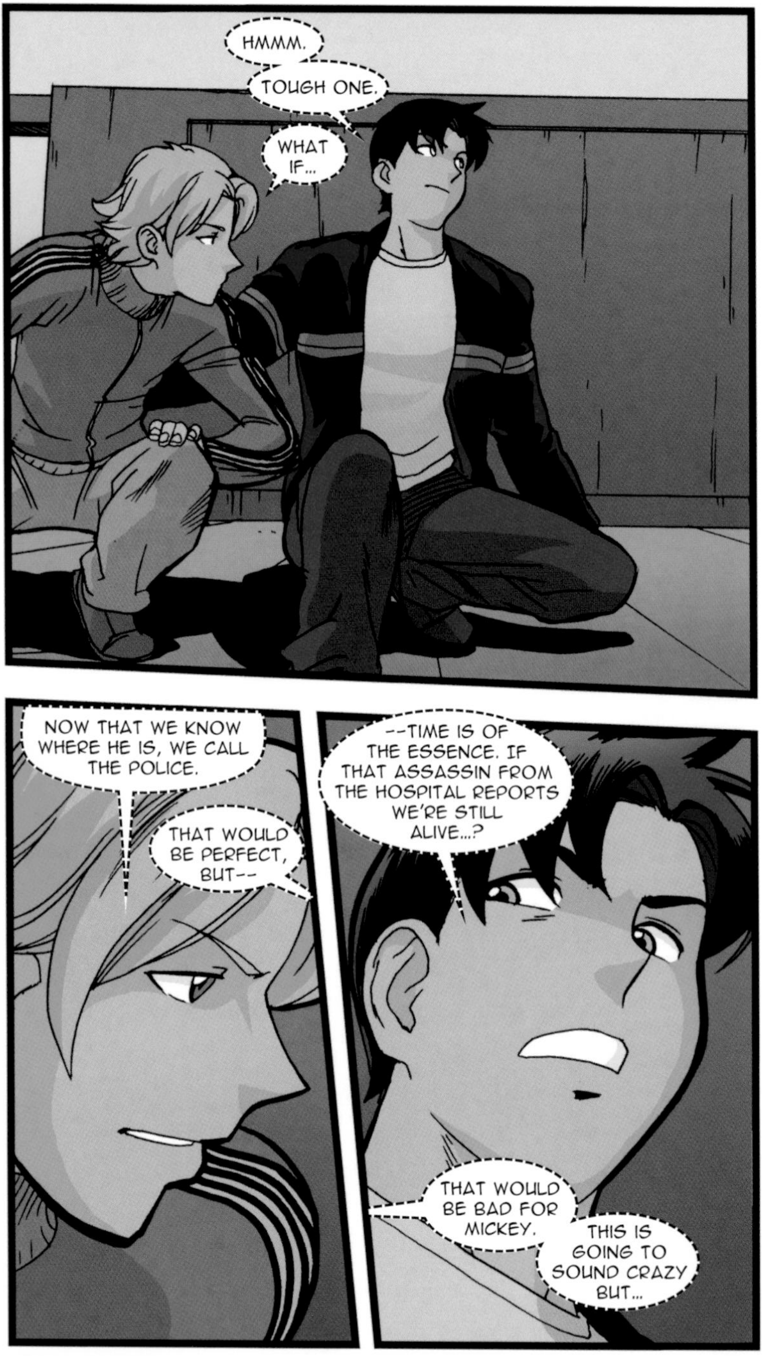
HMMM.
TOUGH ONE.
WHAT IF...
NOW THAT WE KNOW WHERE HE IS, WE CALL THE POLICE.
THAT WOULD BE PERFECT, BUT--
--TIME IS OF THE ESSENCE. IF THAT ASSASSIN FROM THE HOSPITAL REPORTS WE'RE STILL ALIVE...?
THAT WOULD BE BAD FOR MICKEY.
THIS IS GOING TO SOUND CRAZY BUT...

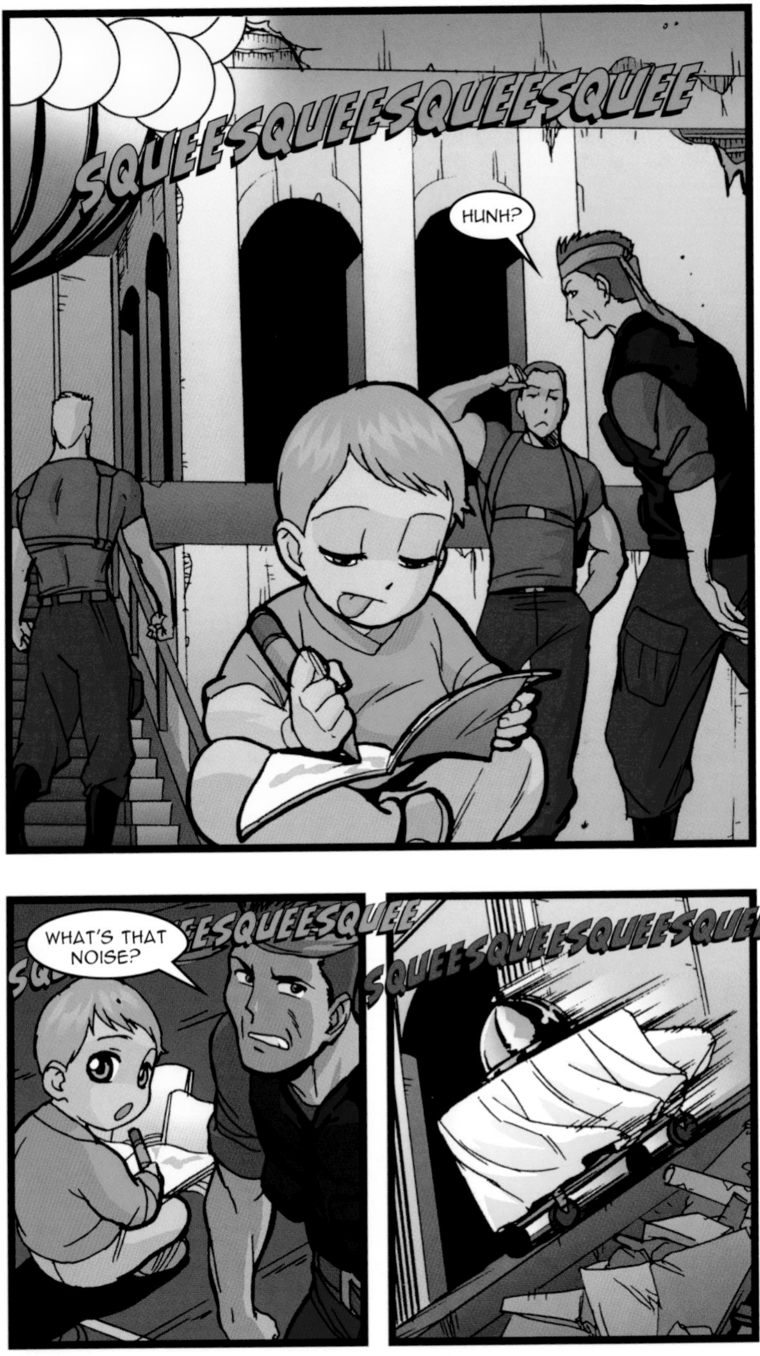
SQUEESQUEESQUEESQUEE
HUNH?
ESQUEESQUEE
WHAT'S THAT NOISE?
SQUEESQUEESQUEESQUEE

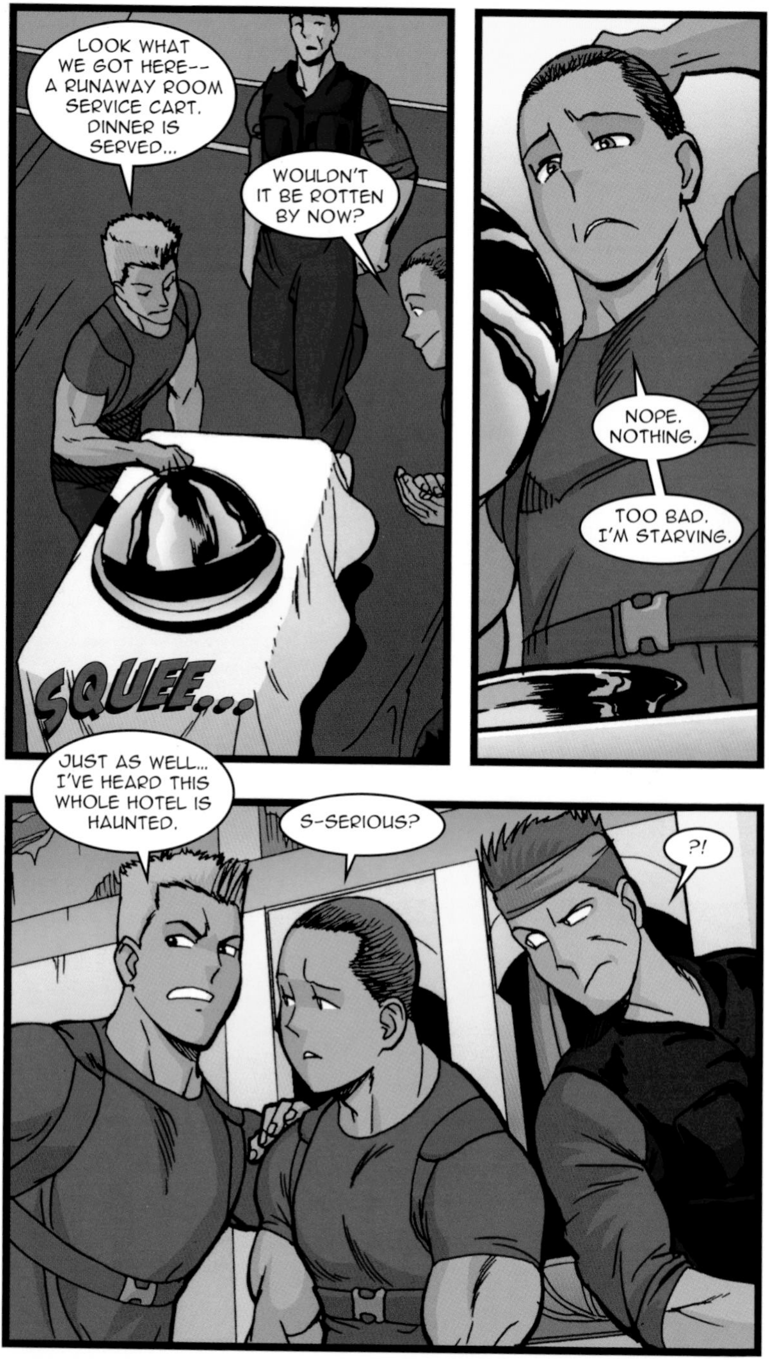
LOOK WHAT WE GOT HERE-- A RUNAWAY ROOM SERVICE CART. DINNER IS SERVED...
WOULDN'T IT BE ROTTEN BY NOW?
SQUEE...
NOPE. NOTHING.
TOO BAD. I'M STARVING.
JUST AS WELL... I'VE HEARD THIS WHOLE HOTEL IS HAUNTED.
S-SERIOUS?
?!

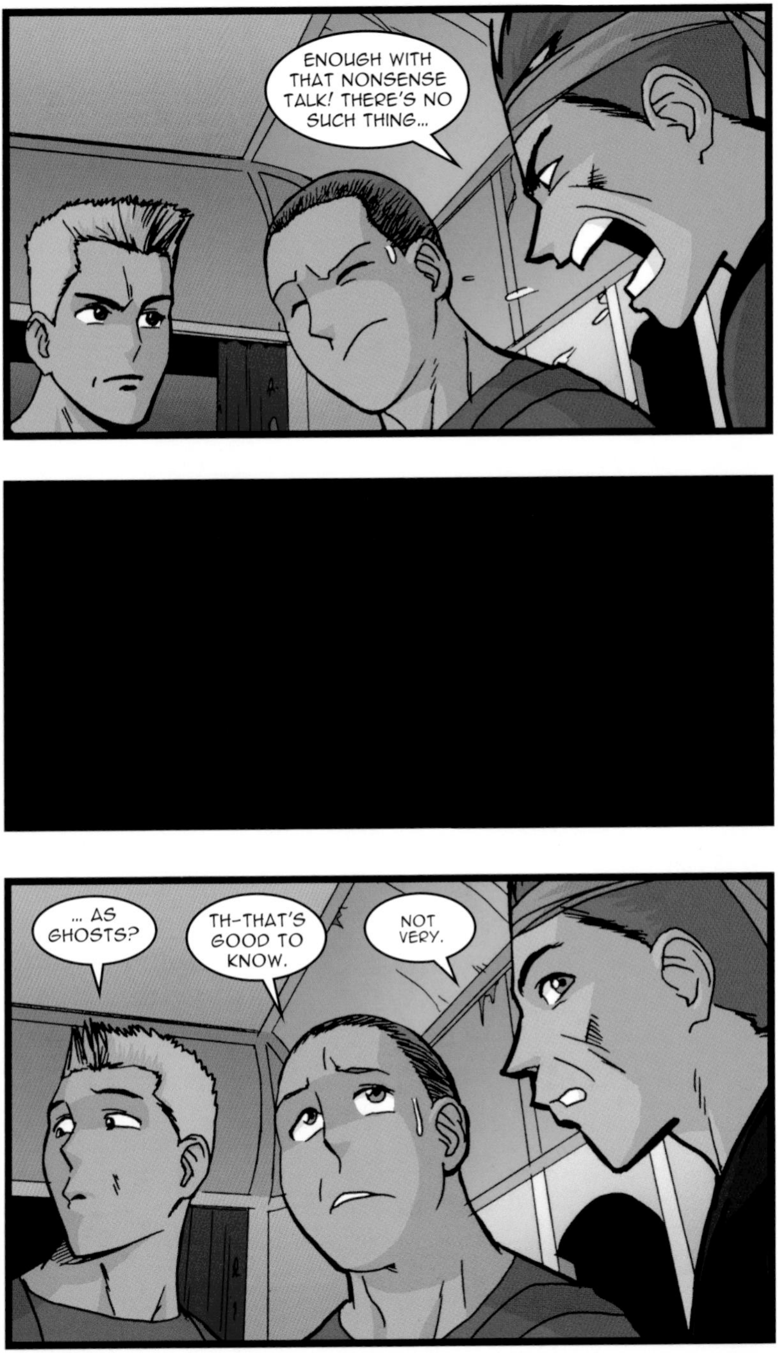
ENOUGH WITH THAT NONSENSE TALK! THERE'S NO SUCH THING...
... AS GHOSTS?
TH-THAT'S GOOD TO KNOW.
NOT VERY.

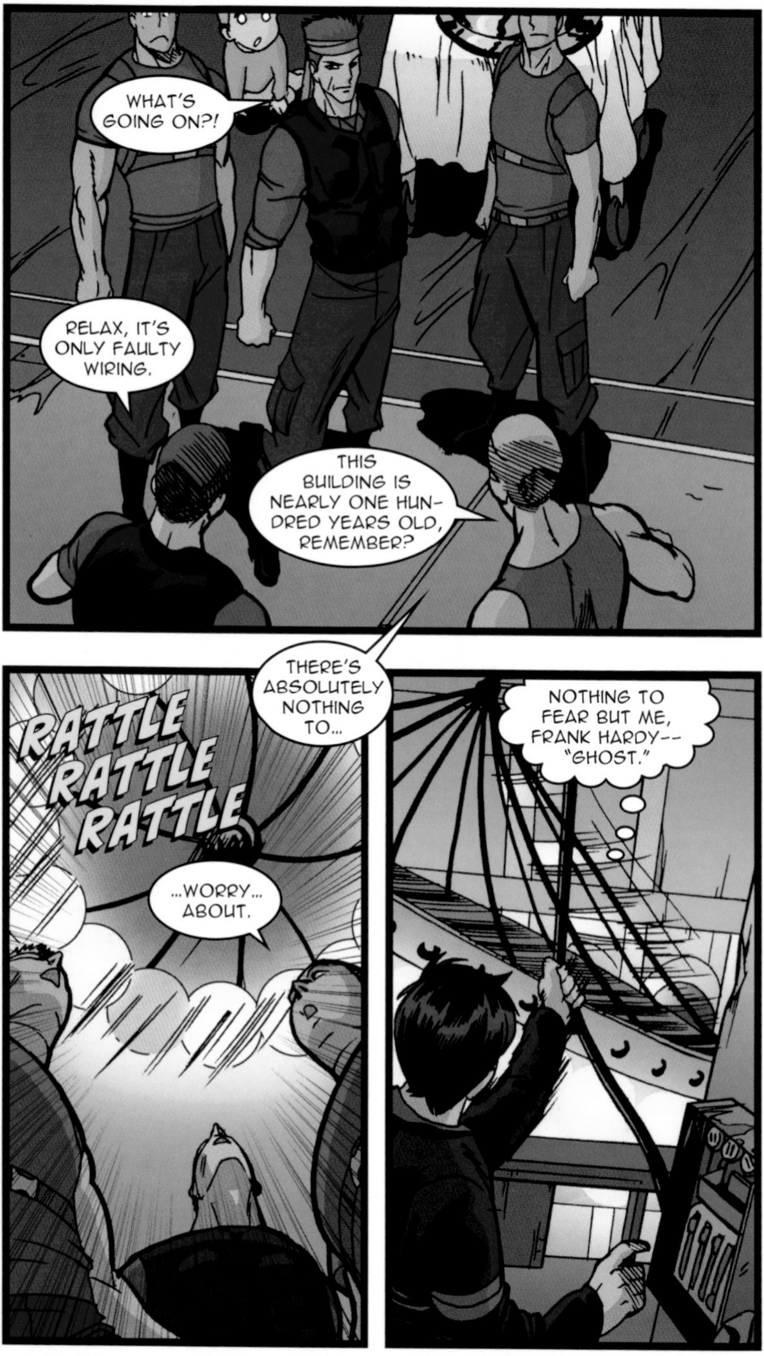
WHAT'S GOING ON?!
RELAX, IT'S ONLY FAULTY WIRING.
THIS BUILDING IS NEARLY ONE HUNDRED YEARS OLD, REMEMBER?
THERE'S ABSOLUTELY NOTHING TO...
RATTLE RATTLE RATTLE
...WORRY... ABOUT.
NOTHING TO FEAR BUT ME, FRANK HARDY-- "GHOST."

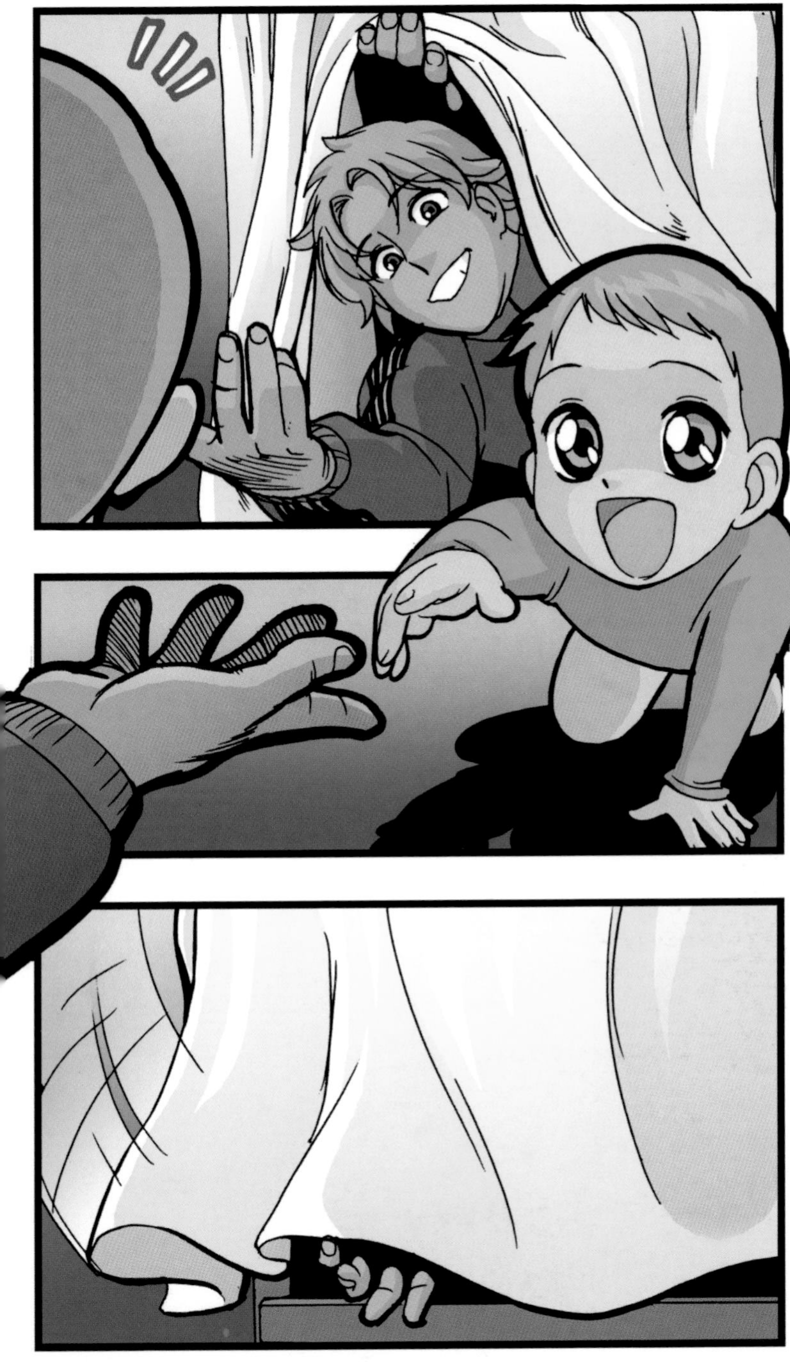

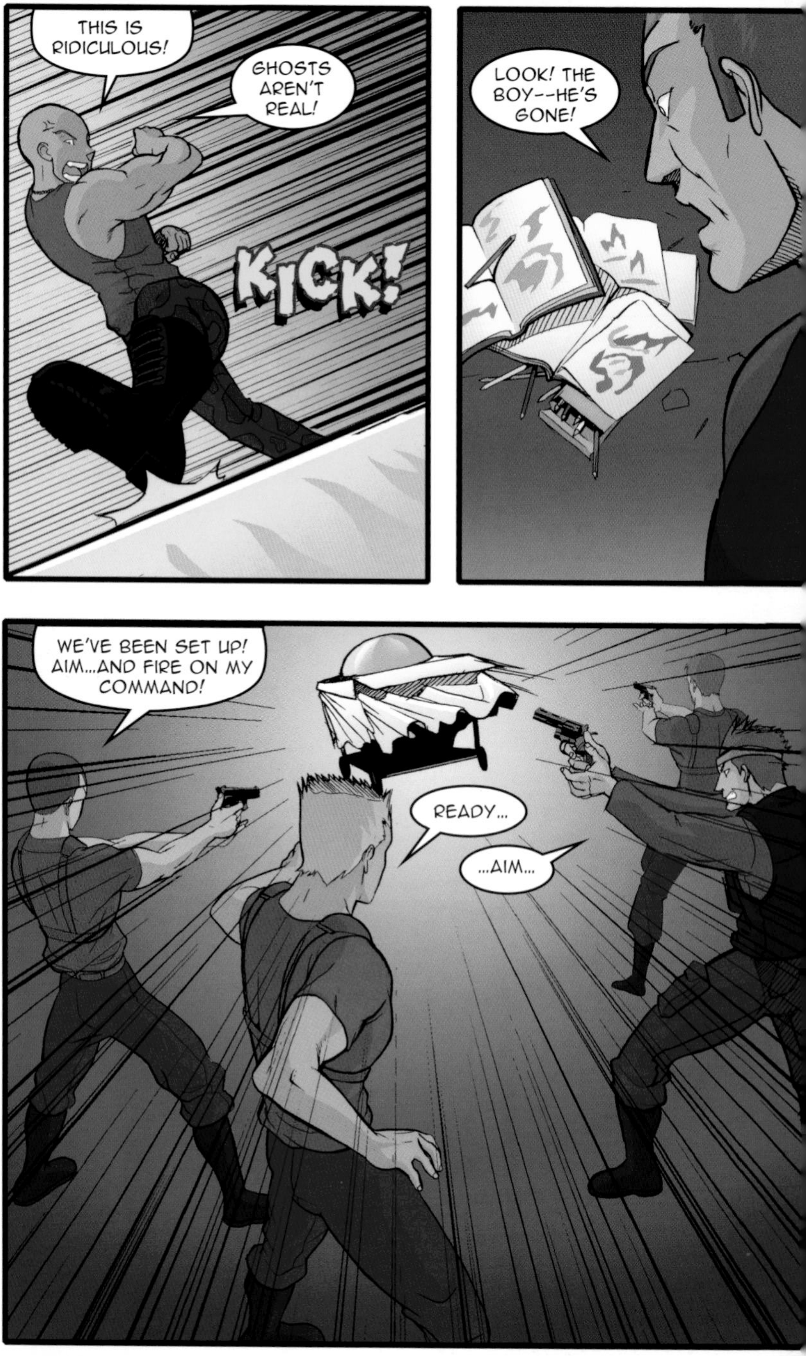
THIS IS RIDICULOUS!
GHOSTS AREN'T REAL!
KICK!
LOOK! THE BOY--HE'S GONE!
WE'VE BEEN SET UP! AIM...AND FIRE ON MY COMMAND!
READY...
...AIM...

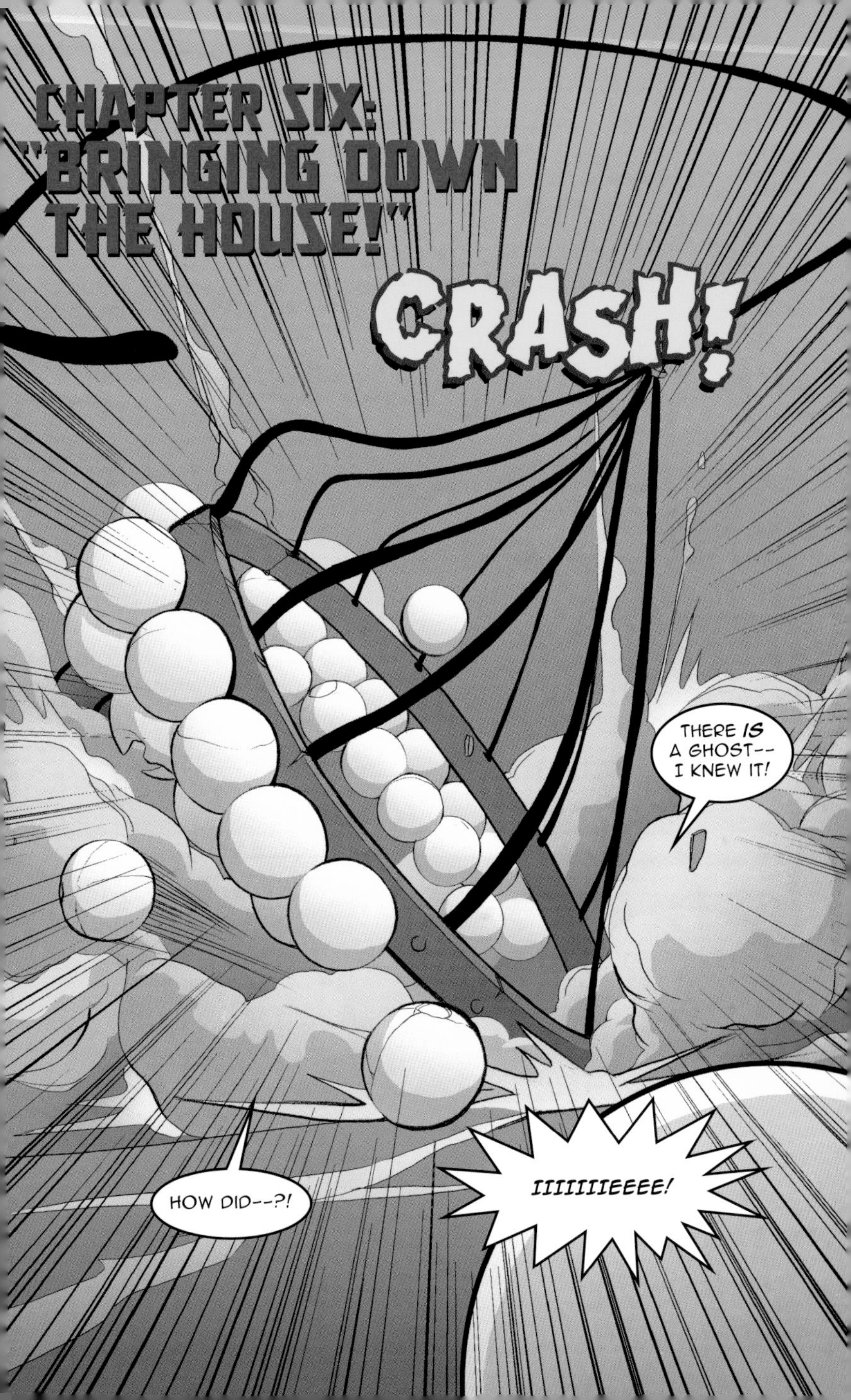
CHAPTER SIX:
"BRINGING DOWN THE HOUSE!"
CRASH!
THERE IS A GHOST-- I KNEW IT!
HOW DID--?!
IIIIIIIEEEE!

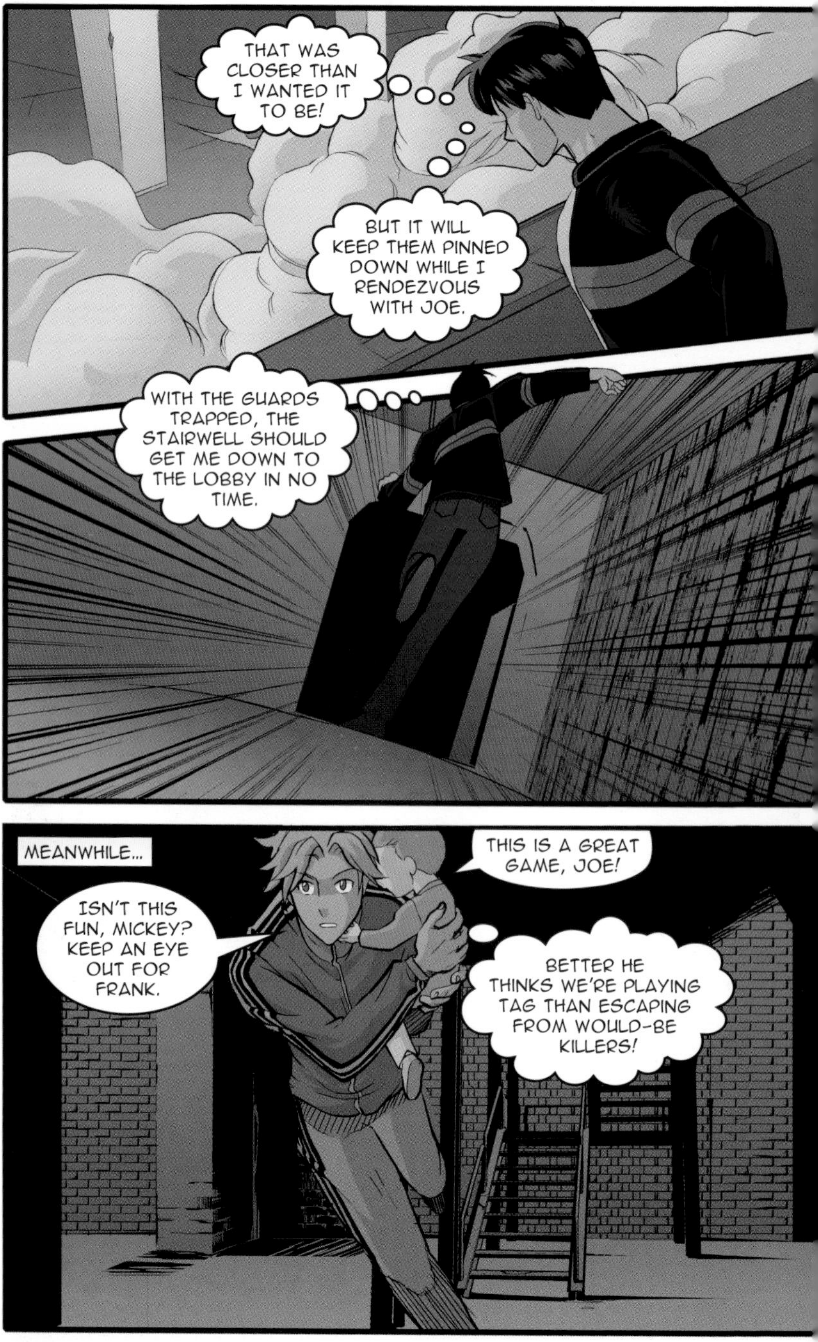
THAT WAS CLOSER THAN I WANTED IT TO BE!
BUT IT WILL KEEP THEM PINNED DOWN WHILE I RENDEZVOUS WITH JOE.
WITH THE GUARDS TRAPPED, THE STAIRWELL SHOULD GET ME DOWN TO THE LOBBY IN NO TIME.
MEANWHILE...
ISN'T THIS FUN, MICKEY? KEEP AN EYE OUT FOR FRANK.
THIS IS A GREAT GAME, JOE!
BETTER HE THINKS WE'RE PLAYING TAG THAN ESCAPING FROM WOULD-BE KILLERS!

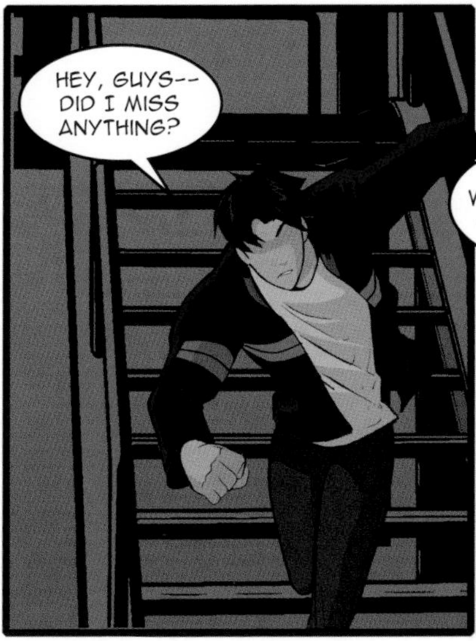
HEY, GUYS--
DID I MISS
ANYTHING?

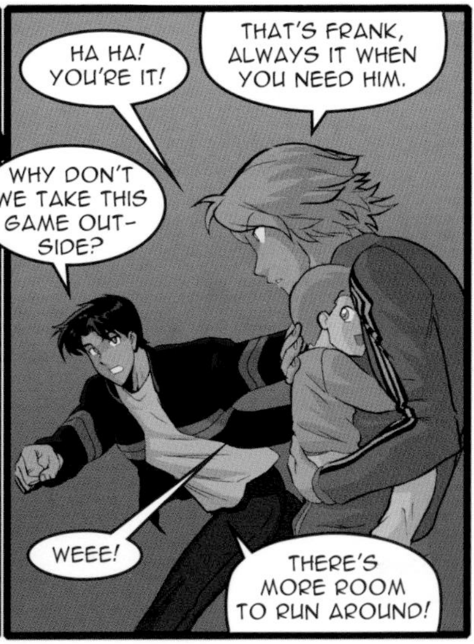
THAT'S FRANK,
ALWAYS IT WHEN
YOU NEED HIM.
HA HA!
YOU'RE IT!
WHY DON'T
WE TAKE THIS
GAME OUT-
SIDE?
WEEE!
THERE'S
MORE ROOM
TO RUN AROUND!

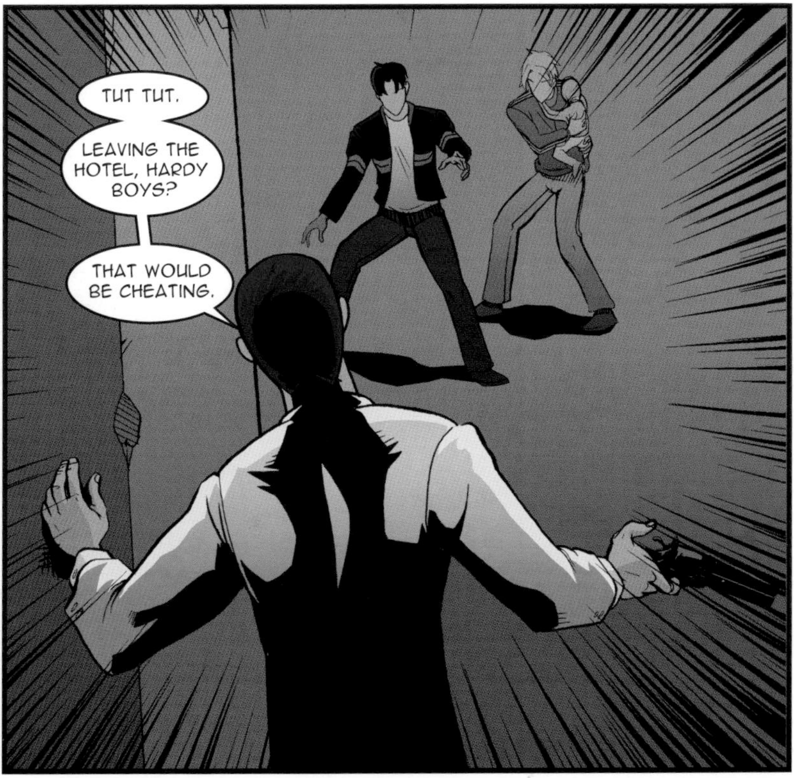
TUT TUT.
LEAVING THE
HOTEL, HARDY
BOYS?
THAT WOULD
BE CHEATING.

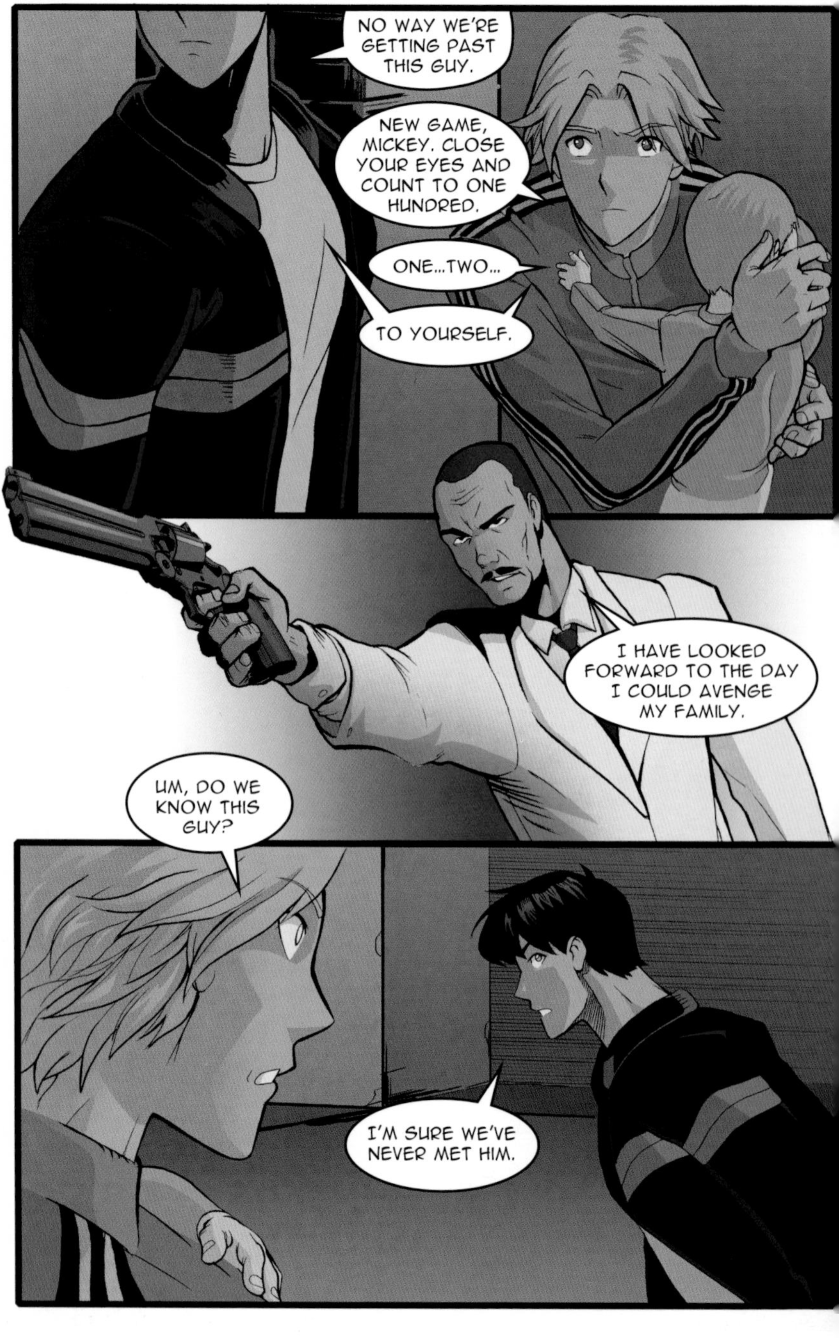
NO WAY WE'RE GETTING PAST THIS GUY.
NEW GAME, MICKEY. CLOSE YOUR EYES AND COUNT TO ONE HUNDRED.
ONE...TWO...
TO YOURSELF.
I HAVE LOOKED FORWARD TO THE DAY I COULD AVENGE MY FAMILY.
UM, DO WE KNOW THIS GUY?
I'M SURE WE'VE NEVER MET HIM.

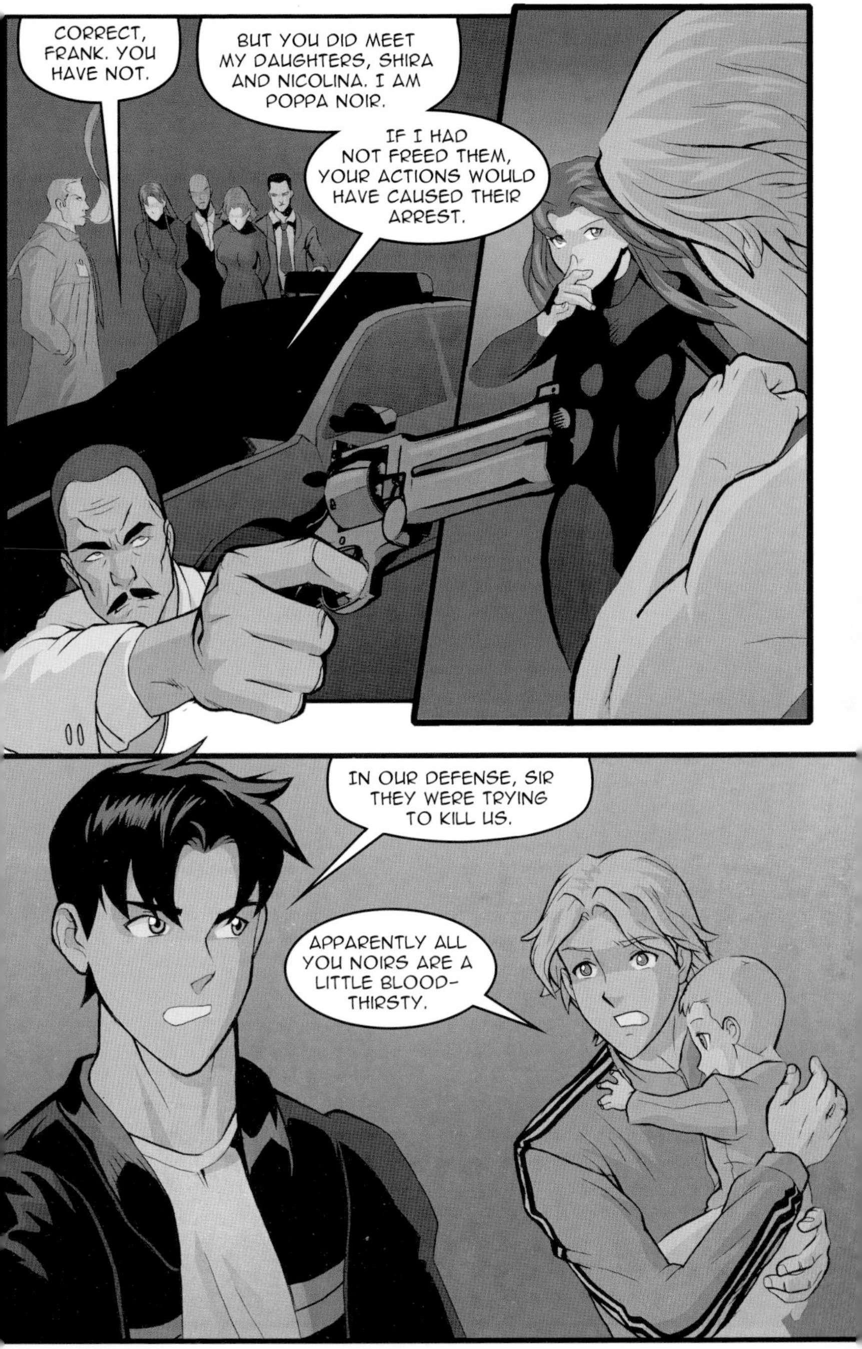
CORRECT, FRANK. YOU HAVE NOT.
BUT YOU DID MEET MY DAUGHTERS, SHIRA AND NICOLINA. I AM POPPA NOIR.
IF I HAD NOT FREED THEM, YOUR ACTIONS WOULD HAVE CAUSED THEIR ARREST.
IN OUR DEFENSE, SIR THEY WERE TRYING TO KILL US.
APPARENTLY ALL YOU NOIRS ARE A LITTLE BLOOD-THIRSTY.

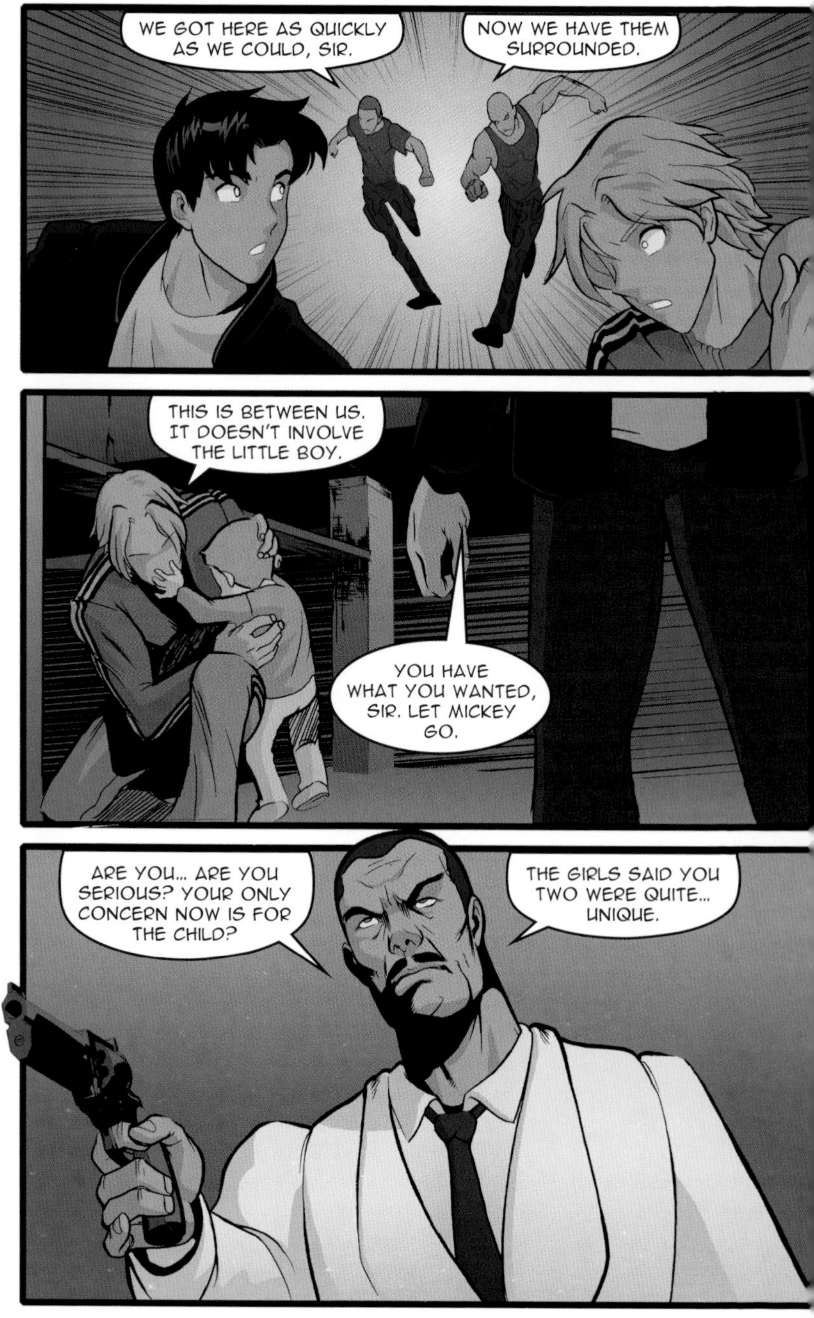
WE GOT HERE AS QUICKLY AS WE COULD, SIR.
NOW WE HAVE THEM SURROUNDED.
THIS IS BETWEEN US. IT DOESN'T INVOLVE THE LITTLE BOY.
YOU HAVE WHAT YOU WANTED, SIR. LET MICKEY GO.
ARE YOU... ARE YOU SERIOUS? YOUR ONLY CONCERN NOW IS FOR THE CHILD?
THE GIRLS SAID YOU TWO WERE QUITE... UNIQUE.

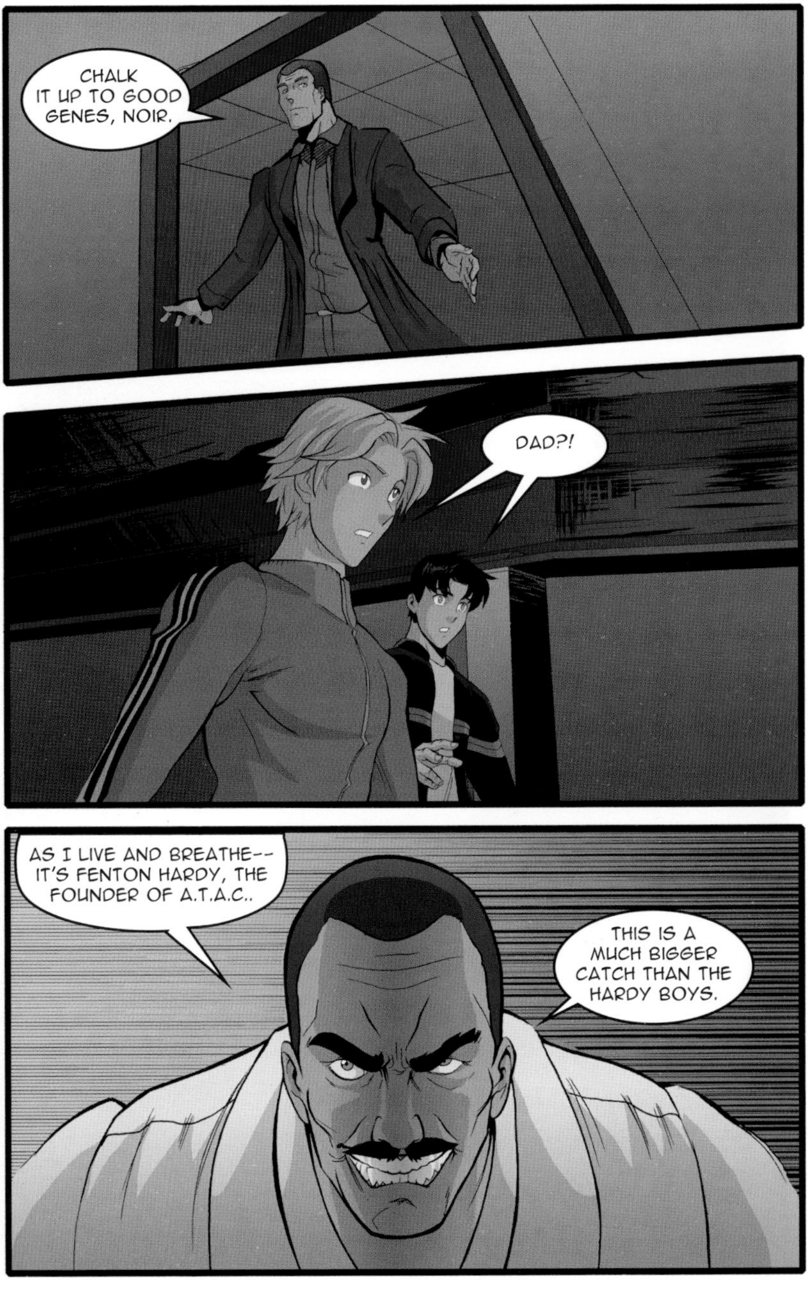
CHALK IT UP TO GOOD GENES, NOIR.
DAD?!
AS I LIVE AND BREATHE-- IT'S FENTON HARDY, THE FOUNDER OF A.T.A.C..
THIS IS A MUCH BIGGER CATCH THAN THE HARDY BOYS.

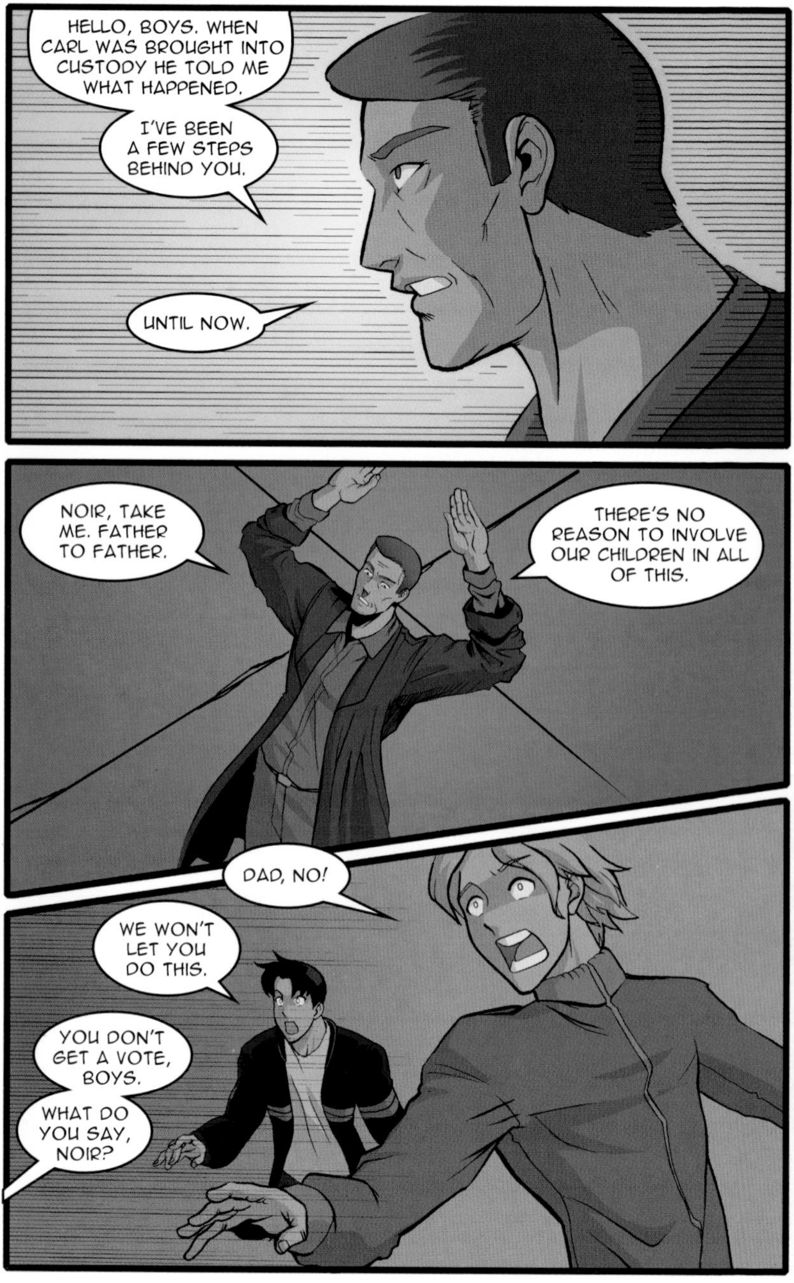
HELLO, BOYS. WHEN CARL WAS BROUGHT INTO CUSTODY HE TOLD ME WHAT HAPPENED.
I'VE BEEN A FEW STEPS BEHIND YOU.
UNTIL NOW.
NOIR, TAKE ME. FATHER TO FATHER.
THERE'S NO REASON TO INVOLVE OUR CHILDREN IN ALL OF THIS.
DAD, NO!
WE WON'T LET YOU DO THIS.
YOU DON'T GET A VOTE, BOYS.
WHAT DO YOU SAY, NOIR?

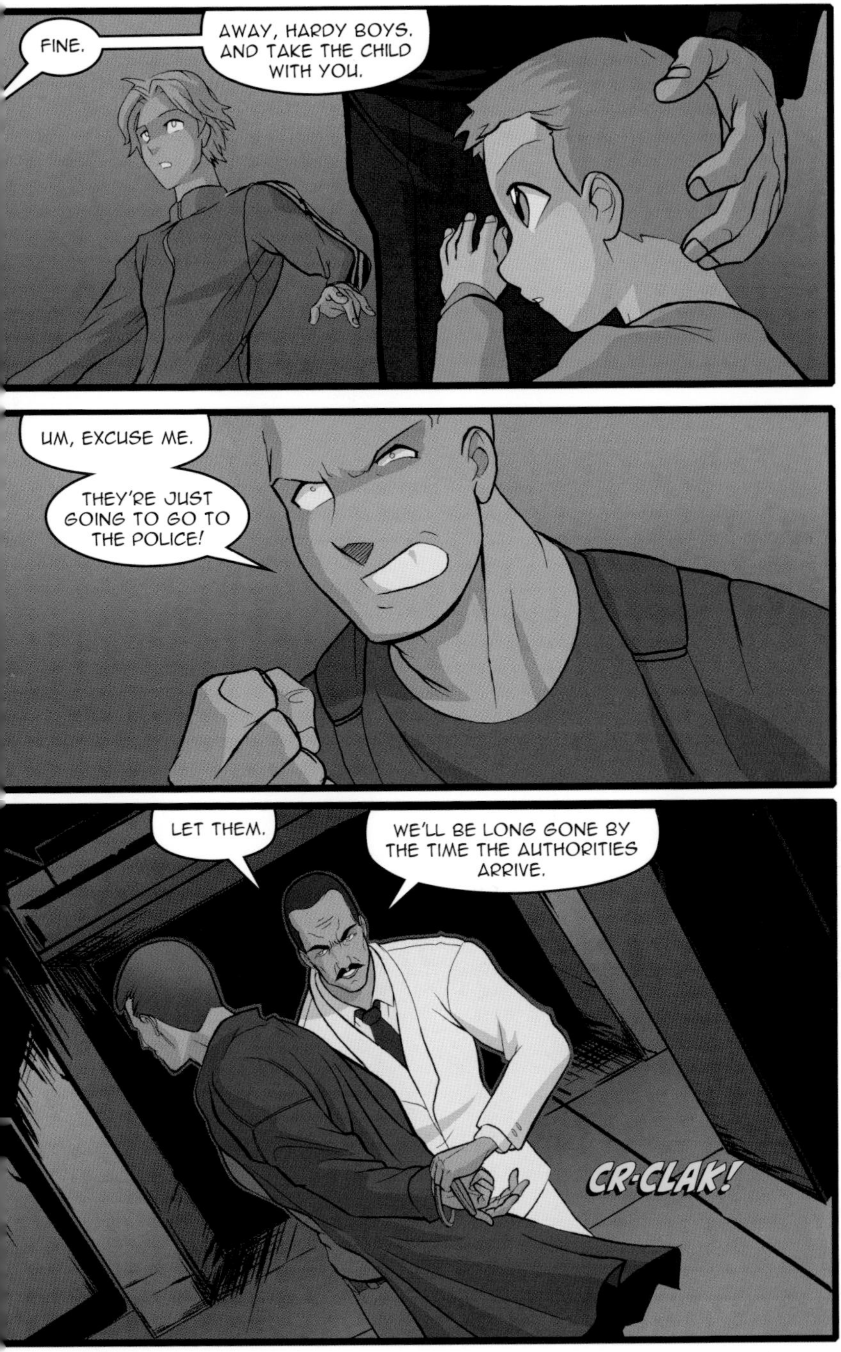
FINE.
AWAY, HARDY BOYS. AND TAKE THE CHILD WITH YOU.
UM, EXCUSE ME.
THEY'RE JUST GOING TO GO TO THE POLICE!
LET THEM.
WE'LL BE LONG GONE BY THE TIME THE AUTHORITIES ARRIVE.
CR-CLAK!

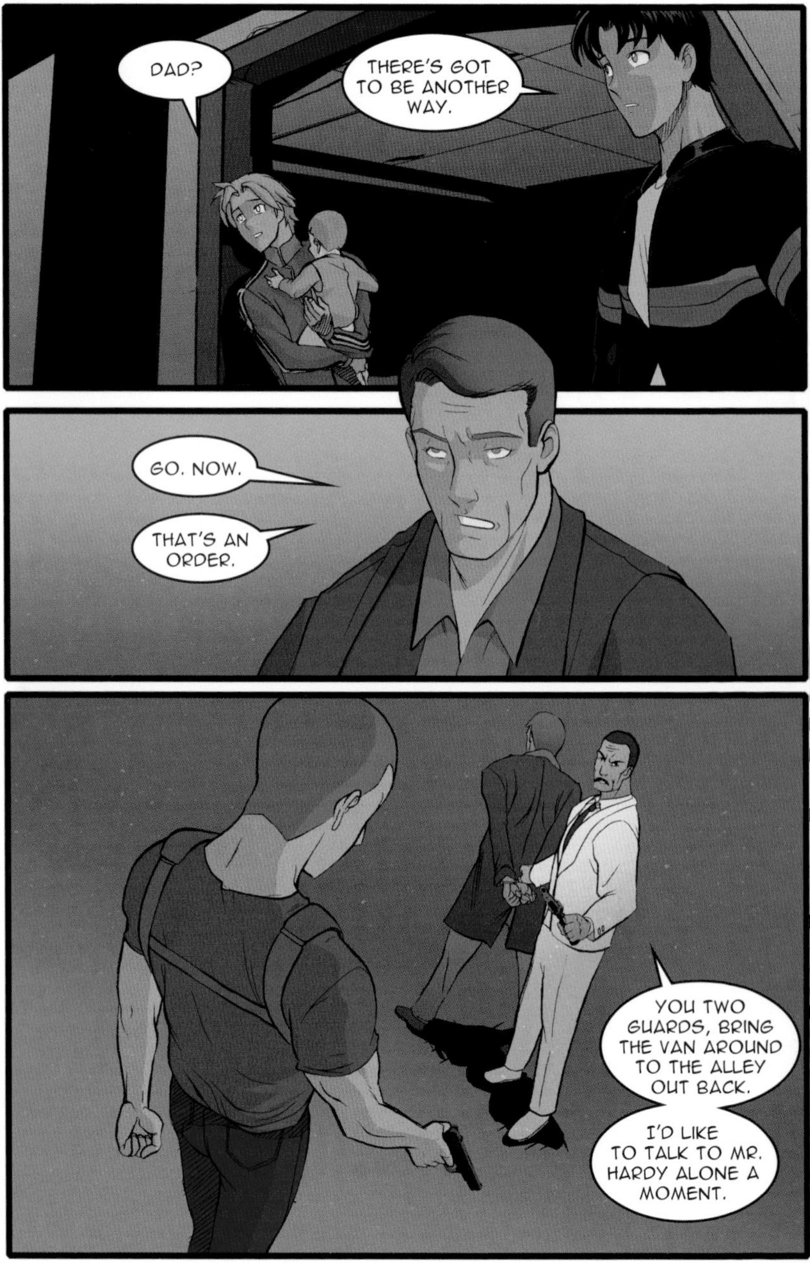
DAD?
THERE'S GOT TO BE ANOTHER WAY.
GO. NOW.
THAT'S AN ORDER.
YOU TWO GUARDS, BRING THE VAN AROUND TO THE ALLEY OUT BACK.
I'D LIKE TO TALK TO MR. HARDY ALONE A MOMENT.

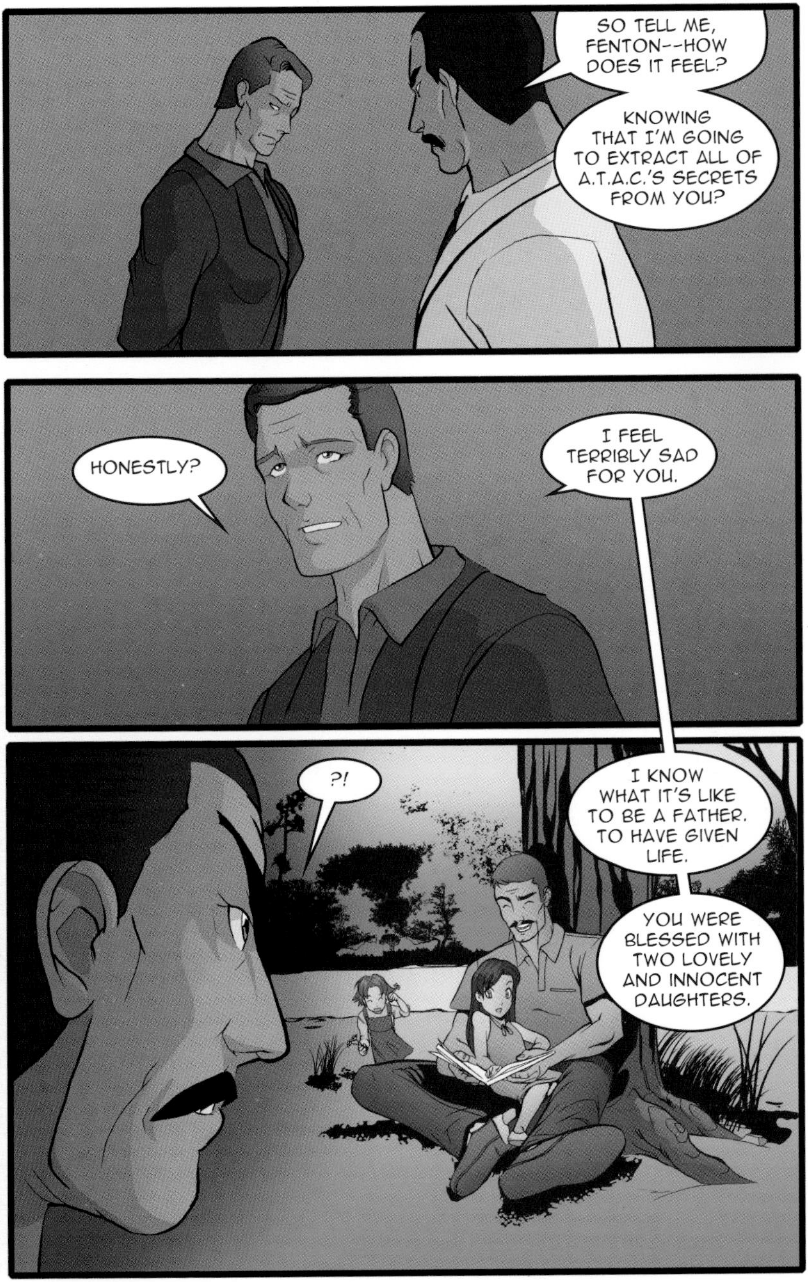
SO TELL ME, FENTON--HOW DOES IT FEEL?
KNOWING THAT I'M GOING TO EXTRACT ALL OF A.T.A.C.'S SECRETS FROM YOU?
HONESTLY?
I FEEL TERRIBLY SAD FOR YOU.
?!
I KNOW WHAT IT'S LIKE TO BE A FATHER. TO HAVE GIVEN LIFE.
YOU WERE BLESSED WITH TWO LOVELY AND INNOCENT DAUGHTERS.

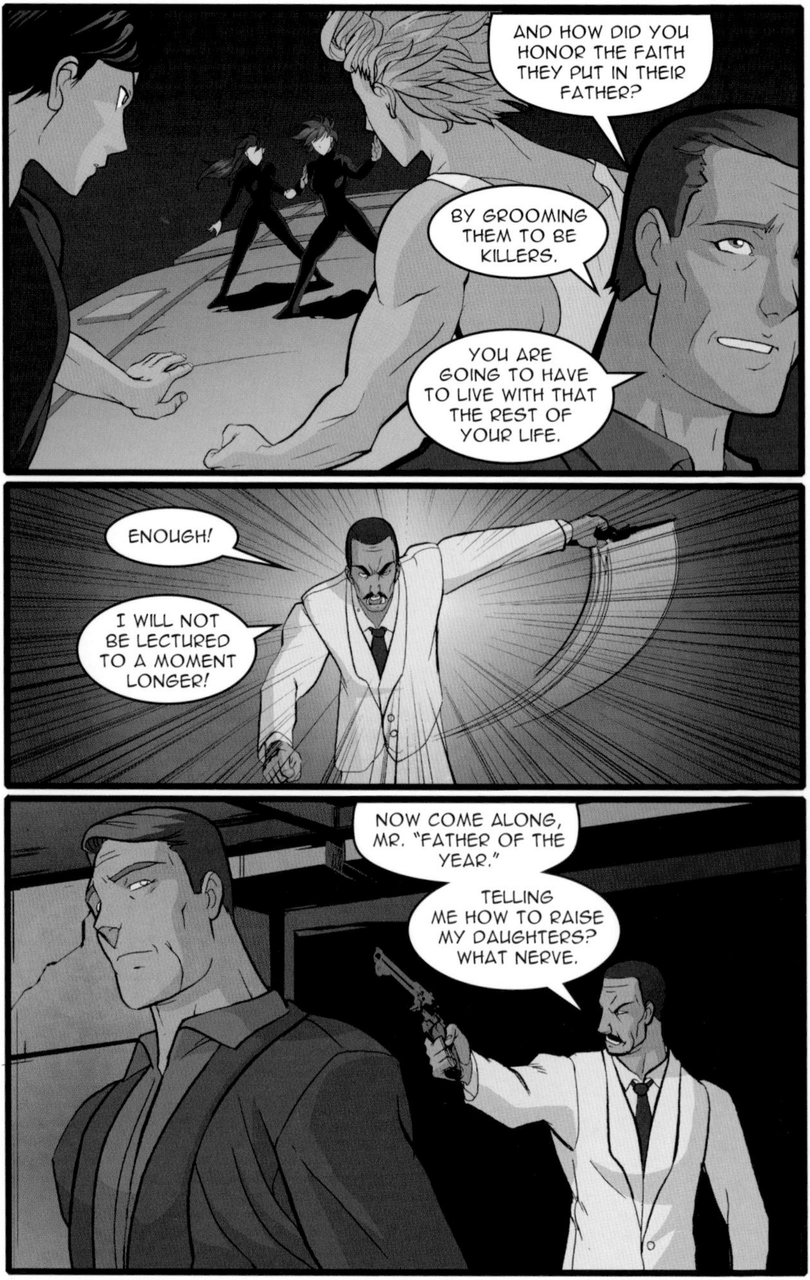
AND HOW DID YOU HONOR THE FAITH THEY PUT IN THEIR FATHER?
BY GROOMING THEM TO BE KILLERS.
YOU ARE GOING TO HAVE TO LIVE WITH THAT THE REST OF YOUR LIFE.
ENOUGH!
I WILL NOT BE LECTURED TO A MOMENT LONGER!
NOW COME ALONG, MR. "FATHER OF THE YEAR."
TELLING ME HOW TO RAISE MY DAUGHTERS? WHAT NERVE.

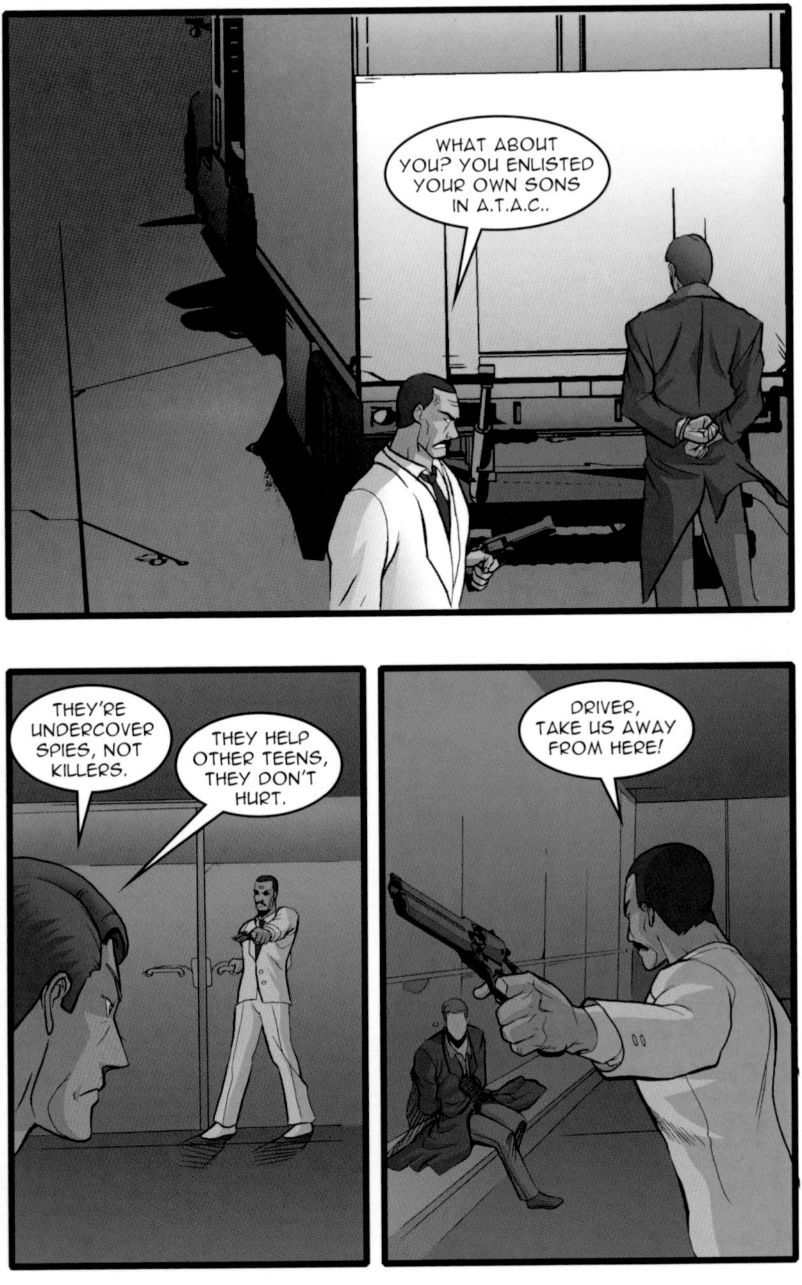
WHAT ABOUT YOU? YOU ENLISTED YOUR OWN SONS IN A.T.A.C..
THEY'RE UNDERCOVER SPIES, NOT KILLERS.
THEY HELP OTHER TEENS, THEY DON'T HURT.
DRIVER, TAKE US AWAY FROM HERE!

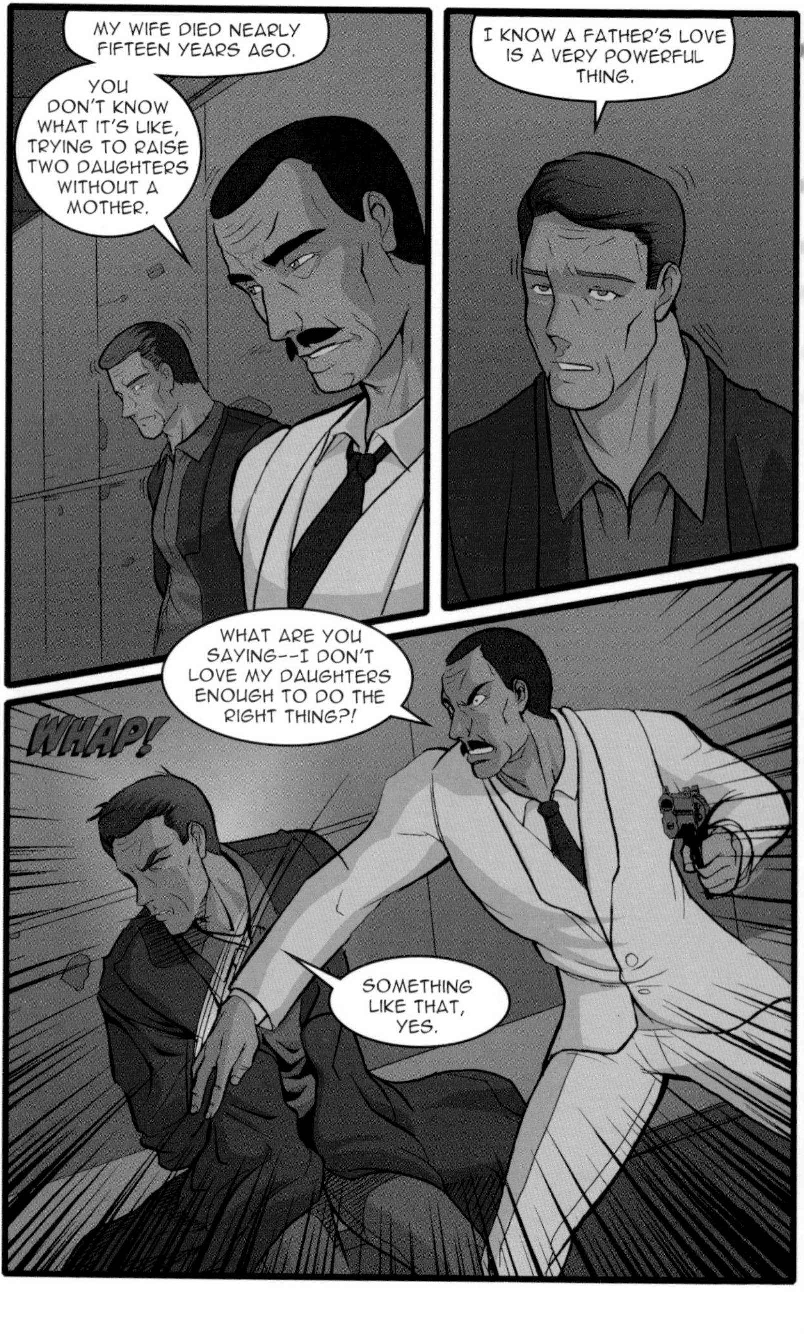
MY WIFE DIED NEARLY FIFTEEN YEARS AGO.
YOU DON'T KNOW WHAT IT'S LIKE, TRYING TO RAISE TWO DAUGHTERS WITHOUT A MOTHER.
I KNOW A FATHER'S LOVE IS A VERY POWERFUL THING.
WHAT ARE YOU SAYING--I DON'T LOVE MY DAUGHTERS ENOUGH TO DO THE RIGHT THING?!
WHAP!
SOMETHING LIKE THAT, YES.

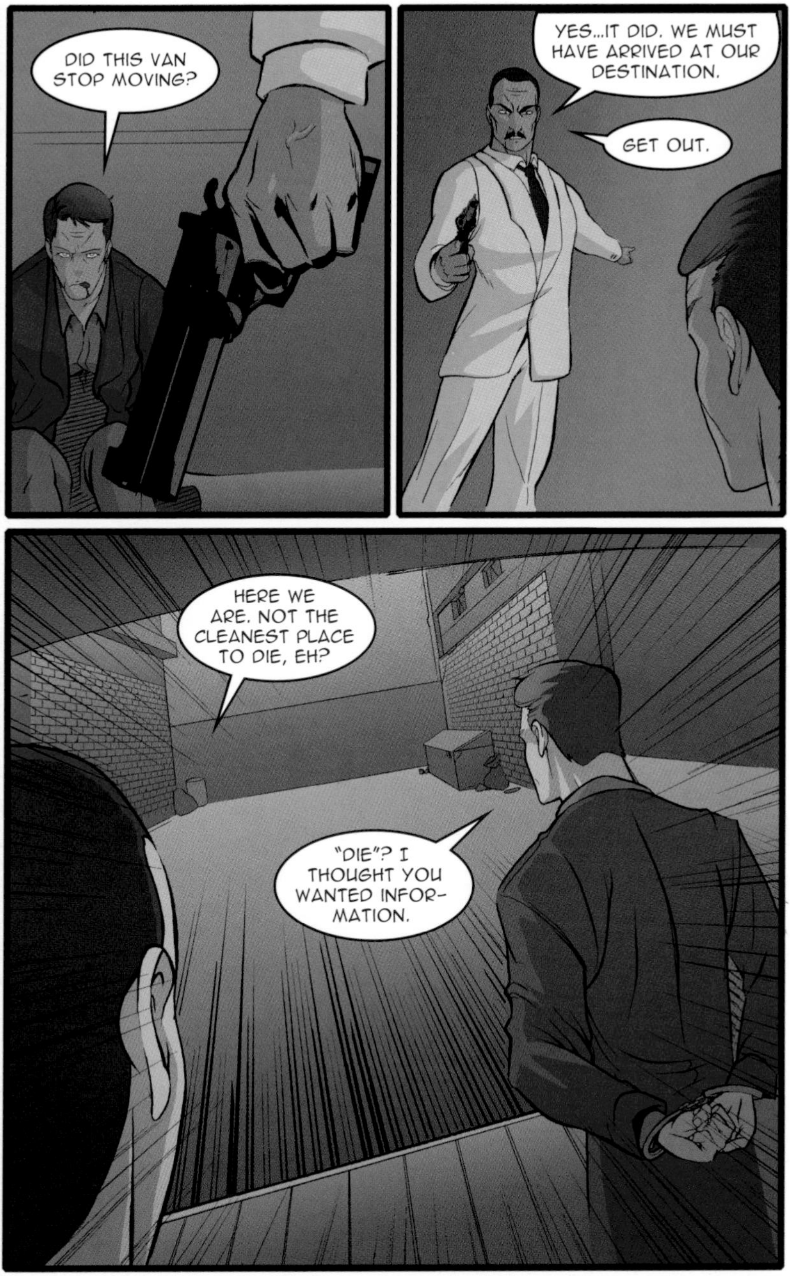
DID THIS VAN STOP MOVING?
YES...IT DID. WE MUST HAVE ARRIVED AT OUR DESTINATION.
GET OUT.
HERE WE ARE. NOT THE CLEANEST PLACE TO DIE, EH?
"DIE"? I THOUGHT YOU WANTED INFOR-MATION.

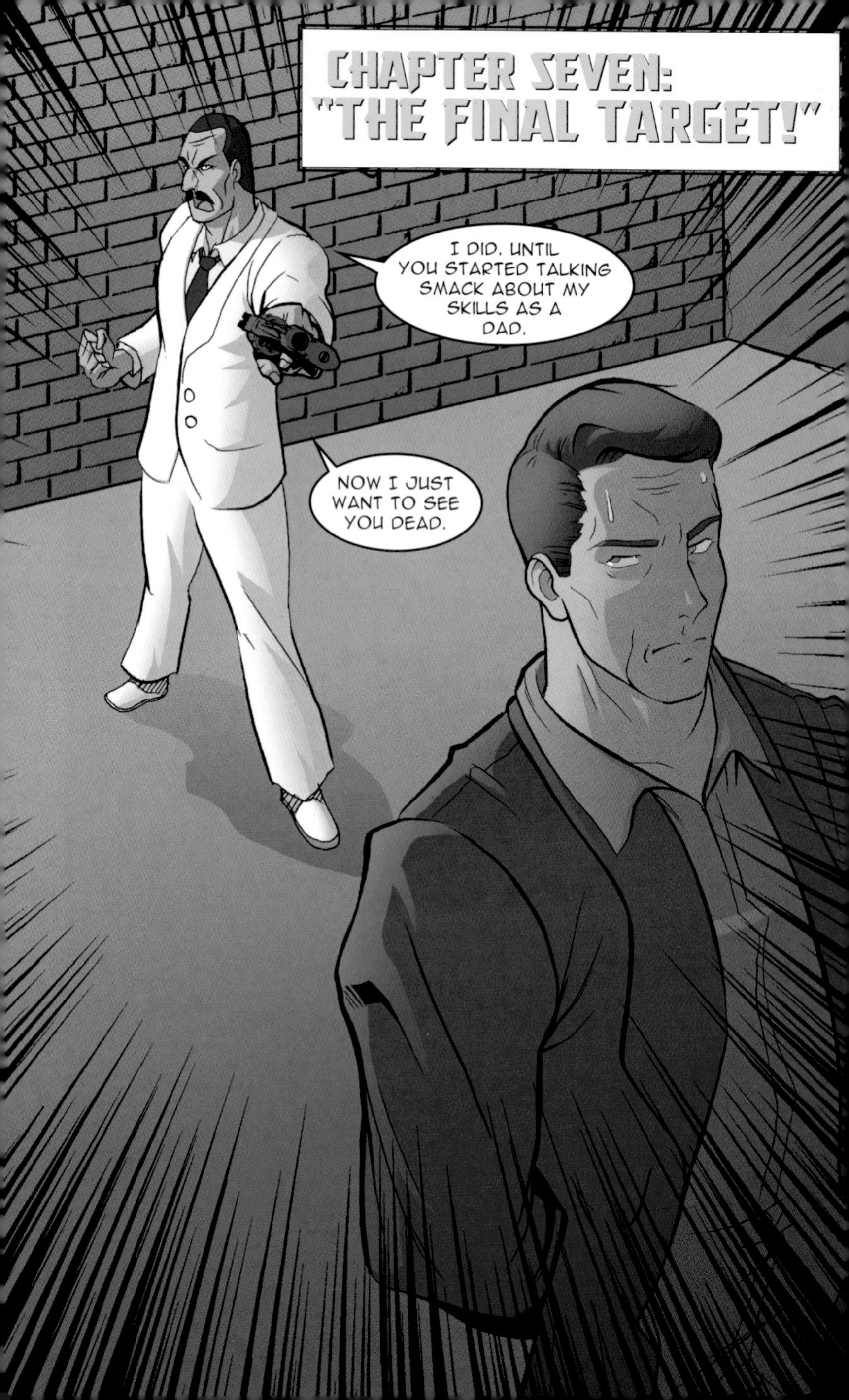
CHAPTER SEVEN:
"THE FINAL TARGET!"
I DID. UNTIL YOU STARTED TALKING SMACK ABOUT MY SKILLS AS A DAD.
NOW I JUST WANT TO SEE YOU DEAD.

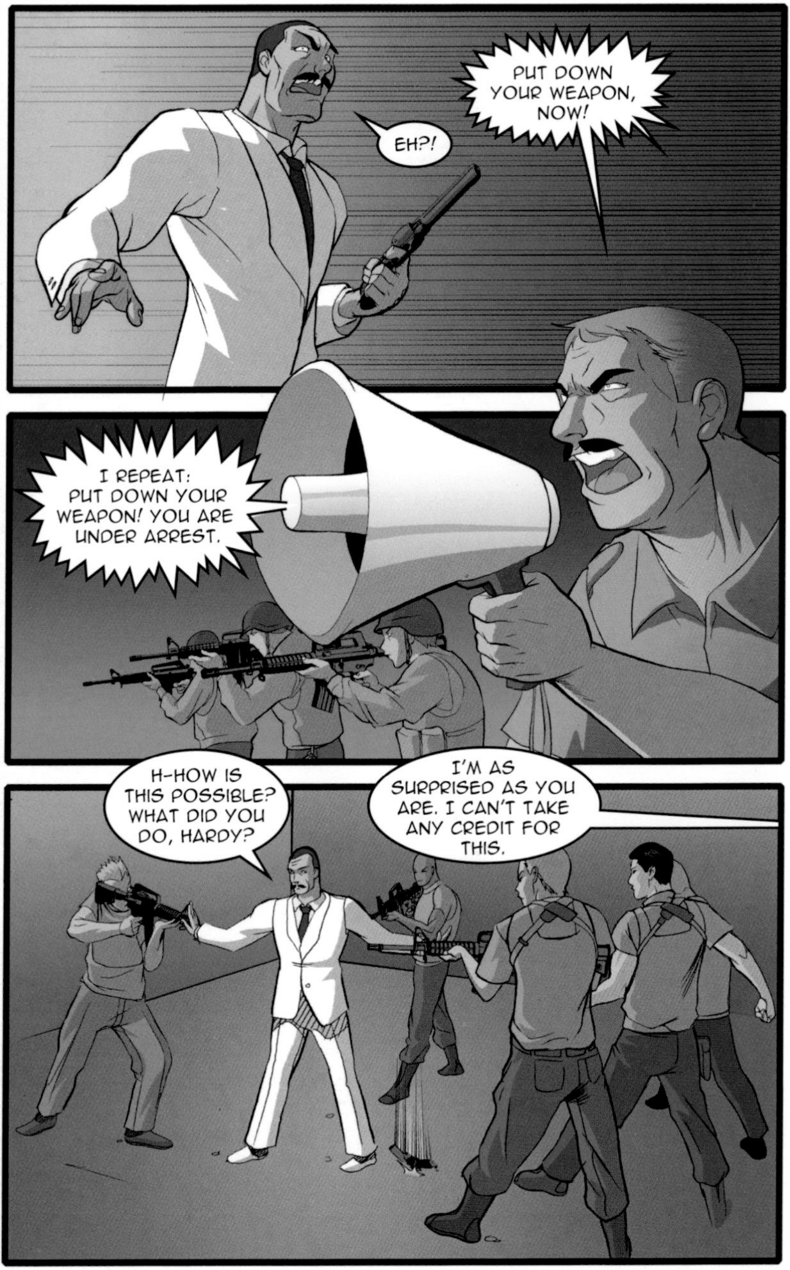
PUT DOWN
YOUR WEAPON,
NOW!
EH?!
I REPEAT:
PUT DOWN YOUR
WEAPON! YOU ARE
UNDER ARREST.
H-HOW IS
THIS POSSIBLE?
WHAT DID YOU
DO, HARDY?
I'M AS
SURPRISED AS YOU
ARE. I CAN'T TAKE
ANY CREDIT FOR
THIS.

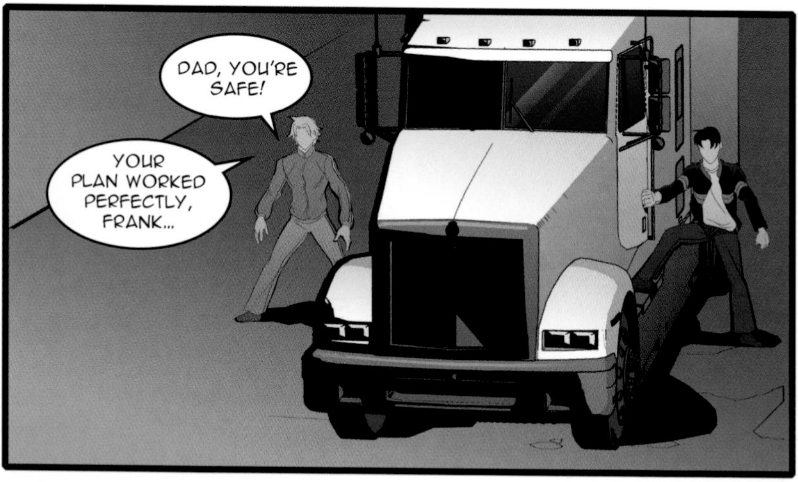
DAD, YOU'RE SAFE!
YOUR PLAN WORKED PERFECTLY, FRANK...

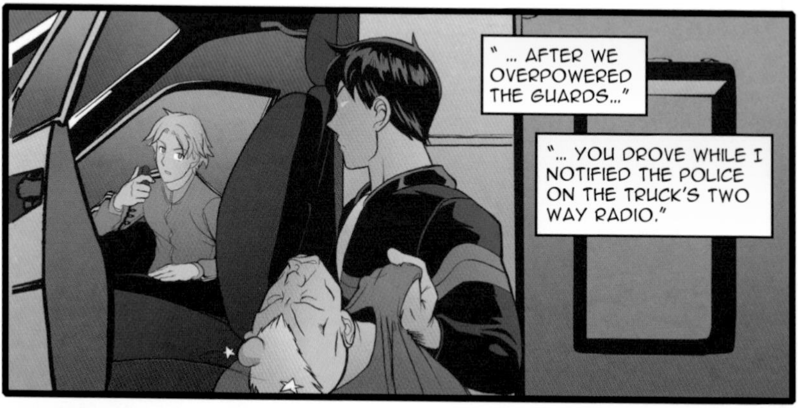
"... AFTER WE OVERPOWERED THE GUARDS..."
"... YOU DROVE WHILE I NOTIFIED THE POLICE ON THE TRUCK'S TWO WAY RADIO."

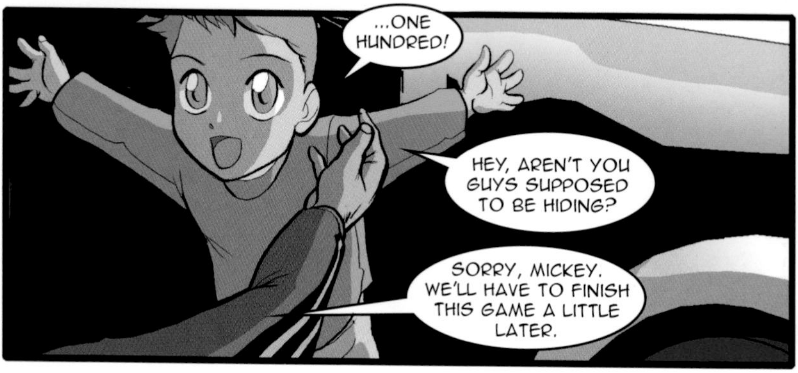
...ONE HUNDRED!
HEY, AREN'T YOU GUYS SUPPOSED TO BE HIDING?
SORRY, MICKEY. WE'LL HAVE TO FINISH THIS GAME A LITTLE LATER.

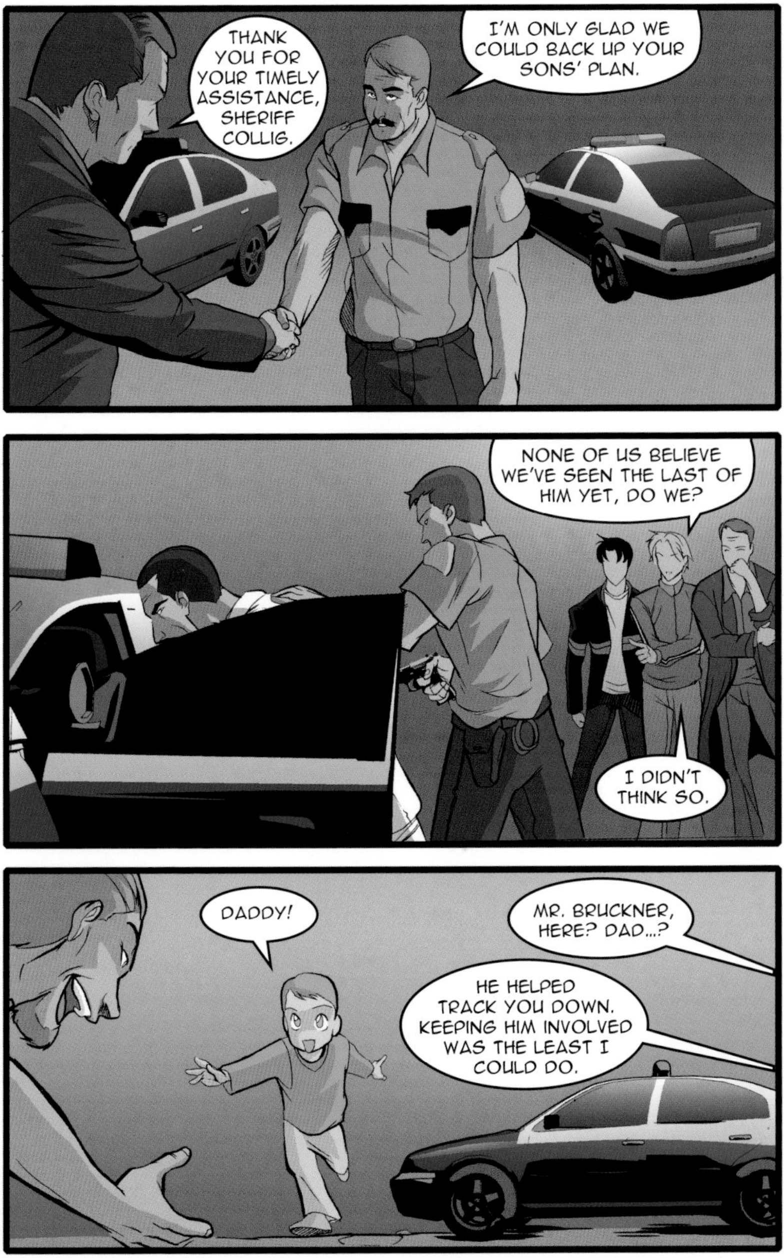
THANK YOU FOR YOUR TIMELY ASSISTANCE, SHERIFF COLLIG.
I'M ONLY GLAD WE COULD BACK UP YOUR SONS' PLAN.
NONE OF US BELIEVE WE'VE SEEN THE LAST OF HIM YET, DO WE?
I DIDN'T THINK SO.
DADDY!
MR. BRUCKNER, HERE? DAD...?
HE HELPED TRACK YOU DOWN. KEEPING HIM INVOLVED WAS THE LEAST I COULD DO.

CHAPTER EIGHT: "FATHER AND SONS"

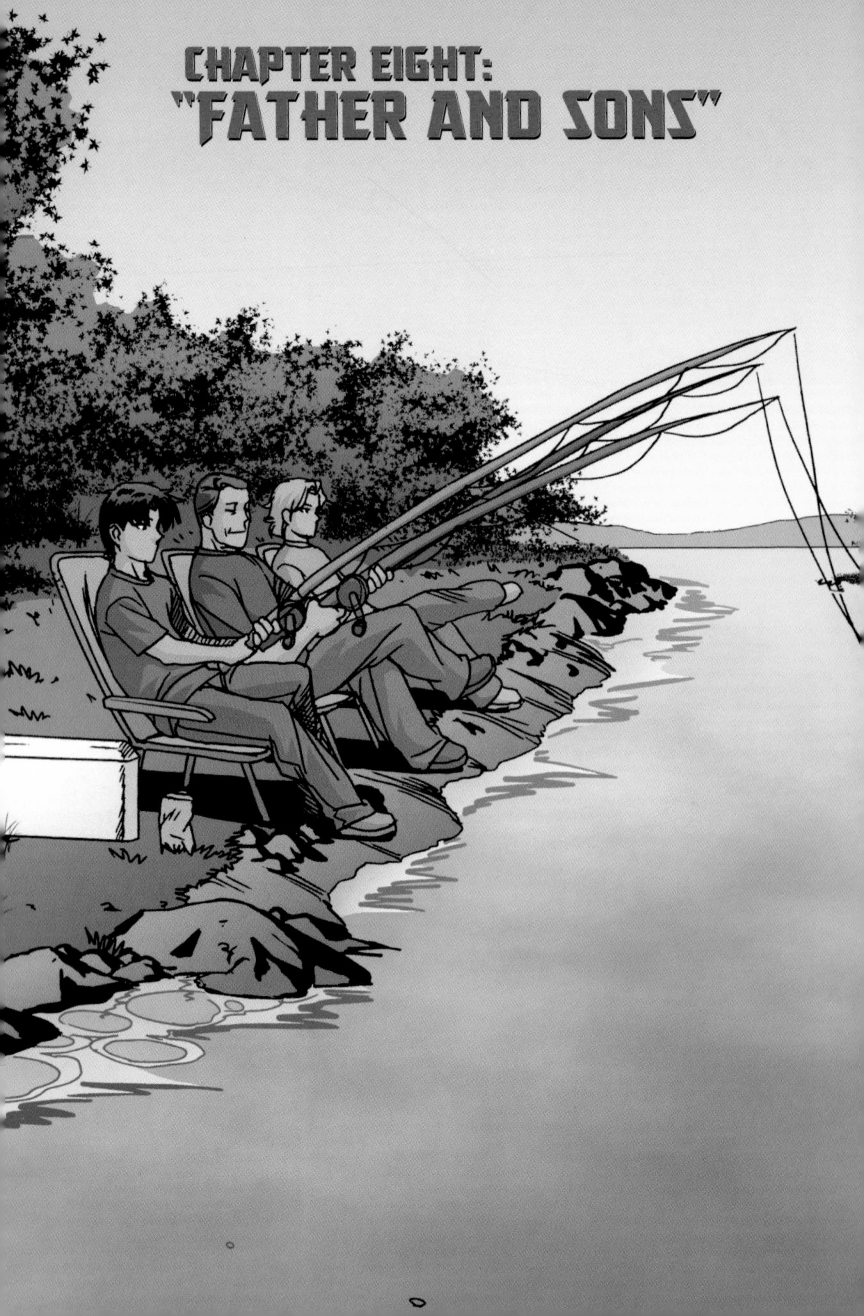

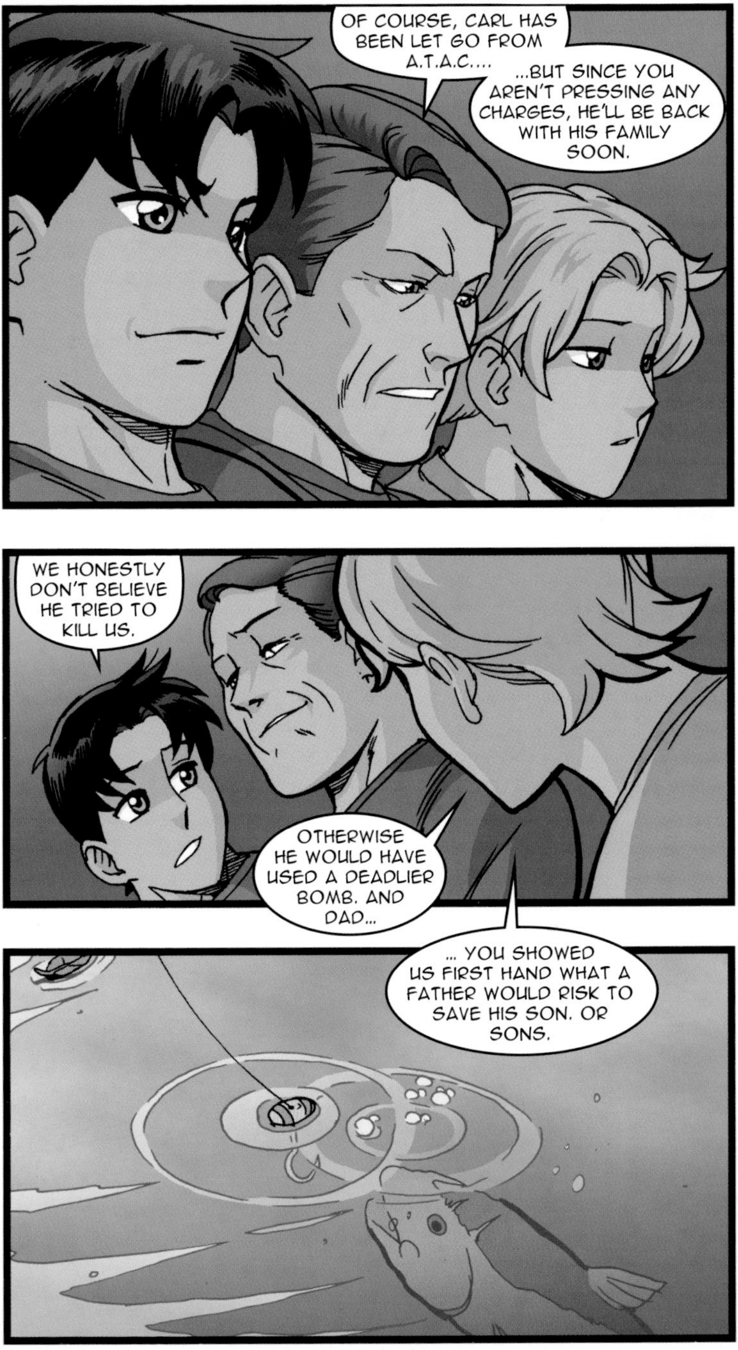
OF COURSE, CARL HAS BEEN LET GO FROM A.T.A.C....
...BUT SINCE YOU AREN'T PRESSING ANY CHARGES, HE'LL BE BACK WITH HIS FAMILY SOON.
WE HONESTLY DON'T BELIEVE HE TRIED TO KILL US.
OTHERWISE HE WOULD HAVE USED A DEADLIER BOMB. AND DAD...
... YOU SHOWED US FIRST HAND WHAT A FATHER WOULD RISK TO SAVE HIS SON. OR SONS.

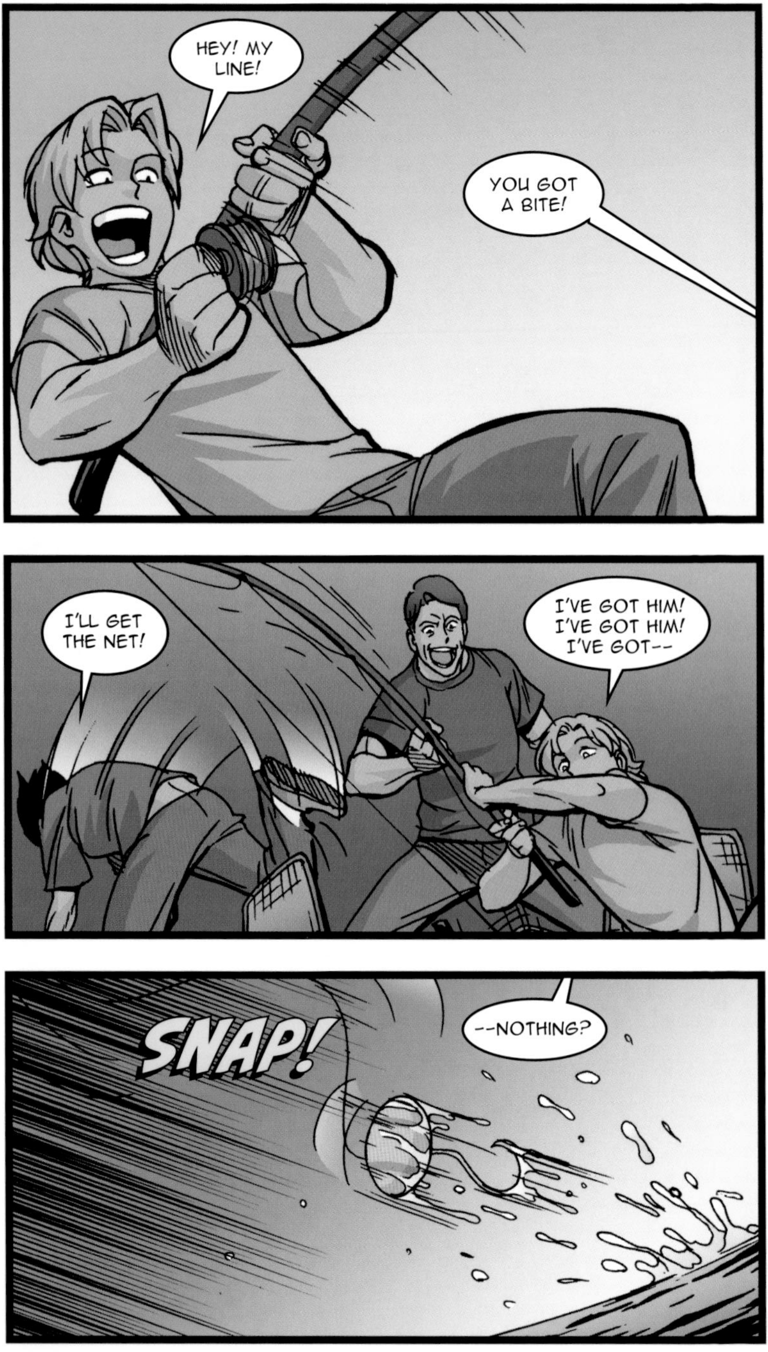
HEY! MY LINE!
YOU GOT A BITE!
I'LL GET THE NET!
I'VE GOT HIM! I'VE GOT HIM! I'VE GOT--
SNAP!
--NOTHING?

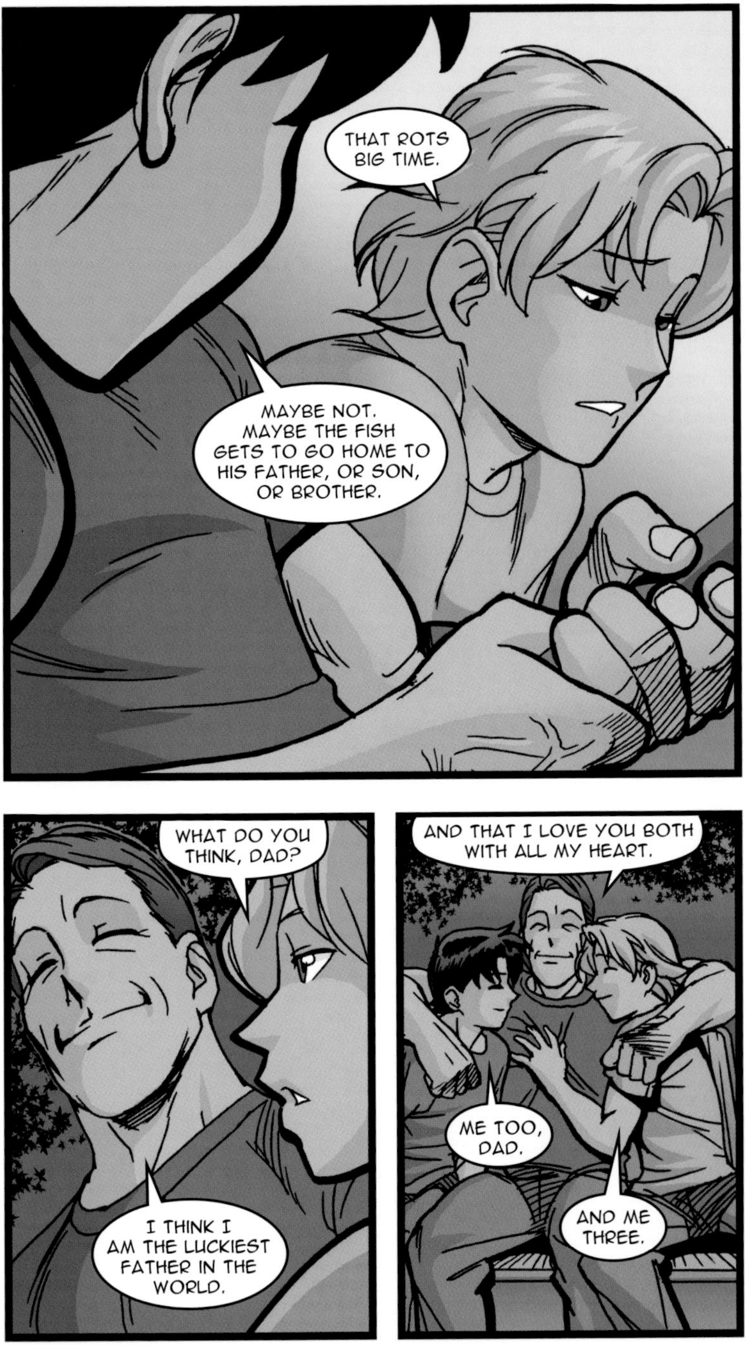
THAT ROTS BIG TIME.
MAYBE NOT. MAYBE THE FISH GETS TO GO HOME TO HIS FATHER, OR SON, OR BROTHER.
WHAT DO YOU THINK, DAD?
I THINK I AM THE LUCKIEST FATHER IN THE WORLD.
AND THAT I LOVE YOU BOTH WITH ALL MY HEART.
ME TOO, DAD.
AND ME THREE.

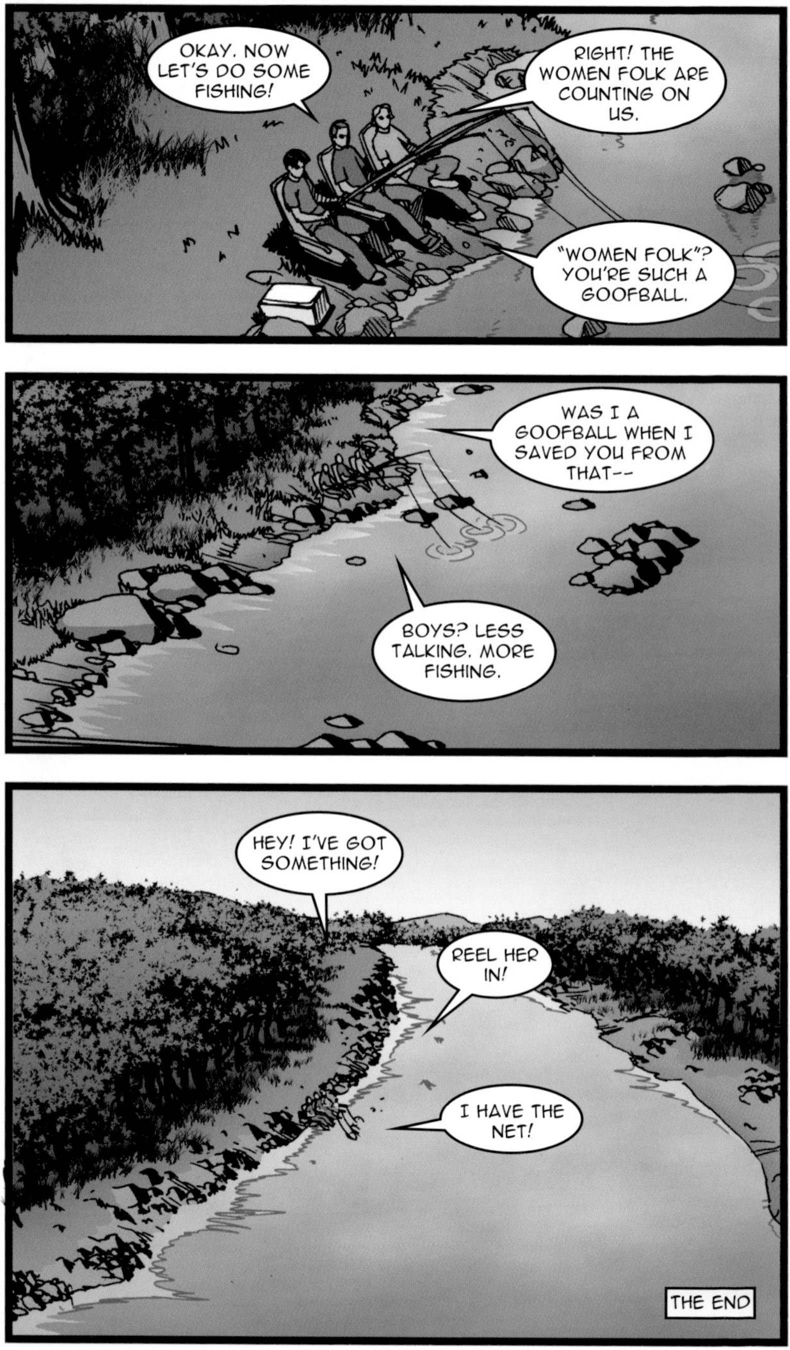
OKAY. NOW LET'S DO SOME FISHING!
RIGHT! THE WOMEN FOLK ARE COUNTING ON US.
"WOMEN FOLK"? YOU'RE SUCH A GOOFBALL.
WAS I A GOOFBALL WHEN I SAVED YOU FROM THAT--
BOYS? LESS TALKING. MORE FISHING.
HEY! I'VE GOT SOMETHING!
REEL HER IN!
I HAVE THE NET!
THE END

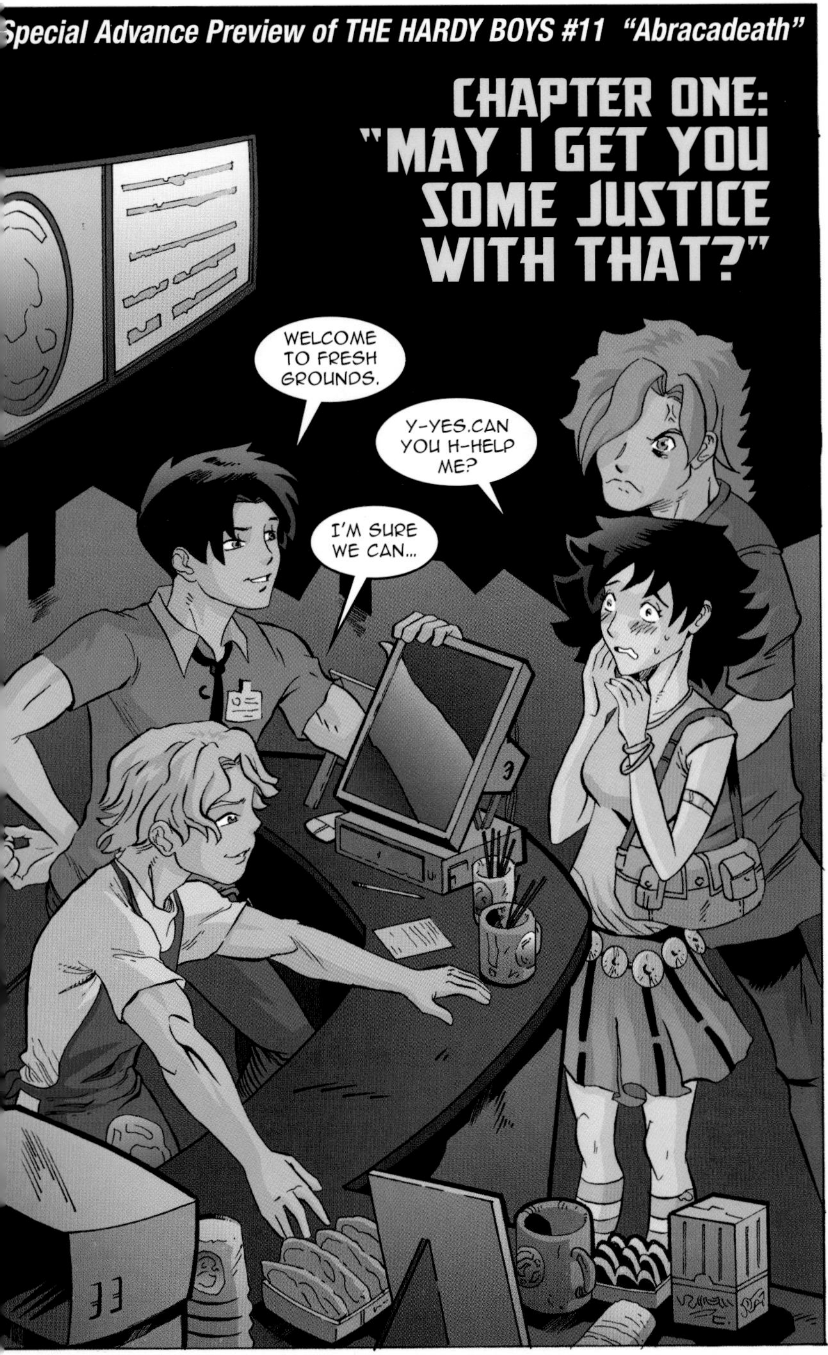
Special Advance Preview of THE HARDY BOYS #11 "Abracadeath"
CHAPTER ONE: "MAY I GET YOU SOME JUSTICE WITH THAT?"
WELCOME TO FRESH GROUNDS.
Y-YES.CAN YOU H-HELP ME?
I'M SURE WE CAN...

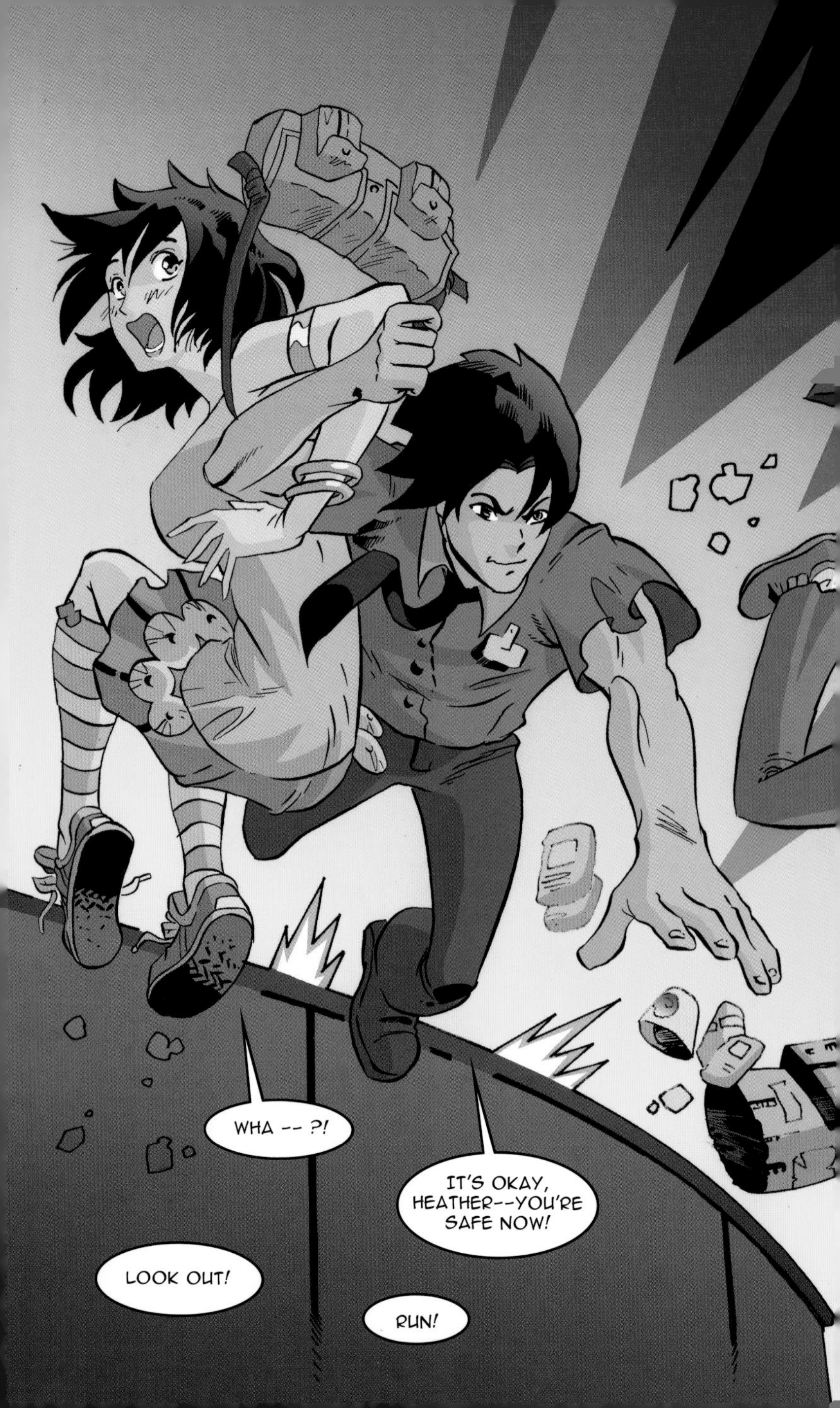
WHA -- ?!
IT'S OKAY, HEATHER--YOU'RE SAFE NOW!
LOOK OUT!
RUN!

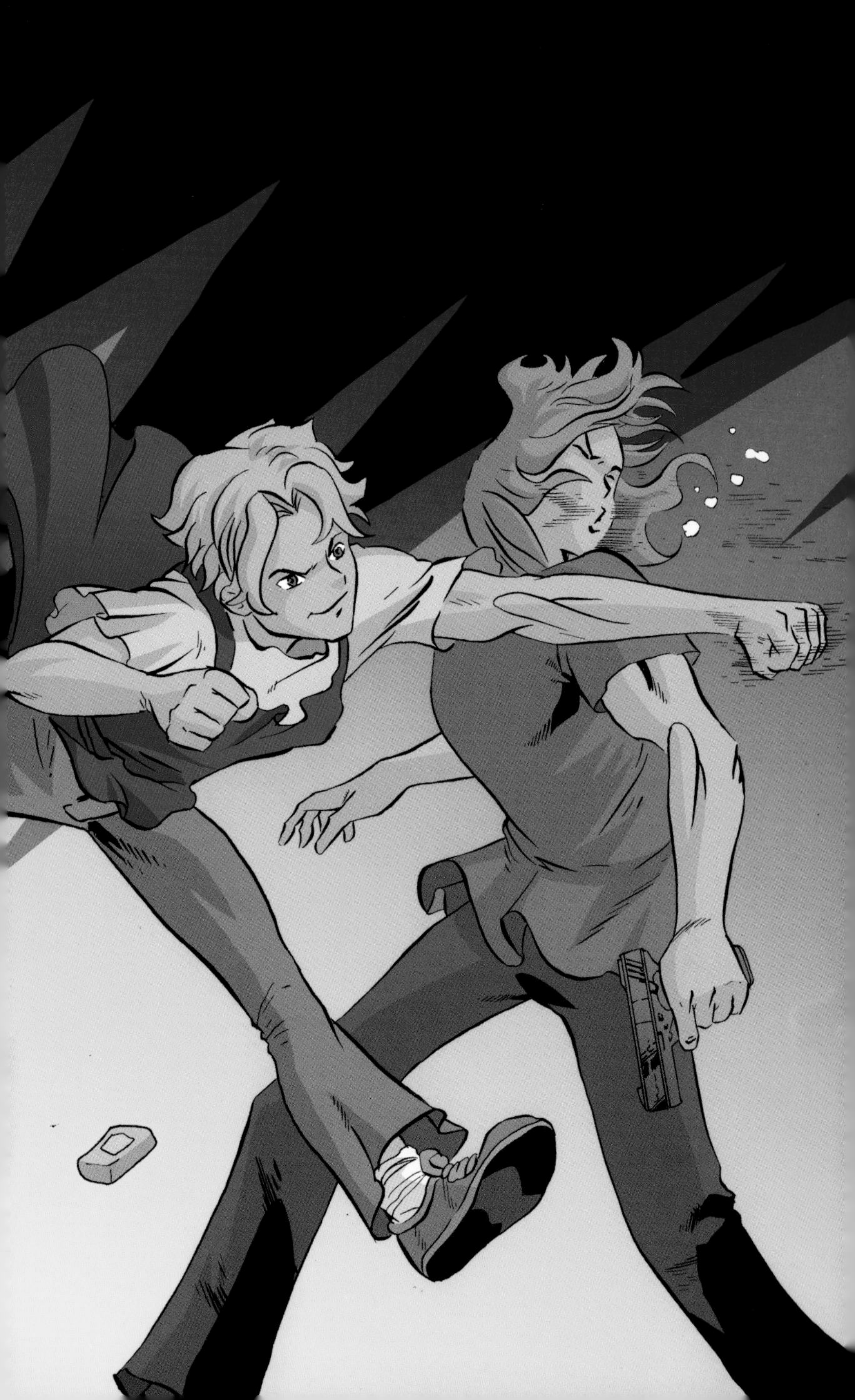

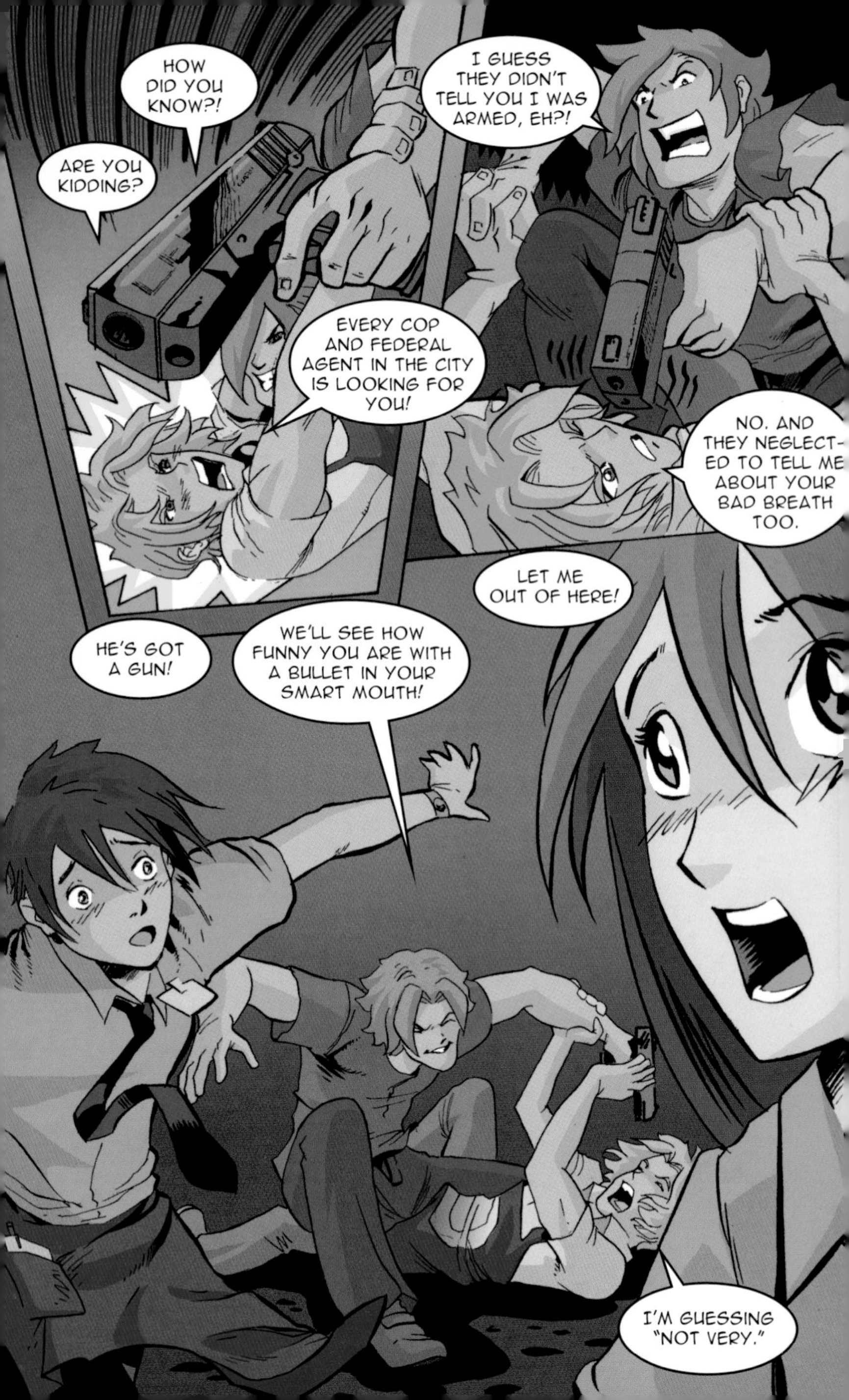
ARE YOU KIDDING?
HOW DID YOU KNOW?!
I GUESS THEY DIDN'T TELL YOU I WAS ARMED, EH?!
EVERY COP AND FEDERAL AGENT IN THE CITY IS LOOKING FOR YOU!
NO. AND THEY NEGLECTED TO TELL ME ABOUT YOUR BAD BREATH TOO.
LET ME OUT OF HERE!
HE'S GOT A GUN!
WE'LL SEE HOW FUNNY YOU ARE WITH A BULLET IN YOUR SMART MOUTH!
I'M GUESSING "NOT VERY."

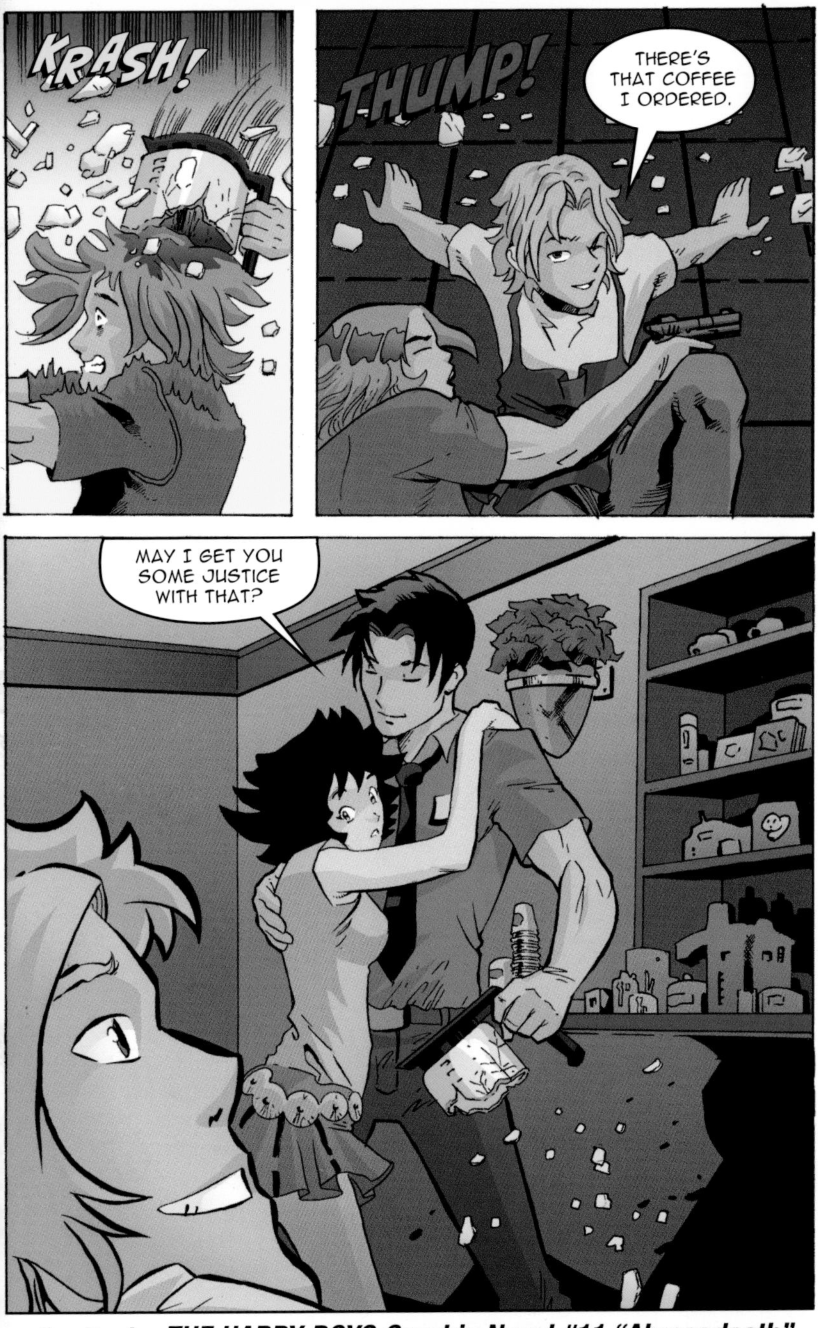
KRASH!
THUMP!
THERE'S THAT COFFEE I ORDERED.
MAY I GET YOU SOME JUSTICE WITH THAT?

Don't miss THE HARDY BOYS Graphic Novel #11 "Abracadeath"

Go Undercover in Paris as Nancy Drew® in

Danger by Design

You, as Nancy Drew, are in Paris to work undercover for a prestigious fashion designer. Minette is all the rage in the fashion world, but strange threats and unwelcome guests are causing her to unravel. It's up to you to stitch the clues together and unmask the mystery in this PC adventure game.

dare to play™

FOR MYSTERY FANS 10 to Adult

Nancy Drew PC Adventure Game #14
Order online at www.HerInteractive.com
or call 1-800-461-8787. Also in stores!
Compatible with WINDOWS® 98/2000/Me/XP/Vista

Created by

NANCY DREW

A NEW GRAPHIC NOVEL EVERY 3 MONTHS!

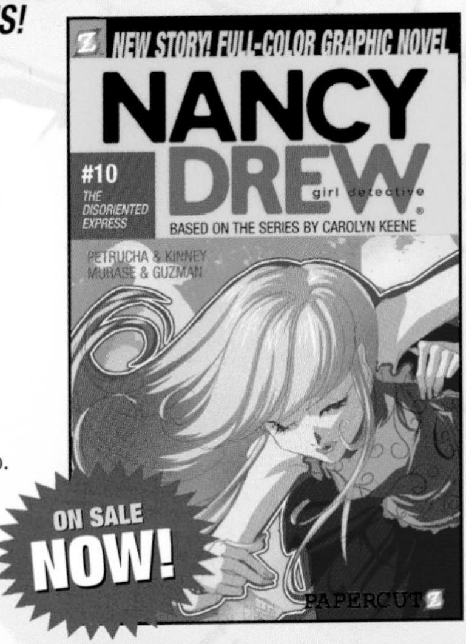
NEW STORY! FULL-COLOR GRAPHIC NOVEL
NANCY DREW
#10
THE DISORIENTED EXPRESS
girl detective
BASED ON THE SERIES BY CAROLYN KEENE
PETRUCHA & KINNEY
MURASE & GUZMAN
ON SALE NOW!
PAPERCUTZ

#1 "The Demon of River Heights"
SBN 1-59707-000-9 pb.
#2 "Writ In Stone" ISBN 1-59707-002-5 pb.
#3 "The Haunted Dollhouse"
SBN 1-59707-008-4 pb.
#4 "The Girl Who Wasn't There"
SBN 1-59707-012-2 pb.
#5 "The Fake Heir" ISBN 1-59707-024-6 pb.
#6 "Mr. Cheeters Is Missing"
SBN 1-59707-030-0 pb.
#7 "The Charmed Bracelet"
SBN 1-59707-036-X pb.
#8 "Global Warning" ISBN 1-59707-051-3 pb.
#9 "Ghost in the Machinery"
SBN 1-59707-058-0 pb.
IEW! #10 "The Disoriented Express"
SBN 1-59707-066-1 pb.
ll: Pocket sized, 96-112pp., full color, $7.95
lso available in hardcover! $12.95 each.
Vol. 1: ISBN 1-59707-004-1
Vol. 2: ISBN 1-59707-006-8
Vol. 3: ISBN 1-59707-009-2
Vol. 4: ISBN 1-59707-013-0
Vol. 5: ISBN 1-59707-025-4
Vol. 6: ISBN 1-59707-031-9
Vol. 7: ISBN 1-59707-037-8
Vol. 8: ISBN 1-59707-052-1
Vol. 9: ISBN 1-59707-061-0
Vol. 10: ISBN 1-59707-067-X

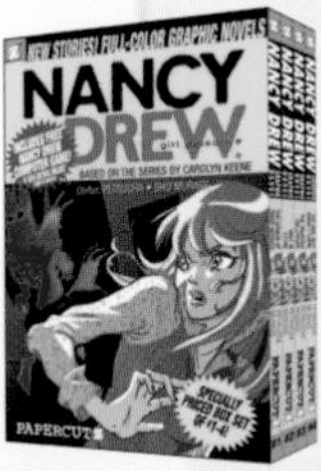
NEW STORIES! FULL-COLOR GRAPHIC NOVELS
NANCY DREW
BASED ON THE SERIES BY CAROLYN KEENE
SPECIALLY PRICED BOX SET OF #1-4!
PAPERCUTZ

Nancy Drew Boxed Set, #1-4
384 pages of color comics! $29.95, ISBN 1-59707-038-6

TOTALLY SPIES!

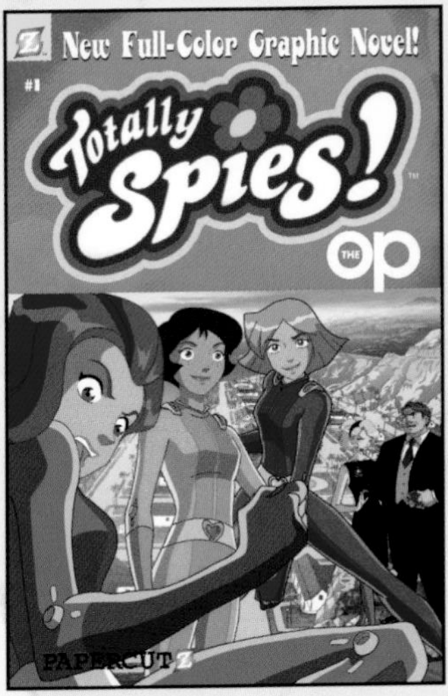
New Full-Color Graphic Novel!
#1
Totally Spies!
THE OP
PAPERCUTZ

#1 "The O.P." ISBN 1-59707-043-2
#2 "I Hate the 80's" ISBN 1-59707-045-9
#3 "Evil Jerry" ISBN 1-59707-047-8
#4 "Spies in Space" ISBN 1-59707-055-6
Each: 5x7 1/2, 112pp., full color paperback: $7.95
lso available in hardcover! $12.95 each.
Vol. 1: ISBN 1-59707-044-0
Vol. 2: ISBN 1-59707-046-7
Vol. 3: ISBN 1-59707-048-3
Vol. 4: ISBN 1-59707-056-4

PAPERCUTZ™

At your store or order at Papercutz, 40 Exchange Place, Ste. 1308, New York, NY 10005, 1-800-886-1223 (24 hours)

MC, VISA, AMEX accepted, add $3 P&H for 1st item, $1 each additional. Distributed by Holtzbrinck

www.papercutz.com

THE HARDY BOYS

UNDERCOVER BROTHERS™

ATAC BRIEFING FOR AGENTS FRANK AND JOE HARDY

The Mummy's Curse

#13: THE MUMMY'S CURSE
Available December 2006

MISSION:

A man has been murdered, possibly over a map to a precious golden mummy. Are there other treasure-hunters trying to find the location of the tomb? Could there be a curse surrounding the ancient mummy and his treasure?

LOCATION:

Cairo, Egypt, and the surrounding area.

SUSPECTS:

Several people on an expedition are suspects. you have to find them before they find the mummy . . . and his treasure!

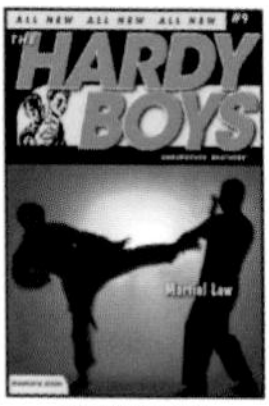

THIS MISSION REQUIRES YOUR IMMEDIATE ATTENTION. PICK UP A COPY OF *THE MUMMY'S CURSE* AND GET ON THE CASE!

WATCH OUT FOR PAPERCUTZ

Hi, Jim Salicrup, Editor-in-Chief of Papercutz here with the latest edition of the Papercutz Backpages.

In case you're wondering exactly what an "Editor-in-Chief of Papercutz" does, here's the answer. Papercutz, as you know, is the name of our company and we publish graphic novels for all ages, such as Nancy Drew, The Hardy Boys, Totally Spies, even The Life of Pope John Paul II... *In Comics!* These graphic novels—comics published in book form—are created by incredibly talented writers and artists, and the guy that works with them to help put it all together is the Editor-in-Chief. Sometimes, the Editor-in-Chief's job is really easy, and all he or she has to do is find great writers and artists and let them put together great comics. Other times, the Editor-in-Chief may help writers work out problems in a story, suggest to an artist how to make a page look more interesting, or just remind everyone when the art and stories are due to go off to the printer so that they can get to your favorite bookstore on time. At Papercutz, the Editor-in-Chief guy is me—Jim Salicrup.

Recently, the Museum of Comic and Cartoon Art presented an exhibit based on my career as a comicbook writer and editor, and they called it "Salicrup's Section," based on the name of my myspace blog. This is really the very first time MoCCA devoted an exhibit to someone primarily known as an editor. Usually exhibits are devoted to great comic book artists, although they recently had an exhibit devoted to Stan Lee, the co-creator of such famous characters as the Amazing Spider-Man, the Incredible Hulk, the Fantastic Four, the Uncanny X-Men, and many, many more, and even though he's one of the best comicbook editors of all time, he's primarily known as a writer. An earlier exhibit focused on Harvey Kurtzman, creator of Mad magazine. Harvey was another brilliant editor, but again, he's probably more famous for his writing and art. I can't begin to tell you how flattering it is to be honored like this, and especially when you consider whom they exhibited before. All I can say is, "I'm not worthy."

If nothing else, such a tribute has inspired me to work harder than ever to make Papercutz a great graphic novel publisher. Let me know how I'm doing by writing to me at salicrup@papercutz.com or Jim Salicrup, PAPERCUTZ, 40 Exchange Place, Ste. 1308, New York, NY 10005. For more information about the Museum of Comic and Cartoon Art go to: www.moccany.org.

Thanks,

Jim

MoCCA

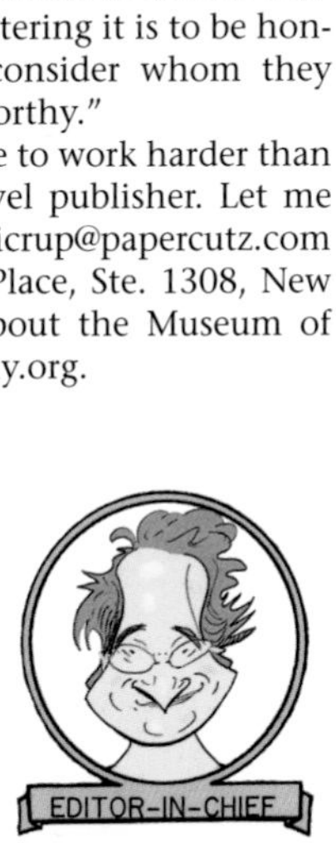
EDITOR-IN-CHIEF

Caricature of Jim drawn by Steve Brodner at the MoCCA Art Fest.

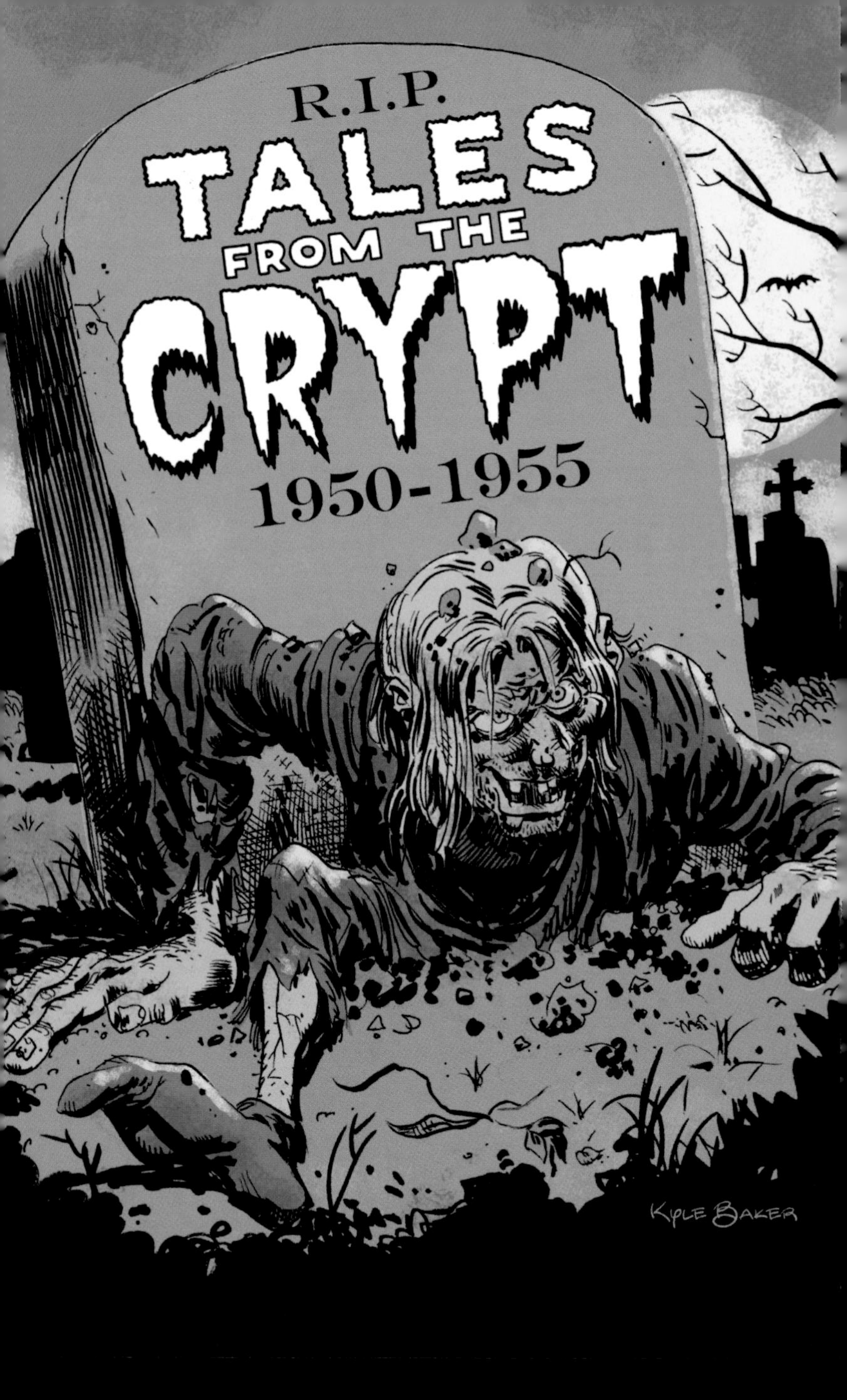
R.I.P.
TALES FROM THE CRYPT
1950-1955
KYLE BAKER

PAPERCUTZ™

presents:
The Return of
TALES FROM THE CRYPT®

It's one of the biggest surprises in the world of comics and graphic novel publishing! Shortly before the 2007 New York Comic Con, Papercutz announced that we would be publishing all-new TALES FROM THE CRYPT comics. After more than 50 years, EC Comics' legendary flagship title returns with all-new shocking suspenstories, narrated by the original Crypt-Keeper, Old Witch, and Vault Keeper. Each issue will feature two 20-page tales of terror in the EC tradition! Reactions ranged from excitement—from fans thrilled to see the most famous horror comicbook ever return after over fifty years–to shock—that it was to be coming from a publisher primarily known for its Nancy Drew and The Hardy Boys graphic novels. Those books contain material suitable for all-ages, but the HBO TALES FROM THE CRYPT series certainly contained a fair amount of adult content.

"People forget that the original TALES FROM THE CRYPT comicbook, published by the legendary EC Comics back in the 50s, was also intended for all-ages, and its primary readership was young boys," Papercutz Editor-in-Chief Jim Salicrup is quick to point out. But that may be exactly what fans find so controversial. The original TALES FROM THE CRYPT comics, featured stories dreamed up by EC publisher William M. Gaines and his editor Al Feldstein, and drawn by Feldstein, as well as Graham Ingles, Jack Davis, Jack Kamen, Joe Orlando, Wally Wood, Harvey Kurtzman, Bill Elder, Reed Crandall,

Johnny Craig, Al Williamson, George Evans, and colored by Marie Severin. CRYPT started a horror comics craze that soon drew the attention of psychiatrist Dr. Frederick Wertham.

Wertham reacted to the popularity of horror comics with children by writing a book called "Seduction of the Innocent," which maintained that comics led to juvenile delinquency and even far worse behavior. Parents were understandably alarmed, and soon the Senate Subcommittee to Investigate Juvenile Delinquency was taking a hard look at comicbooks. EC Comics publisher Bill Gaines spoke before the Subcommittee, but was unable to convince them that his comics were entertaining stories told in good taste. Ultimately, comicbook publishers adversely affected by the negative publicity created the Comics Magazine Association of America which would review comics and award a seal of approval to assure parents that the comic's contents were safe, wholesome entertainment.

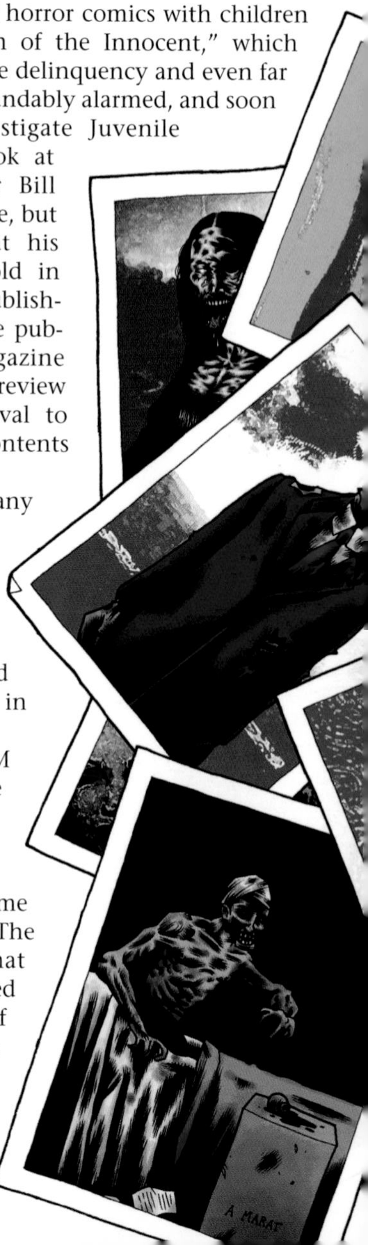

Unfortunately, it was too late for many publishers, who went bankrupt as the negative publicity had hurt sales of comics terribly. EC Comics, tried to hang in there, but despite canceling their horror comics, and creating new titles such as "Valor" and "Psychoanalysis," only MAD comics, in a new magazine format, survived.

The question is, was TALES FROM CRYPT really all that bad? "Of course not!" Salicrup insists. "Ironically, many of the original stories would be approved by today's revised Comics Code. But sure, there were some stories that still wouldn't get by. The point here is that the stories that Papercutz will be creating will be aimed at readers age 10 and up. Instead of excessive blood and gore, we'll be sticking to the TALES FROM THE CRYPT tradition of stories filled with interesting characters, lots of dark humor, and of course, the trademarked EC "shock" endings!"

The first TALES FROM THE CRYPT comic from Papercutz, which will be on sale in comics shops in June, features:

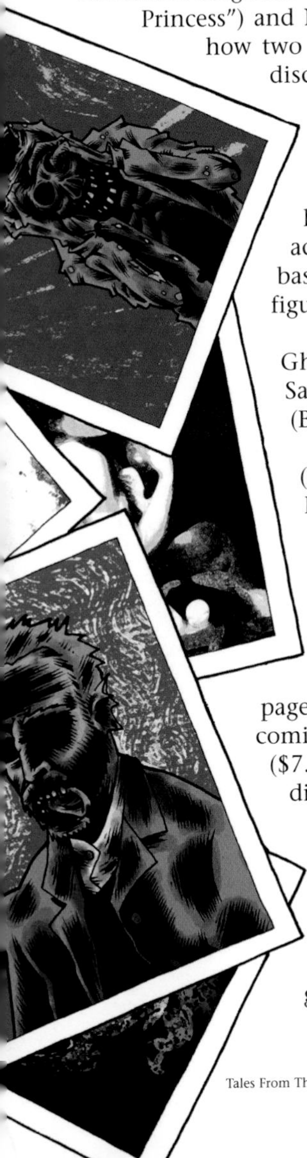

• "Body of Work," by horror author Marc Bilgrey (H.P. Lovecraft's Magazine of Horror, "And Don't Forget to Rescue the Princess") and Mr. Exes (Abra Cadaver). The story reveals how two nosy and somewhat murderous neighbors discover the shocking inspiration for Jack Kroll's creepy "outsider" artwork.

• "For Serious Collectors Only," by Rob Vollmar (Bluesman) and Tim Smith III (Teen Titans Go!). This tale explores how far Thomas Donalley— a middle-aged action-figure collector who lives in his Mom's basement— will go for an ultra-rare Japanese figure.

• Introductory pages featuring the GhouLunatics are written by editor Jim Salicrup and drawn by artist Rick Parker (Beavis and Butt-Head).

• Cover by award-winning artist Kyle Baker (Nat Turner, Plastic Man, Why I Hate Saturn).

Future issues will include stories by Fred Van Lente (Marvel Adventures), Xeric Grant winner Neil Kleid, Stefan Petrucha (The Shadow of Frankenstein, NANCY DREW), Don McGregor (ZORRO), Sho Murase (NANCY DREW), and other great talents. Each bi-monthly issue is 48 full-color pages for an affordable $3.95. Naturally, the comics will be collected in the usual 112 page, ($7.95 paperback; $12.95 hardcover) full-color digest format with more previously unseen stories, the first volume, TALES FROM THE CRYPT "*Ghouls Gone Wild*!" available in bookstores everywhere in time for Halloween.

When reached for comment, the Crypt-Keeper said, "It's good to be back, boils and ghouls—and it's about time! Ahahahah!"

Recently on papercutz.com we featured a special Match Wits with the Hardy Boys promotion. (See, why it's important to drop by our website whenever you can? You never know what surprises you may discover!) Well, the Hardy Boys promotion is officially over, and now...

Papercutz is proud to announce the GRAND PRIZE WINNER of the MATCH WITS WITH THE HARDY BOYS—

JEREMY HAFTEL!

CONGRATULATIONS, JEREMY!

Jeremy's entry was one of several that correctly found the clues requested. Here are the original questions along with Jeremy's answers:

LATER...
THAT POOR SWITCHING AGENT, HE CLAIMS HE JUST PASSED OUT.
YOU SAY "CLAIMS."
DOES THAT MEAN YOU DON'T BELIEVE HIM?
I GUESS THAT SOUNDS SUSPICIOUS, HUH?
MAYBE I'M SEEING A CASE WHERE THERE IS NONE.
THANKS FOR SAVING OUR BACON, HARDY BOYS!
DON'T MENTION IT, SIR.
WE'RE HAPPY WE COULD HELP.

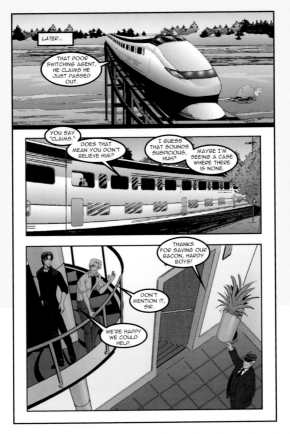

On page twenty-nine, can you find the clue that indicates that there are Hardy Boys imposters aboard this souped-up bullet train? Here's a hint: This is the kind of pointed clue that could only appear in a comicbook or graphic novel. This may be just a simple case of seeing is believing!

Jeremy's answer:
Looking into the window from outside of the train, you see two people who look like the Hardy Boys. They are not talking. The dialogue balloons are coming from other windows where you cannot see the Hardy Boys from the outside. So, it appears that the ones that you can see from outside are imposters.

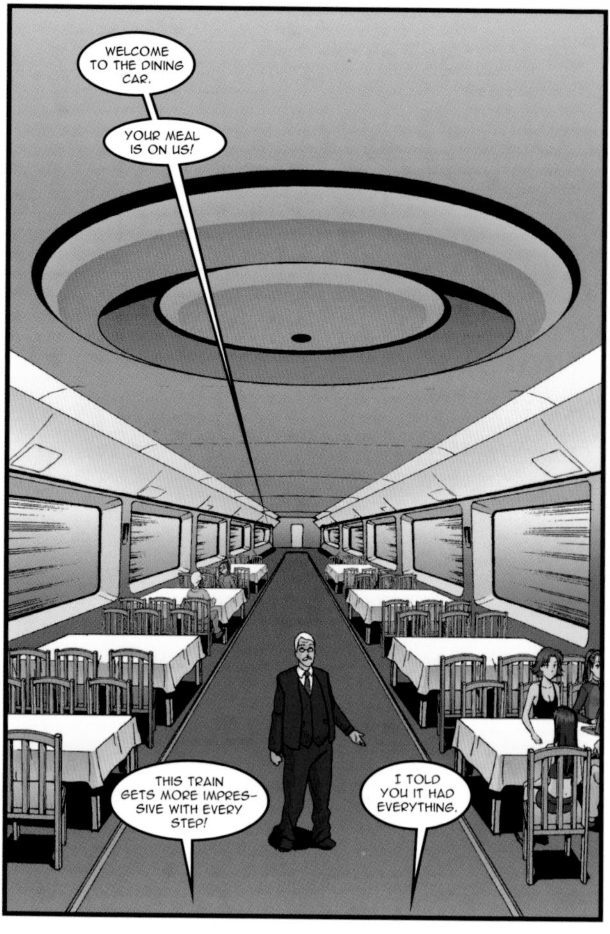
WELCOME TO THE DINING CAR.
YOUR MEAL IS ON US!
THIS TRAIN GETS MORE IMPRES-SIVE WITH EVERY STEP!
I TOLD YOU IT HAD EVERYTHING.

Page thirty has a major clue that something funny is going on aboard this trouble-train! What is it? Here's a hint: If you booked passage on this debut run of this super-duper bullet train, what would you find suspicious by its absence?

Jeremy's answer:
If this is the debut run, you would expect the dining car to be crowded with people and at least some food being served. There is no food, no water and no food servers (and very few people).

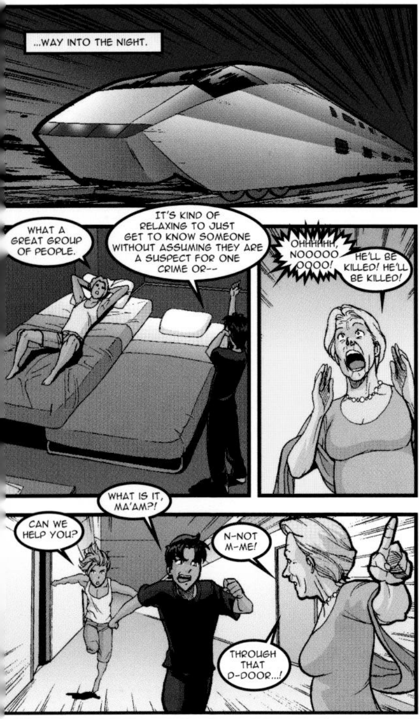
...WAY INTO THE NIGHT.
WHAT A GREAT GROUP OF PEOPLE.
IT'S KIND OF RELAXING TO JUST GET TO KNOW SOMEONE WITHOUT ASSUMING THEY ARE A SUSPECT FOR ONE CRIME OR--
OHHHHHH, NOOOOOOOOO!
HE'LL BE KILLED! HE'LL BE KILLED!
CAN WE HELP YOU?
WHAT IS IT, MA'AM?!
N-NOT M-ME!
THROUGH THAT D-DOOR...!

Here's something you don't see on trains, even super-luxury trains like this one. What telltale clue are the boys overlooking on page thirty-three? Here's a hint: If you ever bunked with a buddy on a train, or even seen a sleeping car on TV or in a movie, you'll spot what's wrong here—unless we caught you napping!

Jeremy's answer:
The word "bunked" makes you believe that the bed should be bunk beds. These beds are not bunk beds and the one on the left looks like it is not supported by anything other than the wall and the other bed which is barely touching it and would not make sense.

Great job, Jeremy! For your efforts you will be rewarded with a guest-starring role as an agent of A.T.A.C. in an upcoming Hardy Boys graphic novel. You'll be helping Frank and Joe make the world a much safer place. Be sure to keep an eye on all announcements at www.papercutz.com for the title and publication date.
Although, Jeremy is our big winner, everyone at Papercutz extends a big THANK-YOU to all of our cunning clue-seekers! We were all knocked out by the incredible response and impressed by the high degree of sleuthing skills evident in each of the entries! Thanks, everyone, for making the Match Wits With The Hardy Boys promotion such a success!

THE HARDY BOYS IN OTHER MEDIA!

While everyone is excited and thrilled by the all-new Nancy Drew movie, starring Emma Roberts, here's an announcement we're sure all Papercutz fans will be equally thrilled and excited by...

Filming may begin in 2008 on THE HARDY MEN, starring Tom Cruise and Ben Stiller!!

According to The Hollywood Reporter, "Mr. And Mrs. Smith" screenwriter Simon Kinberg is currently working on the script for the big-screen comedy, which follows the grown up adventures of Frank and Joe Hardy. Shawn Levy is set to be the film's director.

But let's face it, the movie's still a long time away, probably 2009 at the earliest. Lucky for us there are plenty of Hardy Boys books and graphic novels to enjoy in the meantime. But this also gives us an excuse to celebrate earlier incarnations of the Hardy Boys in other media with the following playlists and episode guides to the vinyl records and animated series.

In September 1969 The Hardy Boys debuted on the ABC television network in an animated series produced by Filmation Studios. To make the show similar to the then-hit animated Archies animated series, Frank and Joe not only solved mysteries, they had a rock band as well!

Here's an episode guide to the animated Hardy Boys TV series produced by Filmation Studios. All episodes were aired on the ABC Network in color and were 30 minutes each, with two mystery stories. The second season was all reruns of the first season's episodes. They were all directed by Hal Sutherland and produced by Lou Scheimer and Norm Prescott. Trying to faithfully adapt an entire Hardy Boys novel into a cartoon that's less than fifteen minutes long would be impossible, so the show's writers loosely adapted original Franklin W. Dixon stories, using story elements from the original series as inspiration.

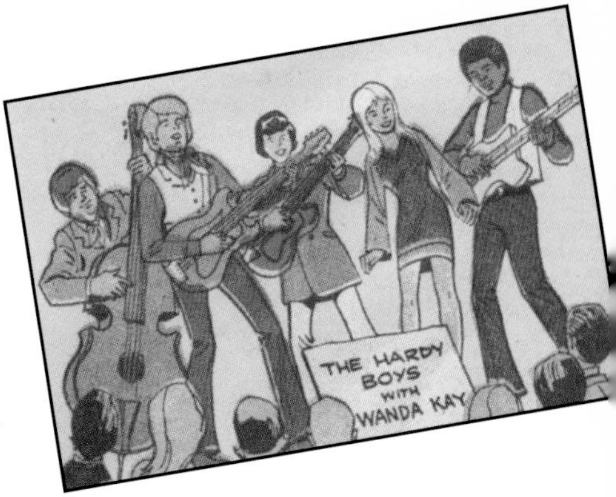
THE HARDY
BOYS
WITH
WANDA KAY

Episode One: (Titles unknown) aired September 6, 1969.
Episode Two: "The Secret Warning" and "The Viking Symbol Mystery" aired September 13, 1969.
Episode Three: "The Secret of the Caves" and "The Secret of the Old Mill" aired September 20, 1969.
Episode Four: "The Missing Chums" and "The Mystery of the Desert Giants" aired September 27, 1969.
Episode Five: "The Mystery of Cabin Island" and "Hunting for Hidden Gold" aired October 4, 1969.
Episode Six: "The Mystery of the Aztec Warrior" and "The Hidden Harbor Mystery" aired October 11, 1969.
Episode Seven: "The Ghost At Skeleton Rock" and "Mystery of the Chinese Junk" aired October 18, 1969.
Episode Eight: "The Shore Road Mystery" and "What Happened At Midnight" aired October 25, 1969.
Episode Nine: "The Sign of the Crooked Arrow" and "The Clue in the Embers" aired November 1, 1969.
Episode Ten: "The Clue of the Screeching Owl" and "The House on the Cliff" aired November 8, 1969.
Episode Eleven: "Mystery of the Spiral Bridge" and "The Yellow Feather Mystery" aired November 15, 1969.
Episode Twelve: "The Mystery of Devil's Paw" and "The Sinister Sign Post" aired November 22, 1969.
Episode Thirteen: "The Melted Coins" and "The Mark on the Door" aired November 29, 1969.
Episode Fourteen: "The Flickering Torch Mystery" and "The Haunted Fort" aired December 6, 1969.
Episode Fifteen: "The Mystery of Wildcat Swamp" and "The Clue of the Broken Blade" aired December 13, 1969.
Episode Sixteen: (Title unknown) and "The Short Wave Mystery" and aired December 20, 1969.
Episode Seventeen: "The Hooded Hawk Mystery" and "The Secret of Pirate's Hill" aired December 27, 1969.

A group of musicians were recruited by Bill Traut and Jim Golden of Dunwich Productions, Chicago with the help of the show's producers, Filmation, to record for RCA and go out on the road to perform the songs live. So Frank Hardy was played by Reed Kailing, of The Destinations—a band that played at the wedding of President Johnson's daughter, Lucy. Jeff Taylor was hired to be Joe Hardy. Deven English was Wanda Kay Breckenridge, a character created for the cartoons. Norbet (Nibs) Soltysiak became Chubby Morton, a character obviously based on Chet Morton. And drummer Bob Crowder, who had played with the Shirelles and others, was Pete Jones, a character created for the cartoons, who was the first regular African-American character on an animated TV series. The musical Hardy Boys band appeared live at the end of the animated episodes, and on the covers of the four Gold Key Hardy Boys comicbooks based on the cartoons.

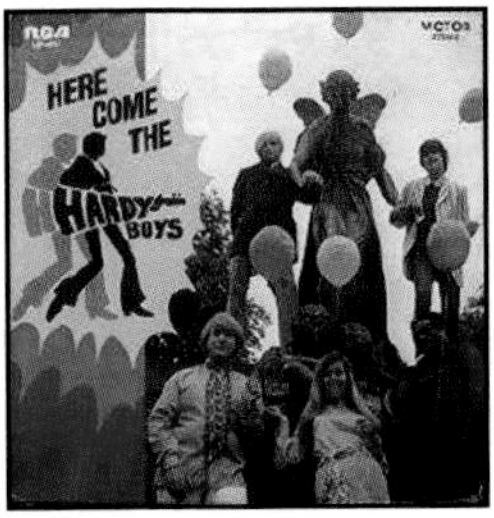
HERE COME THE HARDY BOYS

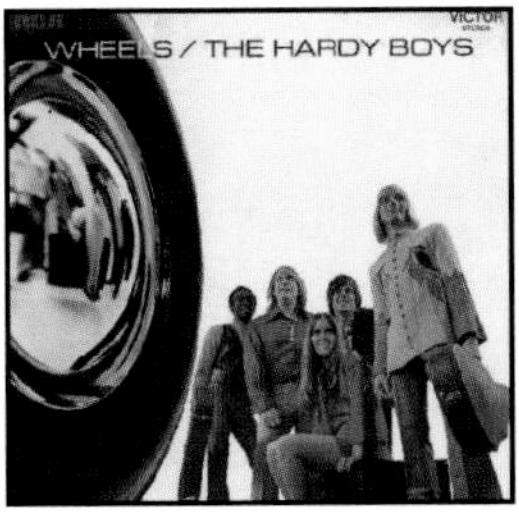
WHEELS / THE HARDY BOYS

Two albums were released by The Hardy Boys, "Here Come The Hardy Boys" and "Wheels." Here are the album covers and the song lists:

Here Come the Hardys
(Theme from cartoon TV series)
Those Country Girls
One Time in a Million
That's That
(I Want You to) Be My Baby
Sink or Swim
Namby-Pamby
My Little Sweet Pea
Sha-La-La
Fees So Good
Love and Let Love
Wheels
Old Man Moses Front Porch Rhythm Band
Carnival Time
Good Good Lovin'
Let the Sun Shine Down
Long, Long Way to Nashville
Love Train
Archie Brown
Where Would I Be
I Hear the Grass Singin'
Baby, This is the Last Time

That last song sure was prophetic, as it truly was the last Hardy Boys song from this groovy band! But who knows? Maybe one of these songs may turn up on the soundtrack to the Hardy Men movie? Stranger things have happened!

PAPERCUTZ ™
Feedback

We've been asking for feedback, and we've been getting it! For example...

Dear Mr. Salicrup,

I just finished reading Nancy Drew graphic novel #7 "The Charmed Bracelet" and saw your article at the end of the book saying you want to hear from your readers.

My name is Nancy, I am 31 years old and I am absolutely crazy about these new ND graphic novels! The first one I read was "Haunted Dollhouse." I really enjoyed the storyline and the references to the original ND series. I also think the artistry is fantastic. I had never even looked at a graphic novel before and only looked into these because they are Nancy Drew. I've been buying the whole series as they come out and I hope they will be around for a while.

I do have a question for you... I just picked up a copy of "Global Warning." I started reading it and realized that the pictures on page 3 are the same as on page 7. The writing makes sense on page 7, but not page 3. Was this a printing error? Just curious...

I look forward to hearing from you...

Sincerely,
Nancy M. DeVault

You're right, Nancy—there was a mistake and that wasn't the correct page. We're presenting the correct page 3 on the very next page.

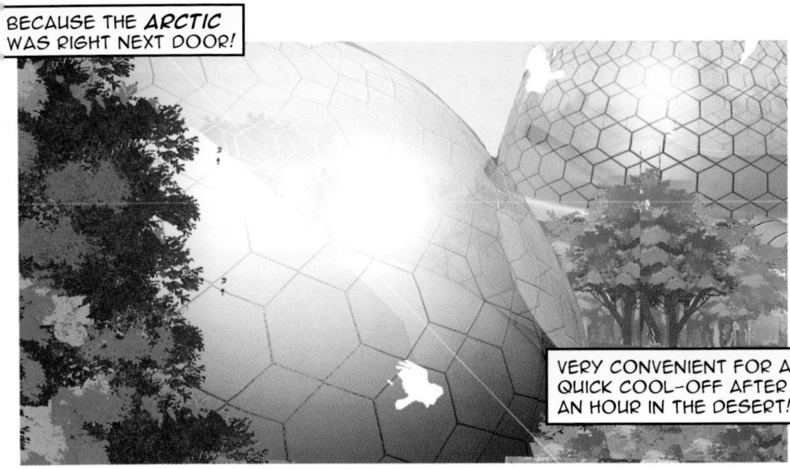
BECAUSE THE *ARCTIC* WAS RIGHT NEXT DOOR!
VERY CONVENIENT FOR A QUICK COOL-OFF AFTER AN HOUR IN THE DESERT!

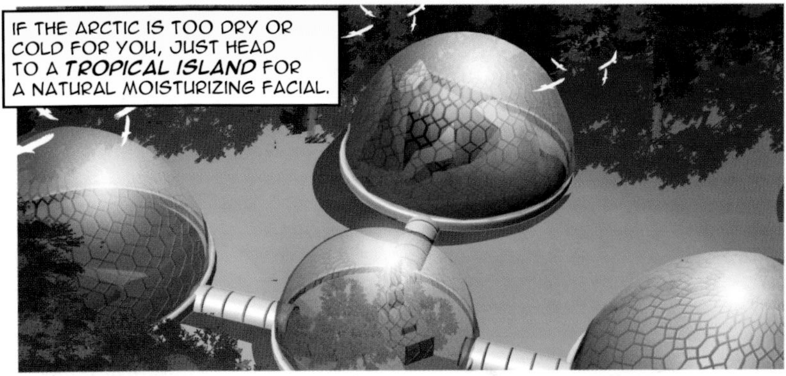
IF THE ARCTIC IS TOO DRY OR COLD FOR YOU, JUST HEAD TO A *TROPICAL ISLAND* FOR A NATURAL MOISTURIZING FACIAL.

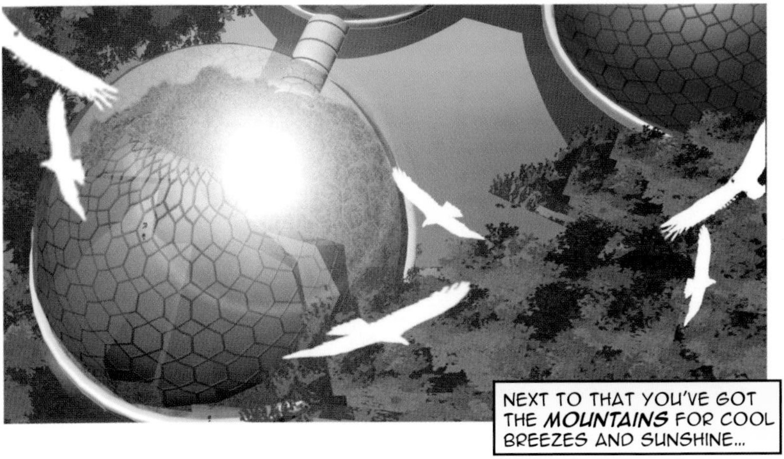
NEXT TO THAT YOU'VE GOT THE *MOUNTAINS* FOR COOL BREEZES AND SUNSHINE...

We hope our Nancy Drew graphic novels will be around as long as Nancy Drew is around. With the new Nancy Drew movie creating a whole new generation of Nancy Drew fans, and considering that Nancy Drew has already been around for over 75 years, all that makes us very optimistic about the future.

We also heard from hundreds of other Papercutz fans. Seems that they're thrilled with the stories, characters, and artwork in all our graphic novels, and the only complaint some have is that we don't come out with more books—that it's tough waiting three months for the next book in a Papercutz graphic novel series. Well, we understand and we'd love to come out with a new book every month, but our artists and writers can only draw and write so fast! There's just no way we can produce our titles any faster and still maintain the excellent level of writing and artwork that you're telling us you love so much.

But hey! We're happy to report that Papercutz graphic novels are also available at many Public Libraries, and we couldn't be happier. As proud as we are of Nancy Drew, Totally Spies, Zorro, The Hardy Boys, and all the rest, we certainly don't want anyone to miss a meal or go broke buying Papercutz graphic novels. So, visit your local Public Library and check us out.

And speaking of libraries, fans want to know where they can buy hardcover editions of Papercutz graphic novels, just like the ones in the libraries. The answer is, you can buy them from your favorite bookstore or direct from Papercutz (see our ads elsewhere in this book). If your bookstore doesn't have any in stock, we're sure they'll be happy to order the books for you. Or check the major online booksellers—they all have the hardcover editions available. We have to admit, we're fans of our hardcover editions just because we love how they look on our bookshelves.

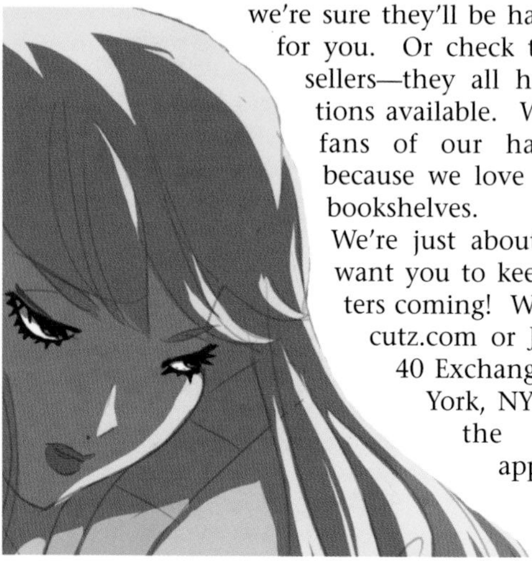

We're just about out of room, but we want you to keep those emails and letters coming! Write to: salicrup@papercutz.com or Jim Salicrup, Papercutz, 40 Exchange Place, Ste. 1308, New York, NY 10005. Thanks for all the feedback—we really appreciate it!